HANNAH HAZE

In Deep

Hannah Haze x

Front covered designed by Marie Mackay

First edition

This book was professionally typeset on Reedsy.
Find out more at reedsy.com

Foreword

You say tomato and I say tomato

I'm a British writer and use British English spelling and grammar. If you do spot any typos in this book, please drop me a line so I can make it right: hannahhazewrites@gmail.com (Or just drop me an email anyway. I love to chat!)

You can find a guide to my omegaverse at the end of this book. If you're new to omegaverse, you may want to take a look.

This book is a sweeter reverse harem omegaverse with one omega, a pack of alphas, and some MM. The main female character mentions problems orgasming in the past. Please visit my website for more detailed content warnings.

Acknowledgement

Lots of thank yous!

Thank you Hannah for sticking with me on this one and pushing me to write those juicy, peachy scenes! Thank you also to my wonderful beta readers Deanna, Linky, Melissa and Whitney for your honesty and feedback — this book is better for your wonderful input. And thank you MaryAnn for your proofreading and editing services.

I'm extremely grateful to Sam Hall for her kind words, encouragement and advice, as well as all the other supportive omegaverse authors. How lucky am I to be writing in a community of such fun, creative people!

To Mr D and Stephy — I appreciate all your support and patience and little sparks of inspiration. It took me a long time to land on a name for this pack but of course Stephy came up with one almost immediately!

This book is set in the fictional city of Studworth inspired by Oxford — one of my favourite places and where I met my Mr D. It's truly beautiful and definitely worth a visit, and I'm grateful it keeps offering me inspiration.

Chapter 1

I'm late.

I peer at my watch, willing the second hand to slow the heck down and give me the few minutes I need to race up these stairs and along the corridor to my class. If I don't get my arse in gear, this will be the third time I've been late this term. My shift at the museum gives me mere minutes to sprint across town in time for my lesson with Professor Michael.

The tutor has a temper like a rhinoceros with a sore head, and I don't fancy the verbal bashing that will come my way if I step through that door any later than 3pm. He already has it in for me. I stick out like a cactus in a rose garden among the perfectly polished students, churned out by the posh private schools. Students whose parents Professor Michael can guarantee will tip him, come the end of term, with a priceless bottle of whiskey or maybe an all-expenses-paid trip to the Caribbean.

Not my parents. They're not even contributing to my fees, let alone my rent.

And then there's the fact I'm an omega, something the professor clearly believes does not belong on his course.

No surprise there. I'm used to that. Cropping up places I shouldn't. Defying people's expectations.

My family always assumed I'd present as an omega, like my

mum, and her mum before her, and her mum before her, and blah blah blah. They've been telling me since I was a little girl what an omega can and can't do. Where they do and don't belong. What they can and can't be.

An omega can't be an astronaut. A rocket scientist. Alone.

Well, maybe they'll end up being right if I don't get up these stairs and into my class.

My rucksack swings from my shoulder, yanking down on my elbow, and I flip it back up, readjusting my grip on my armful of books and continuing to leap the stairs two at a time. I peer up at the dizzying twist of the staircase.

Why couldn't there be a goddamn lift? My heart is pounding in my chest and my lungs are rasping. And why is his room all the way up there in the heavens?

I glance at my watch again. Three more minutes have swept past in a blink of an eye and I don't know if I am going to make it.

Would it be better to skip the tutorial altogether? Except this topic is a tricky one and I could use the lesson to get my head around it. I'm not sure I'll ever understand it otherwise. And I can't fail. I scraped my way into this college by the skin of my teeth and I've been hanging on by my fingernails ever since.

I take another gasp of air, and sprint around the bend in the staircase, running straight into something solid.

For a moment, I wobble on my toes, dropping my pile of books as I flap about, trying to grab something to stop myself from tumbling. My fingers alight on soft material and I grip it. But instead of righting myself, I end up pulling whatever I've grabbed with me as I fall backwards.

I close my eyes and brace myself, ready for the hard impact against my spine. But when I hit the ground, it's not as bad as

I think, arms cushioning my fall and preventing a hard whack. Still, the air is knocked straight from my lungs and it takes a few seconds to breathe again, partly because of the substantial weight pressing down on top of me.

I open my eyes.

I'm nose to nose with a stranger, and it is his large body now pressed down on mine. I blink and then stare straight up into his eyes, a dark emerald green, that have the mesmerising quality of an alpha's.

And then I taste it in my mouth, cinnamon and cedar. Vivid and strong and masculine.

Definitely an alpha.

Shit!

"I'm sorry," I gasp, frozen by his stare. I could wriggle free, but I'm not sure writhing against this stranger when he's pressed on top of me is wise.

A genuine smile spreads across his face and dimples his cheeks. His lips are plush and his teeth white. But this is where the boyish quality ends. His jaw has the brutish cut of an alpha's and he definitely has the physique of one too.

"Are you OK?" he asks, making no effort to move.

"Yes, I'm fine." I bite the inside of my cheek, trying to prevent myself from taking a deep inhale. Doing that would have my eyes rolling back in their sockets. His scent is delicious. "I think you broke my fall."

"You're welcome." He doesn't move. In fact, he appears quite comfortable as his gaze flickers across my face. "You're an omega," he states simply.

"Yes." I swallow. As usual, I took my blockers this morning to mask my own scent, but up-close they're pretty useless. I shift a little, but he doesn't seem to notice, his eyes continuing

3

to roam from my face down my throat and to the neck of my top.

A slight frown creases his forehead. "I thought I knew all the omegas at Crestmore College."

If I wasn't trapped underneath him, I'd shrug. I never bothered joining OmegaSoc when I started as a fresher last term. It seemed cliche and suffocating to me. I'd been the only omega at secondary school, and I didn't want it to be the factor that continued to define me here at college. I was aiming for a new start and a new me.

So far, I've gone unnoticed by avoiding the omega and alpha haunts and using blockers. Now that I've literally run into an alpha, my cover is blown.

His frown deepens as he examines my face more closely. Then he shakes himself from his thoughts and carefully rolls off me, jumping to his feet and holding out his hand.

Ignoring his help, I scrabble up onto my hands and knees and gather my scattered books back into a pile.

"I'm sorry for pulling you over," I say, as I brush myself down and shuffle past him, restarting my race up the stairs.

"Wait," he calls after me.

But even if I wanted to, I can't. I am definitely late now. My watch declaring the time as 3pm exactly and two more flights of stairs still to climb. "I'm sorry, I'm late."

I can hear him calling after me, but I keep running, not halting until I'm outside the professor's door.

I pause, my hand on the handle, and catch my breath. Then, with what I'm sure is a flushed and sweaty face, I slip into the room and find a seat at the back of the class. Professor Michael glares at me over the top of his half-moon glasses, but for once, he says nothing.

Perhaps that's because I reek of alpha.

Professor Michael is an alpha himself, bonded to an omega an eternity ago, but an alpha nonetheless. If I can smell the scent, then so can he.

In fact, as I sink low in my chair and subtly sniff my shirt, I realise I'm completely bathed in it.

Did that alpha do that deliberately?

I glare at the professor from the back of the room as he chalks up a particularly nasty equation on the blackboard. White dust sparks up into the air as he attacks the board, loud squeaks making the other students cringe.

He's probably delighted to smell an alpha all over me. He probably thinks that means I have a 'beau'. Someone who'll be bonding me and whisking me away from his class before the term is finished.

I won't be sorry to disappoint him. I'm here to stay, to finish this course and go on to bigger and better things. I'm not here to score some alpha, some tyrant who'll dictate my life for me while I pop out his kids. If I wanted that, I would've relented to my mum's demands and enrolled in one of the special omega colleges, the ones where they teach you how to be the perfect omega mate.

Not that I could ever be that.

Not that I want to either.

I let out a long sigh. The numbers and the symbols blend into one another and the professor's voice becomes one long hum. Bigger and better things – like a job at the International Space Agency – aren't going to happen if I can't understand these equations first.

I spin my pen around in my fingers and inhale, realising immediately what a mistake that is. The alpha's scent rushes up my nose, making the gland at the back of my neck tingle. I roll my shoulders, trying to dissolve the sensation. When I get back to my dorm room, I'm going to have to scrub myself from head to toe and burn these clothes.

Although I have to admit, the scent is intoxicating, like floating in a warm, scented bath of aphrodisiacs.

Which is precisely why I have to stay away from alphas.

It's too easy to be seduced.

Chapter 2

Have you ever had the feeling that someone is watching you? Like you can feel the weight of their stare upon your skin?

Your body senses it before your mind. You squirm in your seat, shift on your feet, your skin heats. You look up, but you realise you imagined it. No one is watching you. Everybody's gaze is fixed elsewhere. You go back to what you were doing, but that same sensation returns.

It's a familiar sensation for all unmated omegas. Someone, somewhere is always watching us.

Today is the fourth time I've sat studying in the library, certain I'm being watched. I roll my neck, my eyes sweeping the other desks, looking for whoever it is who's fascinated by me.

Back home, I was repeatedly catching people's attention, no matter how hard I tried to shrivel into the background. I was one of the few omegas in a town dominated by betas. Like the rest of the world. We omegas and alphas are a dying breed.

Here in Studworth – a city a million times bigger than my sleepy hometown – I hoped there'd be more of us. More chances to be lost in the crowd. My small frame isn't an obvious giveaway, but my scent is. Which is why I use blockers to try to disguise the aroma. A strategy that never worked at home. Everyone knew what I was. There was no hiding.

Usually, those whose attention I capture aren't so hell bent on disguising their interest. Typically, it's an alpha who has no problem striding over and making his intentions clear.

"Come with me, Omega. And I'll fucking rut your brains out."

Yeah, I've heard that plenty.

However, this time, my skin doesn't crawl in the way it usually does when I feel myself being watched. I sniff the air subtly, my attention fixed on the textbook in front of me. A hint of cinnamon flavouring the air. Something nice, interesting, but far too faint for me to get a real hold of it. Just a teasing taste.

I turn my page, running my finger down the neatly typed text, pretending to study the content. Then I flick my gaze up.

This time, I catch my observer red-eyed. For a fraction of a second, my eyes lock with a pair of emerald ones before they dart away.

Ha. I fucking caught him. Perhaps now the pervert will be ashamed enough to stop his staring. Except, almost immediately, his eyes return to mine, and he holds my gaze. A smile that dimples his cheeks spreads across his face, and it's my cheeks that flush as I drop my gaze back to my book.

It's him. The alpha I knocked off his feet two weeks ago. I haven't seen him since our encounter on the staircase, although I've thought of him. His scent. His emerald eyes.

I lean closer to my friend, Sophia, beside me.

"Don't look," I whisper, trying my best not to move my lips, "but who's that guy straight ahead, about two tables away?"

Sophia knows everyone, not just in our faculty, but across

the whole college and probably the city too. She also knows everything they are doing. I'm constantly amazed by the endless numbers of people who stop and say hi to her as we rush to lectures or head out to a nightclub. I suppose it's because, unlike my grubby, comprehensive background, Sophia went to the most exclusive private school in the country. The school is known to pump out Prime Ministers and billionaires. How we ended up friends, I'm still not sure. She took a shine to me on my first day here and placed me firmly beneath her wing.

Sophia ignores my instruction, and lifts her head to stare straight ahead.

"Why?" she asks me. I want to tug on her arm so that she stops staring, but Sophia doesn't understand the concept of subtlety. She doesn't need to. Rich betas can look where they like without ramifications.

"I just want to know," I hiss.

"Zane Amir. "

She turns to address me and I raise an eyebrow. Of course, I don't know who he is.

"Honestly, Rosie, sometimes I think you exist in this clueless bubble. How can you not know who he is? He's one of *The Crew*."

I stare at her blankly. Is that meant to mean something to me?

"The Crestmore Crew, the varsity rowing team. Please tell me you've heard of the boat race? The one held every summer between the top colleges? It's huge. The colleges invest loads in their teams, where winning is more important to them than their damn academics and research."

"Yes, I know about the boat race." Not that I've ever watched it on TV. Whereas no doubt Sophia spends every race on the

9

banks of the Thames, sipping expensive champagne. Rowing is one of those posh sports that only people with money can afford.

I shrug and drop my eyes back to my textbook. Members of the rowing team are treated like football players or pop stars in this college. Why one has taken up staring at me is anyone's guess.

Sophia nudges me with her shoulder. "Do you like him?"

I can hear the tease in her voice. She's been trying to set me up ever since we met. She seems obsessed with getting me laid, says I should live a little. But I don't need that distraction. This college is my ticket to brighter and better things. Men and sex are a distraction I can't afford. Not that I've had much luck with either.

"He's an alpha, you know," Sophia adds.

"Yes, I know," I say in a bored voice, scribbling in my notebook.

"And he's coming this way."

"What?!" My eyes jump up to find Zane strolling towards our desks. I let out a squeak of alarm and rearrange my book.

"Hi," he says as he reaches us, flashing us both with his charming smile.

"Hi Zane," Sophia pipes up, kicking me under the table. "How are things?"

"Alright, considering."

"Considering what?"

"Took a tumble on the staircase a few weeks ago."

My gaze leaps back up to him. He's staring right at me.

"Oh god," Sophia said, "did you hurt yourself?"

"A little bruised. I'm not sure about the other party."

"Other party?" Sophia repeats in confusion.

"Soph," Zane said, "who's this?" He gestures towards me and butterflies flutter in my stomach.

"This is Rosie." Sophia wraps an arm around me and squeezes. "Isn't she gorgeous?"

I groan.

But Zane doesn't respond to the question. His smile twitches and he simply says, "Nice to meet you, Rosie. And good to see you, Soph." Then he turns and walks away.

We both watch him go, and then Sophia pinches my arm. "What was all that about?"

"I have no idea."

"He was literally drooling all over you, and you could barely look at the guy. That's Zane Amir. I think his family owns most of London."

"I don't care, Sophia."

Sophia rests her elbow on the desk and leans her cheek against her palm. "How can you not care? The man is at least six foot five and he rows. Have you ever seen a rower's abs?"

"Still not interested, Sophia." Although, maybe I am, just a little.

"I wish I had your self-control."

"No, you don't." I pinch her back. "You don't even need to be here studying. This all comes naturally to you. You can afford to be out screwing around."

"You're a good influence on me. That's what my mum keeps saying. Try to be more like Rosie. Focused, dedicated."

"You make me sound so boring."

"You know what they say – all work and no play ... You could play with Zane."

"Soph!" I flip to the next page of my book. "Do you think you could explain this to me again?" I ask, pointing to an equation.

"I didn't understand it in lectures."

"Sure." She shuffles the book around and runs her eyes over the problem. "Zane Amir," she mutters to herself. I can hear the amazement in her voice and I have to confess I feel it too.

Chapter 3

My room in the halls of residence is the cheapest kind. It's barely bigger than a box with one window, one cupboard, one desk and one narrow single bed. It's painted the same beige they've used throughout the college, and the heater rumbles as it spews out warmish air.

It's why we spend most of our time hanging out at Sophia's. Hers is five times as big, with an actual bathroom, kitchenette and lounge.

We're there, curled up on her sofa, reading through our lecture notes for a test the next day, when there's a knock on her door.

We both look up.

Sophia shrugs at me as if to say she's not expecting anyone, hops up, and skips over to the door

A small man wearing jeans and a hoodie stands in the doorway. I don't recognise him, but of course Sophia does.

She squeals in delight and hugs the man in tight, dragging him into her room.

"Harrison!" she yelps. "I haven't seen you in ages. Not since last summer."

His eyes flick towards me and then he drops down onto the

sofa.

"How's it going Soph? You liking university?"

"Loving it. You? I haven't seen you around."

"Been training hard."

Sophia heads over to a cupboard in the corner and picks out some tumblers and a bottle of rum. She pours the dark liquid into each glass and passes them round.

"Rosie," she tells me, "this is Harrison. Our big brothers are, like, the best of friends. Harrison, this is Rosie. We're on the same course."

"Physics?"

We both nod and he whistles in a way that signals he's impressed.

"Nice to meet you," I say, taking the glass Soph offers me. The straight rum tickles my nose, but I take a little sip anyway.

Harrison lifts his glass. "To big brothers."

"May they always stay out of our business," Soph adds.

Harrison chuckles at that and takes a long gulp.

"So, to what do I owe this visit?" Soph asks him. "I mean, it's great to see you, but …"

"I'm here on an errand."

"Oh god. Not my brother checking up on me?"

"No, nothing to do with him. It's actually to do with Rosie."

"Me?" I gasp, looking at Sophia. She cocks her head.

"Rosie?"

"Yes, I heard she was likely to be here."

"Why do you want to see me?" I try to rack my memory. Have I met this guy somewhere before? I'm sure I never have.

"I have an invitation for you."

I gape at him.

"What? Who from?"

"*The Crew* wants to invite you to go to their house and hang out."

"*The Crew* is inviting Rosie to hang out?"

"At their pack house, yes."

"Oh my God!" Soph cries, clapping her hands together and bouncing up and down, making the springs of the sofa squeak. "Are they interested in her?"

"Seems she's caught their eye."

My gaze swings from my friend to this messenger. I'm confused. What does this mean? Why has a pack I've never heard of sent this guy around to ask me to hang out?

I stare at my friend in confusion.

"They want to fuck you, Rosie."

"They?" I swallow down bile rising in my throat. What is she talking about?

"*The Crew* is an alpha pack. Zane, who we met the other day in the library, he's one of them," Sophia says slowly.

"Zane, Duncan, Ollie and Seb," Harrison adds.

"Do you know what that means?" Sophia asks me.

"Yes," I snap. I've heard tales of some alphas choosing to live this way, forming strong lifelong bonds with other alphas and living together as a family unit. I've never come across one in reality, though.

"But why have they sent you?" I ask Harrison.

He smirks. "They're doing things the old fashion way, I guess. They know approaching an omega directly can put them in a difficult spot. It can be intimidating. They like to send me as a go-between to set things up."

"I'm not interested," I growl, and Harrison's eyes widen.

"Are you insane, Rosie? This pack is legendary. They are the hottest guys at this college. Think of the fun you could have."

Except it wouldn't be fun. Not when they work out they were wrong about me.

I frown at her and turn to Harrison. "You do this often?" I've been approached for sex before, but never through a third person.

"Yeah. They're good friends. I went to school with some of them." He chuckles. "You're the first one to turn an invitation down."

"Exactly! I'm not interested in being a toy to a bunch of alphas. Their plaything. I don't want to be chewed up and spat out."

Sophia giggles. "I'd love to be chewed up and spat out."

I scowl at her. "You know what I mean."

"At least think about it," she says.

"They're solid guys," Harrison adds. "And they're picky. They don't just ask any and every girl to hang out."

I shake my head. "Am I supposed to be flattered?"

"I think they're on the look at for an omega, for their pack."

"So they want a trial run, do they?"

Harrison chuckles again. "What'd you want me to tell them?"

"To go to Hell!" I snap.

Harrison simply nods and passes his half drunk rum to Sophia.

"I gotta go Soph, got practice, but let's go for a drink sometime soon."

"Sounds good." She follows him to the door. "Don't mind my friend. She can be a bit of a prude."

"I am not a prude," I call out.

"Tell Zane and the others I'd be happy to hang out."

"Unfortunately, he's not interested in betas like us." He

kisses her on the cheek.

"Were you two a thing?" I ask as the door closes.

"We've slept together a few times, but we never dated. Why? Do you think he's cute?"

"Soph!"

She flops back next to me on the sofa. "You just turned down *The Crew*! I can't believe you did that. Aren't you even a little bit curious?"

"You have no idea what alphas are like to omegas. You think they're these big hot dudes, but they're possessive and dangerous. I'm not interested in getting caught up with one – let alone four."

"Sometimes I think you're scared to have fun."

"I have fun!"

"When was the last time you had an orgasm that involved someone else?"

Does fantasising about someone else count? Because otherwise the answer is never. I'm not a virgin, but the guys I've been with have never made me come.

Maybe that's half the reason I stay away from alphas. The one and only alpha I've been with concluded there was something wrong with me.

Omegas are made for sex. Orgasming is meant to be as easy as breathing to us. But not for me. He couldn't make it happen.

"I'm happier this way," I tell her. "Honestly." And I am. I don't need the heartache of another alpha telling me how broken I am. I'm happy enough focusing on my studies and working hard.

Alphas are a whole heap of trouble I don't need.

"It's always been a fantasy of mine to be with two men at the same time," Soph says, swirling around her drink and gazing off into the distance.

"That sounds intense. And possibly damaging."

"Doesn't it?" she says with a smile.

I roll my eyes at her, but when I'm back in my room later that night, I google alpha packs. I find a video of an omega writhing between the bodies of two alphas. She looks trapped, helpless, completely powerless to their will, and I know I've made the right decision.

Chapter 4

After my message back to the pack, I think that'll be the end of things. After all, alphas don't like bratty omegas or rejection.

But I couldn't be more wrong. Two days later, Zane is there on the stairs waiting for me. Right where we collided.

"I said no," I tell him as he smiles at me brightly, those green eyes glinting and his cheeks dimpling.

"No?" He blinks at me in confusion. I guess he assumed Harrison had the message wrong. He's probably not used to being turned down. "Care to explain–"

"I don't have to give a reason."

"OK." He nods slowly as if he's trying to decode my words.

I snort and keep walking. "I'm not interested in *hanging out* with a pack of alphas."

His gaze flickers across my face, taking me in. "I'd like to take you on a date. Just us. If you're not interested in meeting my pack, that's fine."

I stop in my tracks and look at him. I didn't think that was how things worked in a pack. I thought relationships were interconnected. I can't help but think he's lying.

"No thanks."

I start climbing the stairs again and he follows me. His scent races up the stairs and into my nostrils, making me a little lightheaded.

"Not even one date? Jeez. You're a hard customer."

"It's not personal. I'm not interested in dating right now. Or anything else," I add quickly before he gets the wrong idea.

"Shame," he says with a hint of disappointment. I'm tempted to look back at his face, to glance at those deep green eyes, but I force myself to keep walking. "I've never met an omega who smelled as sweet as you."

I blush, hoping he doesn't see the colour in my cheeks and know how much that compliment pleases me. Try as I might, those omega instincts lurk inside me, regardless.

* * *

To my astonishment, he shows up at the museum's coffee shop next.

"Are you stalking me?" I ask him, frowning.

"Yes," he tells me.

"I could report you to the college administration."

He grins. We both know he's untouchable. Star of the rowing team. They'll turn a blind eye to just about anything he does. "If I order a latte, do you promise not to spit in it?"

"Maybe."

I turn away from him. Keeping my resolve, not falling for his charm, is easier with my back to him. His scent hangs like a temptation in the air. I scoop fresh coffee groundings into the machine, heating the milk with a hiss.

"I actually came to ask you something non-date related."

I rest a cup beneath the machine and let the coffee filter down.

"What?" I ask him.

"I hear you tutor maths."

I peer over my shoulder at him. "Yes." It's another way I make extra cash. I have a few kids from the local school who I teach, plus one or two college students too. "Why?" I ask him suspiciously.

"I'm looking for someone who can help me."

I pour the warmed milk into the cup and spoon foam across the surface. Then I sprinkle cocoa on top and hand it to him. His fingertips stroke against my knuckles as he takes the cup and I pretend not to notice. Pretend that the feel of his skin against mine doesn't set it tingling.

"What are you studying?" I ask him.

"Medicine."

He's going to be a doctor? Why does that make him a hundred times more attractive?

"Then why do you need a maths tutor?"

"We have a maths module coming up which I need to pass."

"I don't think I can help you."

"How much do you charge?"

"Ten pounds an hour."

"I'll pay you twenty, and I'll come to yours." He hands over his card to pay for his coffee. "I'm serious, Rosie. I can't afford to fail this module. And my maths is ..." He stares at me with a sad puppy-look in his eyes. My stomach flips and I can't say no. I can't let him fail medicine. Not when he's going to be a doctor and help people.

I know it's a bad idea, but the money and those eyes make it too difficult to resist. I press his card to the machine, letting it beep.

"OK. We can do a trial session." I shuffle on my feet. "I doubt

I'll be able to help."

"I know you will. How does tomorrow at seven sound?"

I nod my agreement. "But the library. Not my room."

"You're the tutor."

"I'm very strict," I tell him.

"I hope so. Can I have your number then?" He grins like he just won a point in a game and I roll my eyes. I reel it off and tell him to message me a sample test paper.

"See you tomorrow, Rosie," he says with a wink and I try to ignore the way my stomach swoops again.

* * *

To my surprise, he's already there in the library when I arrive on Tuesday evening. It's pretty empty. Tuesday night is half price at the nightclub in town and most college students will be heading there tonight.

It's eerily quiet and his scent particularly potent. I approach the desk cautiously. He looks up and smiles, his eyes darting with what looks like appreciation, down my form.

I shiver. I can't deny the effect he's having on me. Perhaps it was a bad idea to come here. But now I'm here, I don't want to go.

I pull out the chair beside him, scooting it back so there's no chance of us touching.

"Hi, sugar," he says.

"You call all your tutors sugar?"

"No comment," he laughs and I wonder how many tutors have succumbed to the charm of an alpha like Zane.

I wonder if I will be the next.

I wonder if that would really be such a bad thing.

It is. It won't work out between us. I'm a broken omega. In the end, he'll reject me.

I pull out the questions I've prepared from my bag and spread them on the desk. "I thought we'd start with these."

He drags his chair closer, the legs scraping against the floor.

"This one?" he asks, peering over my shoulder, his warm breath brushing against my cheek, leaving me to imagine how warm his lips would feel.

I daren't move. I don't want to pull away from him, but the temptation to lean towards him is tantalising.

He reaches around me and takes a hold of the paper, positioning it in front of him. His eyes dart across the rows of equations and I take the opportunity to study his face. He has a fine line of stubble across his chin today and I have an urge to brush my fingers across it.

"Hmmm," he says and I jolt. He doesn't meet my eye, but a smile flickers across his face as he picks up a pen and twists it around in his fingers.

"Do you need me to talk you through it?" I ask, my voice a little shaky.

He shakes his head, then begins to scribble on the page. I follow his answer.

"That's right," I say. "Do you—"

"Got anything harder?" He adjusts his chair and the outside of his bare arm brushes against mine, setting more tingles darting across my skin. For a moment, I remember how it felt to be trapped beneath the weight of his body. I swallow, twisting my hair from my face.

"Let me see." I flick through the pages of questions I'd prepared for this tutoring session. I'd expected to spend most of the hour on the first few pages. I didn't think he'd be able to answer the question that easily. Finally, I find something more challenging and once again he swivels it towards him. His leg jiggles under the table and I can feel the vibration of it through the library floorboards. Then he taps the pen against his mouth, forcing my gaze to rest on his plush lips, "I can talk you through how to–"

His pen meets the paper and he scribbles down the answer. I check my notes. It's correct. He flicks through the final questions until he reaches the last one and then studies it, making a few scribbles before showing me his answer. It's correct again.

Leaning back in his chair, he crosses his arms and grins at me.

"I don't think you need a maths tutor," I tell him.

"Nope, but thank you for helping with my confidence."

I shake my head, repressing a smile. "Bullshit. You know, I could have been helping someone who actually needs my help and earned some money."

"I'm going to pay you," he tells me.

I peer at my watch. Fifteen minutes have passed. "You owe me five pounds."

"I'll pay you for the entire hour."

I shake my head. I'm not a charity case.

He reaches into the pocket of his jeans and pulls out his wallet. Then, flicking it open, he finds a fiver and hands it to me. I try not to notice the big wad of notes in there. More money than I've ever held in my purse for sure.

I hold the note up to the light. "Just checking if it's real."

He laughs. "If it's not, I'm screwed."

"It is."

He leans forward and rests his elbows on his knees.

"So, seeing as you have the next forty-five minutes available, how about I take you on that date?"

"A forty-five minute date?"

"One drink? Or if you're a fast eater, I can buy you dinner."

I don't answer him. Instead, I collect up my things. He watches me silently.

I want to go for a drink with him. Despite his cocky attitude, I like him. He's warm and funny, and, yes, hot. Really hot. And he's going to be a doctor.

What harm could one drink do? Sophia's right. I am allowed to have fun.

When I've zipped up my bag, I glance over at him. "Forty minutes," I tell him. "And just a drink." I don't want him thinking he's won me over just yet.

I expect him to smirk in satisfaction but he nods and jumps to his feet, holding out his hand like he'd done on the staircase. I take it this time and he tugs me gently to my feet. The tips of his fingers and the pads on his palm are calloused. From the rowing, I guess.

Keeping a grip on my hand, he walks us out of the library and onto the street.

An early spring breeze rustles past us and the sky shines brightly with an almost-full moon. Earlier it rained, and small puddles litter the pavement, reflecting the silver light. Zane's hand is warm wrapped around mine and I'm stupidly glad he hasn't released it.

I should probably pull my hand away. I'm only encouraging him.

And this isn't going to go anywhere.

It's only one drink.

Chapter 5

To my surprise, Zane doesn't lead me into a noisy sports bar, but a quiet cafe decked out with an endless number of plants, their leaves trailing from pots on the walls and down towards the floor. Meditation music with soft bells and low notes plays out as well as the quiet hum of conversation from the few other customers in here.

He leads me to a booth near the back, sitting himself down on the bench opposite me.

"I thought we were going for a drink," I say. This doesn't look like the kind of place you can order a glass of wine.

"I had training today and I've got training first thing tomorrow. I've got to be careful what I have." He swivels the menu card around to me. "Know what you want?"

I run my eye down a long list of fruit and vegetable smoothies and my nose scrunches up.

"What?" he chuckles.

"It all sounds –"

"It's good for you."

"Broccoli smoothie is good for you?"

"Yep – as long as they don't add loads of extra sugar."

"Hmmm ..."

"Want me to choose something for you?"

"As long as it has no broccoli or carrots in it, yes."

He shakes his head and slides out of the booth, going to order at the counter.

I watch him chat with ease to the server, noting the way she looks up at him through her eyelashes and fiddles with her hair. I bet they know each other.

He smiles at me when he returns and my stomach does that uncontrollable flipping thing. It's like magic. Like a magic switch. He smiles at me, my stomach responds. How is that possible?

"How often do you train?" I ask him when he's back into his seat.

"Every day."

"Every day? You don't get a day off?"

He cocks his head and examines me. "You know it's really competitive, right? If I'm not prepared to train every day, there'll be someone else who is."

I chew the inside of my cheek. Everybody else knows this stuff. But everyone else comes from a different world.

"Do you like it? The rowing, I mean?"

"Mostly," he chuckles, "Sometimes I fucking hate it. It can be brutal out there on the river in winter. But this time of year, it's really beautiful down there. You been out on the river?" I shake my head. "You never gave rowing a go? I thought everyone at least tried it in their Freshers' week."

"Not me."

"I'll take you."

The waitress arrives with two large glasses filled to the brim with a pink, thick liquid, so I'm saved from responding.

Zane slides mine towards me. I give it a cautious sniff.

"I promise it's not going to kill you."

27

"It might give me indigestion for a week!"

He laughs. "Try it, Omega."

My eyes leap to him at the sound of that name. He must see the shock on my face because he lifts a palm.

"I'm sorry, it just slipped out. It's kind of hard to be around you and not be thinking about the fact you're an omega. You smell so sweet."

My cheeks burn furiously, and I dip my head and take a long gulp of the cold drink. Strawberries dominate the flavour and I lick some from my bottom lip.

"I use blockers," I tell him. In fact, I've taken a whole fuck load before coming to meet him tonight.

He shrugs. "I've gotten good at picking up scents beneath blockers. It's both a blessing and a curse," he chuckles.

The waitress arrives again, balancing a tray by her shoulder, and starts to place dishes in the space between us on the tabletop.

"This was meant to be one drink," I tell him, quirking my eyebrow.

"I'm sorry, I'm starving and the food here is amazing."

I stare down at the dishes, a combination of breads and vegetables and dips. The aroma reaches my nose and my stomach grumbles.

He tears a piece of bread between his fingers and plunges it into the wet-looking puree. "Try this one." I can't resist. I haven't eaten dinner yet and my stomach rumbles again at the thought. Zane grins. "Are you hungry or growling at me?"

"Hungry," I admit.

He smothers the other half of the bread in the dip and lifts it to my mouth. "Try it."

The smile fades from his face and his eyes are locked on my

mouth. I suddenly feel hot. I should push his hand away and make a joke. This can't go anywhere. It'll only end in disaster. But I want him to place the food in my mouth. His eyes are intense. I can't drag my own gaze away from his face. I open my lips and carefully he slides the flatbread between them. His thumb brushing the wet side of my mouth. My stomach swoops and I'm sure my eyelids flutter.

We're frozen like that, the bread resting in my mouth, his fingers touching my lips, and my pulse starts to drum in my throat.

"Eat it, Omega," he whispers and I obey, closing my mouth. For a fleeting second, I capture his thumb between my lips, and then I chew, the flavour savoury in contrast to the fruity drink and strongly infused with garlic. "Good, right?"

I swallow and nod. Then, quickly, I grab a handful of what look like vegetable fritters.

He takes one too, snapping it in half between his sharp alpha teeth. "Where are you from?" he asks me.

"A little town just outside Manchester. Can't you tell by my accent?"

"I had an inkling. I like your accent. It's cute."

I ignore the compliment. "How about you?"

"London. My parents are both bankers so it's the only place to be unless you're gonna live in New York or something." He takes a long draw on his straw. "And what do you do for fun, Rosie?"

"Fun?" I crinkle up my nose. I've been working so hard to keep up with my course, there hasn't been a huge amount of time for fun. "I guess I hang out with Sophia. And back home I used to hang out with my sisters."

"Sisters?" he says, emphasising the plural.

"Yeah, there's five of us. I'm the oldest."

"Sounds intense."

"No more than four alphas living together, I'm sure."

He smiles. "Yeah."

I lean back in my seat and chew on the fritter as I look at him. He's wearing a casual Ralph Lauren shirt with the sleeves rolled up, jeans, and trainers. I'm sure his outfit costs more than my rent.

"What?" he asks me, jerking his chin in my direction.

"Just trying to figure you out."

He peers down at his watch. "Well, you've got five minutes. Then my time is up."

Wiping grease from my fingers, I take a long gulp of my drink and then I slide out of the booth. "That was incredibly yummy. Thanks."

He hurries to stand up. "You're seriously leaving?" Amusement dances in his eyes.

"I've got somewhere else to be."

"You going to let me take you on a date again?"

The waitress is watching us from the counter. Her mouth rotates as she chews gum and a blue light from a phone shines from beneath her, lighting up the underside of her chin.

"I don't know." It's the truth. I don't. I should thank him and then keep the hell away from him. But every time he touches my skin – just those accidental brushes – he flicks a match against flint and fire rushes across me.

It's as if my body lies dormant, waiting to be stirred into life by his touch.

"I can work with that," he says nodding. "I have to warn you, I'm pretty persistent. When there's something I want, I usually get it."

That heat crawls up my neck and bleeds into my cheeks. "We'll see," I say, but I have a premonition he will be proven right.

* * *

He messages me later that night wanting to know that I'm home safely, and then he's there waiting at the foot of my stairs in the morning.

"I thought I'd walk you to lectures," he says simply, taking my rucksack from my shoulder and slinging it over his own.

One of the other girls on my floor pushes through us, her eyes widening when they lock on Zane.

"Don't you have a lecture of your own to get to?"

"Not until later this morning."

"And how did you know I had a lecture now?" I start to walk, and he strolls easily alongside me.

"I asked around. I've never been to the Physics block. I'm curious."

"It's more exciting than it sounds."

I find the elastic in my hair and untwine it, letting my hair shake loose about my shoulders. It's practical to have it tied back but it makes my face look longer and for some reason I care about how I look right now with him.

The pavement is busy with other students, some walking in small groups or in pairs, others alone. As Sophia lives outside the college's accommodation, I tend to meet her in the lecture hall, which means I'm usually one of the ones walking alone. It's strange to have someone by my side, his hand finding the small of my back several times as he moves to the side, letting other students pass us on the path.

The roads are busy too, so I can't smell Zane's scent over the traffic fumes, although his palm when it touches me is warm even through the light cotton of my shirt. I want it to stay there. I want it to slip beneath the fabric and touch my actual flesh.

What is wrong with me?

"This is really stupid," I tell him. "We're not living in the fifties. I can carry my own bag." I attempt to wrestle it off his shoulder. But he snatches my hand away and grips it in his own. He smirks at me as if he just won a prize because now we're walking hand in hand.

"I didn't take you for a holding-a-girl's-hand kind of guy," I mutter when I fail at yanking my hand from his.

"I have no idea what that means."

"Never mind." Although, I like it. I like the sensation of his hand wrapped around mine.

"I'm trying to win you over."

"Win me over to what?"

"The idea of going on another date with me."

"If I said no, would you honestly respect that and leave me alone?"

He stops and with my hand still in his, I halt too. Someone swears at us from behind, then swerves around Zane.

I look up into the alpha's face. It's serious but not stern. There's a kindness to the set of his mouth and his eyes.

"You haven't told me no." I told his pack's go-between no, but he seems to have forgotten that. "Do you want me to leave you alone, Rosie?"

I notice he doesn't call me omega. He knows it would be unfair when he's asking me a question like this.

My eyes fall to his chest, where the letters of the Crestmore rowing team stretch across his shirt.

"No," I confess. "But I'm not sure about this either."

"We can take this slowly."

I snort. Since when have an omega and an alpha ever been able to take things slow. The urge to fuck, to knot, to breed, is too damn strong.

He squeezes my hand and my gaze drops lower to where his fingers wrap around my smaller ones.

"Agree to another date and I promise I'll be good until then. I won't disturb you." His weight shifts from one foot to another. "It has to be a proper date this time. At least two hours."

I can't help laughing and my eyes are drawn back to his face. The sight of him hits me afresh. He's so good-looking it's almost blinding.

Slowly. We can take things slowly. I can do that. Enjoy his company for a bit before he discovers the truth.

"Fine." I tell him. "That sounds doable."

"Thursday night. Eight o'clock. I'll pick you up."

"OK."

He licks his tongue along his bottom lip and then swings my bag off his shoulder and thrusts it into my chest.

"What?" I say, grabbing it quickly before it slips to the ground.

"I'm staying out of your way," he tells me, spinning on his toes. "Like you said. I'll see you Thursday, Rosie."

I'm speechless. I watch him disappear into the sea of people.

Thursday. I'm already wishing the days away.

Chapter 6

Sophia lies out on my bed, propped up on her elbows and watching me as I fling tops from my drawer and on to the floor.

"I thought this date was no big deal," she says in an amused tone that irritates me.

"It isn't. I'm not sure you could even call it a date."

"Did he call it a date?"

"Yes," I mumble.

"Then it's a date."

I hit the bottom of the drawer and swear. Where the fuck is it?

"And so what exactly are you doing?"

"Looking for my halter top."

"Oh!" Sophia says and when I throw my head around to glare at her, she's repressing a smile.

"What?"

"It's just if this date is no big deal, why are you searching for that top?"

I stick my tongue out at her. The top is the nicest thing I own and always earns me compliments. So what if it's the thing I want to wear tonight? So what if I want Zane to admire me in it?

I'm trying my best not to untangle the thoughts in my head, to ignore the nagging voice in my ear that keeps asking what the hell I'm doing, to play down the butterflies fluttering in my stomach.

It's just a date. It doesn't mean anything. If anything, it'll be good. He'll realise I'm not an omega worth pursuing and I'll realise he's one of the stuck up boys who think too much of themselves. Certainly, not a guy who should have triggered these damn butterflies.

I move on to my wash basket, cursing as I fling more clothes onto the floor in a bid to dig right down to the bottom.

"You're not actually going to wear it if it is dirty, are you?"

"No, I'm ruling it out." I scoop the pile of clothes back in the basket with an angry huff.

"Wardrobe?" Sophia slides off the bed and walks to my cupboard flinging open the doors and sorting through the hanging articles. I wish she wouldn't. My wardrobe is about a quarter the size of hers and the items in there are mostly treasures I discovered in second-hand stores or charity shops. There's a slight musty smell to it that I've tried my best to remove with fabric softener and potpourri.

Sophia doesn't seem to notice. She stops at a summer dress, blue, with spaghetti straps and a slight flare to the skirt.

"How about this?" she suggests. "You'd look amazing in this, Rosie. And it's flirty but not too dressy."

I take it from her hands and hold it up. "I don't know." It would reveal an awful lot of skin. The alpha already makes me feel exposed when I'm with him. I'd feel practically naked in this.

"Trust me. I am an expert at dates. I've been on hundreds."

"Doesn't that make you the opposite of an expert?"

She bumps me with her shoulder. "I like to keep my options open." She pauses. "You should too. Zane is hot and rich and a sports star and he's going to be a doctor. Fucking hell, Rosie! But you don't have to plump for the first alpha that comes sniffing around."

"Who said I am?" I may not be as experienced as Sophia when it comes to men and dating but that's from choice. And nothing more. I've not wanted to date. And no one has tempted me into changing my mind.

Not until Zane.

"Sorry, I'm not trying to be rude or anything. I'm just saying, you're gorgeous, Rosie, and intelligent. You can have any guy you want, if you want."

I laugh. "I'm not sure that's exactly true, but thanks."

"It is true. Wear the dress. I promise you'll have him walking funny all night."

I give her a big push and she falls back onto the bed, laughing.

"*I* may be the one having to deal with issues like that," I confess. "He makes me feel things ..."

Sophia stops laughing and lifts her head to stare at me. "Oh shit, this is serious. What sort of things?"

"Like my whole body might catch on fire when he looks at me."

"Wow," Sophia says, flopping her head back against the mattress as I pull off my denim shorts. "I'm not sure I can help you. I've never met a guy who does that to me."

"You've dated plenty of hot guys before, though."

"Yeah, and girls," she reminds me, "and they turn me on. But I've never experienced anything like that."

"Shit," I mutter, working the blue dress over my head.

"You have to call me straight after this date. I want to hear about every single detail."

"I doubt I'll have anything to tell. I'm sure he's going to realise I'm not his kind of girl."

Sophia throws a cushion at me. "Bullshit!" I chuck the cushion back at her and find my brush, dragging its teeth through my wavy hair. "No one who looks at you with that much heat is going to lose interest that quickly ... Maybe when he gets to know you and learns about what a giant geek you are, he'll have second thoughts."

"Oh god," I moan, burying my face in my hands.

"I'm joking," she laughs, before jumping from the bed and taking the brush from my hand. "Want me to do your hair?"

Gently, she untangles my hair. "So, how about the pack? Is that invitation still open?"

"I told him I'm not interested in a pack and he said that was fine. I guess he can date outside the pack or something if he wants."

"Hum," Soph says, gripping the brush between her knees and dividing my hair into sections. "I don't think things work like that with a pack."

* * *

I guess Sophia is right about the dress, because when I meet him at the bottom of the stairs, Zane's eyes do a long sweep of my body from my toes to the top of my head, and for a moment I feel like I'm drowning in his gaze as he soaks up every millimetre of me.

"Duncan, I gotta go," he says into the phone by his ear, ending the call and pocketing the device.

"Hi," I croak out, trying not to gulp down that scent of his, which seems even more intense tonight.

His eyes meet mine. They are dark and already my skin tingles as if responding to some unseen power they possess.

"Fuck, Rosie," he grumbles, shaking his head.

"What?" I ask, frowning.

"I have a suspicion you're going to want me to behave on this date and then you come out looking like this. I'm not sure if I'll be able to keep my hands off you."

My frown grows deeper. I don't think I want him to behave. I think I want to find out what not behaving looks like.

But I don't say anything. I stand there, meeting his gaze.

He takes a cautious step towards me, as if testing the waters, and then another.

He takes my hand, squeezing his hot fingers around my palm and bends to whisper in my ear. His scent engulfs me, strong and virile. "My chat is going to go to shit on this date. All I'm going to be able to think about is taking this dress off."

"What happened to taking things slow?"

He leans back and the heat seems to die in his pupils. "You're right, I'm sorry." He blows out a hiss of air, his cheeks expanding, then flattening. "Shit. I'm sorry." Collecting himself, he shakes his head ever so slightly, and then, avoiding my eye, leads me from the hall of residence.

"I warn you now," he says, his pace fast so that he's a stride in front of me, tugging me along, "I'm planning to completely woo you. You're going to agree to lots more dates after this one."

I understand what he means when we reach the restaurant he's booked. It's one of the most expensive in the city, with a walled garden at the back full of the delicate white flowers of jasmine and the accompanying floral aroma. Water trickles from a fountain in the middle of the garden and fairy lights twinkle in among the vines that crawl up the ancient walls.

It's magical. A place where fairies and elves should dine, not mere human beings like us.

I catch glimpses of eye-watering prices as menus are whipped away from me, and Zane orders our food and wine.

"I don't get to choose?" I ask.

"Not tonight."

"I like choice. I like options."

"Good to know." A smile hovers on his lips.

"I've never been somewhere like this before."

"Also good to know." He leans across the table. One lone candle flickers between us and he pushes it to one side. "If I'm honest, I have this deep urge to spoil you. If I'm really honest, I've had this urge ever since you ran into me. I want to spoil you and make you feel good."

My cheeks heat but I don't think he can see in the dim light.

"I don't know what to say."

"Tell me the truth, exactly what you're thinking."

"Exactly?"

"Yes." He reaches across and brushes his knuckles across my cheekbone. "I've been living in my pack for nearly two years now. One thing you learn quickly is the need to be up front and honest. You can't keep secrets. You can't assume everyone knows how you're feeling. You have to tell them."

"It sounds complicated."

"It's not. I love my brothers, and they love me too. Our bond is unbreakable. There is nothing simpler."

I nod, although I don't understand. I've heard of alpha packs but I've never met one before. They are rare. And the dynamics involved with that many people have always sounded complex.

"So tell me what you're thinking."

"I'm thinking that I don't know what I think of that," I laugh.

"Explain," he tells me.

I run my fingers through my hair, trying to make sense of my own feelings. "My parents love me, although my mum can be … overbearing. I don't want to give the wrong impression about them, they've made sacrifices for me. But I've never exactly been spoiled. I had to earn my keep and work hard in my family. And, I guess, I'm not sure if being spoiled would be utterly fantastic or completely cringeworthy and uncomfortable!"

"There's only one way to find out." I bite my lip. "If you'll let me."

My gland tingles in my neck and his fingertips have brandished my cheek. I close my eyes and let the air from my lungs escape. When I open my eyelids again I find myself staring straight into those bottomless eyes. I know he's snaring me in, carefully, slowly, winding in the line. I'm caught.

The waiter arrives with a bottle of red but Zane waves him away and pours the burgundy liquid into my glass. It sloshes against the sides before settling in the bottom. Pinching the stem between my finger and thumb, I lift the wine to my nose and sniff. The bouquet is rich and fruity and much heavier than anything I'd usually drink.

"Trust me," he says, noting my hesitancy, "once you've tried good red wine, you'll never want to drink anything else."

I wonder how he knows that, then remember the banker parents.

He watches as I lift my glass to my lips and tip, letting the liquid run into my mouth. The taste is strong and I blink as it dissolves onto my tongue.

"Good?" he asks.

"Hmmm," I admit. "What did you order us to go with it?"

"Steak."

"Steak?" I splutter. "How do you know I'm not vegetarian? You never asked."

"Are you?"

"No, but I could've been."

"The steak here is the best. And I rowed for two hours today. I'm allowed the fatty protein."

His phone beeps then and he tugs it from his pocket, and reads the messages across the screen before typing a reply, his thumb moving rapidly.

"Do you always message other girls on a date?"

He grins although his eyes remain on the screen. "It's my pack. There are a few things we have to sort out about training tomorrow." He lowers his phone. "But here, you have my full attention."

The food arrives almost immediately, and I have to admit, he's right. The steak is divine, especially complimented with the wine. I've never eaten anything quite like it, certainly not this good. Even hanging out with Sophia I've never eaten so well.

He eats much faster than me, explaining he's always famished after training. When he's finished, he sits back, sipping his wine and observing me eat. I cut the steak into tiny pieces. Taking my time, wanting to make it last, both the amazing taste of the food and this moment with him.

"You eat like a rabbit," he says.

"A carnivorous rabbit."

"Should I just have ordered you a carrot to nibble?"

"No, this was ..." I close my eyes and swoon, and satisfaction passes over his face. "Are we allowed dessert?" I pat the

41

napkin against my lips. "Or will it interfere with training?"

"What do you want? Let me guess, something with chocolate."

"No," I shake my head, smiling at him and causing a smile of his own to blossom across his face.

"What then?"

"Something lemony?"

"Lemony?"

"Yes. I like a little sour with my sweet."

He orders me a lemon cheesecake and laughs as I moan and groan my way through the dessert. It's the most beautiful piece of food I've ever seen. More art than pudding, with tiny curls of white chocolate, sprigs of mint and swirls of raspberry puree. The cheesecake itself melts in my mouth, and I don't think I've ever eaten anything as good.

"Do you use food to seduce all your women?" I ask him as I pull the spoon from my mouth, sucking every last miniscule of the cheesecake from it.

He leans forward. "I'm not big into seducing women."

I guess he doesn't usually have to bother. Is that why he's been so determined to pursue me? I'm probably a rarity. An omega who's turned his pack down.

He examines my creased brow. "What?"

"Nothing."

"Tell me." He grabs my cheesecake and pulls it to his side of the table. "Or no more."

"That's just mean!"

"But effective. Out with it."

"I like you, Zane," I say, giving him the honesty he wants. "But I'm not sure about this. If I trust it." I hesitate. "If I trust you."

His eyes widen as if he can't quite believe my words.

"Why don't you trust me?"

"Hmmm, apart from the fact you just stole my desert." I capture the plate between my fingers and drag it back in front of me, taking another large forkful before he can steal it again.

"Seems a minor crime."

"Uh uh. This is the best cheesecake I've ever eaten. Stealing it is a very big crime."

"What else?" he asks, jerking his chin in my direction. "What else don't you trust?"

I meet his gaze and hold it. "Your intentions."

He laughs. "You have me there, Omega. My intentions are not pure at all."

"But why me?" I blurt out, unable to keep my curiosity at bay.

"Why not?"

I plunge my fork into the lemon cream and sink it right down to the base before snapping a piece off. "Is it because I turned you down?"

I lift the piece to my mouth and my gaze back up to him at the same time.

He leans closer, capturing my hand and swivelling the fork around to meet his waiting mouth. He clamps his lips around the fork and that heat swims low in my belly as I slide the implement from his mouth.

"Partly," he says once he's swallowed. "That is part of the appeal. But there's a lot more to my attraction to you, Omega."

I manage a stiff nod. "And what about your pack? I'm not interested in being part of a pack and can you really date me in that case?"

"It's early days." His eyes sparkle with amusement. "I'm

not asking you to marry me. Let's just see where this goes, huh?"

"I can do that." In fact, it sounds perfect to me. Nothing serious. Just two people enjoying each other's company.

One lone piece of cheesecake remains on my plate. I scoop it up and now the plate is empty. The meal is over.

I'm not sure what comes next. But my body is needy to find out.

I feel a little light-headed from the wine and his scent and the nerves cascading through my blood. The next few minutes seem to pass in a blur. The dishes are cleared away. I try to pay my half and Zane refuses. We walk through the courtyard. And then we're out on the dark, empty street.

I stare at him, an arm's length away. He stares back at me.

I think I'm floating.

"I'm going to kiss you," he tells me, taking a step towards me. I take a step away.

I don't know what I'm doing. I don't know what I want.

Except I do.

I want him.

Every fibre of my body screams with need for him.

He keeps coming, and I force myself to halt, to let myself go, to be overwhelmed, engulfed, smothered by him.

And in the next moment, his hand grips my waist, and the other slides into my hair, and he's bending down, his breath rustling against my face before his warm lips meet mine.

My heart pounds in my chest.

My gland sears in my neck.

My body aches to be touched.

His mouth slides against mine and I lose myself completely.

44

Chapter 7

He keeps his word. We take things slow. Only a kiss that first night.

But it's enough to leave me burning in my room alone that night. Did I make the right decision? Should I have invited him in, let him have me, extinguished any flames before they took hold?

Instead, I'm alone and frustrated. I don't feel this way often. I'm too busy with my studies and my work, and I'm pretty efficient at smothering those omega longings. The longing to be kissed, to be held, to be touched, to be ravished.

I think of his kiss now, tracing my slightly swollen lips with the tip of my finger, reliving the feel of his mouth against mine, of his strong arms encasing me, of his cinnamon scent and the thud of his heart.

I remember how his knuckles skimmed down the outside of my arm, and I mimic the action with my own hand, closing my eyes and remembering everything.

A pulse beats between my legs. What would it have felt like if his hand had strayed lower, to my thigh, to the waistband of my knickers, to where I'm wet and throbbing now?

I touch myself there, believing they are his fingers parting my folds and finding my clit, caressing it lightly and circling it with care. My skin flushes and I sigh.

I've never fantasised about a real alpha before. The men in my head have always been fictional. But now I make myself come with Zane in my head; his deep green eyes, his warm breath, and his gravelly voice in my ear. "*Sweetheart*," he groans as I buck against my own fingers, plunging them inside myself, wondering what it would feel like to take him.

When the aftershocks fade and I lie sweaty on my tiny bed, I stare up at the ceiling, at the crack running from one corner to the next.

This is dangerous. Am I already in too deep?

* * *

I can't stop thinking about him, but when he doesn't call the next day, I wonder if perhaps he isn't as into me as I thought.

Sophia rolls her eyes and reminds me of the first rule of dating. "Never call the next day." She examines my face. "Did you agree to a second date?"

My stomach falls. "No, we never discussed it."

"But he said other encouraging stuff ..."

"He said he wanted to spoil me."

Sophia smiles. "He'll call."

"Couldn't I just call him?"

She considers this idea. "Fuck it, if you like him, why not. Show him you're not some meek omega. That you know what you want."

"I'm not sure if I know what I want," I mutter.

"One way to find out." Sophia points to my phone and I type Zane a message, thanking him for the date and hinting that I'd like another. I receive a reply almost immediately, and we arrange to meet up in the centre of the city early next week.

I spend the next few days in a skittish, flustered state. A typical bloody omega. Rather than the sensible woman I want to be, tackling difficult mathematical equations and impressing my professors with well-thought-out answers, I'm doodling Zane's name on my notebook and reliving his kiss over and over. I feel fifteen, not twenty.

It's just because it's new and exciting. This insanity will pass. And so will this fling.

The date destination is a surprise. I wait for him outside Highnam's department store wearing a black tea dress with pink rosebuds that Sophia lent me. I'm a few minutes early, and I chew my thumbnail as I scan the people heading home at the end of the day.

Finally, I spot Zane sprinting through the crowd, swerving past people. He spots me, waves and runs towards me. When he stops, he's not even winded, but his dark hair has flopped into his face.

"Sorry," he says, brushing it back. "We had a pack meeting that overran." His eyes flit all over me. "You look beautiful, Rosie." Then he kisses my cheek and takes my hand.

"A pack meeting?" I say as we walk along the pavement. "That sounds very official."

He chuckles. "It is a bit anal but Seb insists on it, says there are some things we have to discuss and work through. I suppose he's right. Four alphas living together can become complicated."

I'm curious about his pack and how it works. There are so few packs and the relationships seem different in each. "Does your pack know you're taking me on another date?"

"Yep."

"And that's not a problem?" Do they feel aggrieved I turned down the group offer, but am now seeing one of the pack mates?

Zane turns to look at me. "Why would they care?"

"You're allowed to date people outside the pack?"

"Yes," he says, looking a little puzzled. "We can make our own decisions, although obviously, we consult one another. I suppose if any of my pack mates really objected to a girl, I'd end the relationship, but I can't see anything like that happening."

He squeezes my hand, and I notice his scent seems especially strong in the chilly spring evening.

"Where are we going?"

"Ahhh," he says, "be patient, we're almost there."

Are we going to one of the nightclubs in the city centre? There are a few exclusive ones frequented by alphas. I bet someone like Zane can get in easily. I look down at my cute dress. Perhaps I should've gone for something more sophisticated.

But then he's leading us away from the shops and restaurants and into a side street lined with cherry trees, heavy pink blossoms weighing down the branches. We pass through a square and stop outside an unfamiliar building. I read the sign. *Studworth City Aquarium.*

I peer back at Zane quizzically.

"It's open late and they serve drinks," he explains, winking and tugging me through the heavy doors.

Inside, he buys us tickets and a glass of wine each. Then, still holding my hand, he walks me into the aquarium.

Walls of glass line a long passageway, and the light sparkles a deep blue. Beyond the glass tropical fish of all shapes and sizes, colours and patterns, glide through the water. When I look up,

I see the water extends over our heads as well, surrounding us completely as if we really are swimming deep under the ocean.

"It's beautiful," I whisper.

"Yeah, and peaceful. I find it a good place to unwind."

"You have trouble unwinding?"

"Sometimes medicine can be tough. The things you see ..."

I nod, stroking my thumb over the back of his hand.

I never understood the appeal of holding hands. But now I do. This innocent touch is electric.

A stingray drifts above us and we watch, its spindly tail dragging through the water.

"I've never travelled outside the UK," I admit. "I'd love to go snorkelling."

"My family has a boat that's moored in Greece. The snorkelling there is incredible."

I take a sip of my wine. How many houses, boats, and cars does his family own?

A shoal of fish darts around us, and we pause, Zane coming to stand behind me and resting his hands on my waist. He nuzzles into my neck, and I lean my head to one side, allowing him the full slope of my throat.

He takes a deep inhale of my scent, and my gland tingles with the proximity of his mouth. I have a sudden urge to ask him to kiss it. But it's intimate. Too soon. And people are milling around us.

"I've been thinking about you," he whispers into my ear as bright yellow fish soar around us.

"I've been thinking about you too."

"Good things, I hope," he chuckles. "Or are you still having doubts?"

I think I will always have doubts. It took numerous battles

and going against my mum's wishes to get to Crewmore College. I don't want to throw it away. Especially when this could end as quickly as it's started once he learns the truth about me.

"I just want to take things slow," I answer.

I am a coward. What I really want is for him to press me up against this glass and kiss me hard, to touch me. But then what? He'll discover the truth. And so I'm going to prolong the inevitable.

"Rosie, can I ask you something personal?" I nod my head, suddenly nervous. Has he worked it out? Is there something about my scent? "Are you a virgin?"

"No."

"Did something happen to you then?"

"No," I say, squirming slightly in his arms.

"But your experiences haven't been great?" I don't answer, and he kisses the tender skin under my ear. "A lot of men are shit in bed."

I laugh, the tension bubbling out of my throat. "And how would you know that?"

"Experience"

I snap my head towards him, peering at his face. In the dark, his features are hidden, but I think he's serious. "You've slept with other men?"

"Yes." His hand strokes my hip bone.

"As an experimental thing ..."

"I'm bi, Rosie."

"Oh," I say.

We're both silent, and then he asks, "That isn't a problem, is it?"

"No." Then a thought occurs to me. "Are you sleeping with

any of your pack mates?" I still don't understand how their pack works, if it's all brotherly love or something more.

"Yes," he says without hesitation.

"Who?"

"Duncan. "

"Only Duncan?"

"Yes."

"Does he mind you seeing me?"

"No. He's pleased for me, pleased I've found an omega. That's how our pack works. If Duncan wasn't happy with our relationship, I'd quit it." He tickles my lower back. "Are you OK with it?"

Do I have any cause not to be? This is only our second date. And I knew I was seeing a pack alpha. There was always a possibility he was sleeping with some of his pack mates.

"I don't think so. But I don't know. Two weeks ago, I didn't even want to consider dating. Now I'm dating someone who already has a boyfriend ..." I nibble my bottom lip. "And sometimes you invite girls around to hang out with *all* of you?"

"Yes, that's also how our pack works. We enjoy sleeping with the same omega." His fingers curl around my waist. "Is that something you think you'd be interested in, Rosie? I mean, if only for your heat." He buries his nose in my hair. "I bet you smell amazing in heat."

I freeze.

Heat.

With an alpha, it always comes down to the heat. Always. Always there at the front of their mind.

I lean my head away from him and twist around in his arms to meet his gaze.

A pack is the last thing I want. A bunch of alphas trying to

51

control and constrain me. No thanks.

And, anyway, I couldn't handle the stigma and the prejudice associated with being a pack's omega. Don't I already face enough of that as it is?

I have my dream. The one I tattooed on my wrist so I won't ever forget. I don't need more hurdles in my way.

Reach for the stars, Rosie. Don't let anyone hold you down.

"One alpha is more than enough for me," I tell him.

Chapter 8

He takes me on another date, and another, and he seems to know not to push me. As much as my body craves his touch, I'm still flittish. We both know if he pushes me too quickly, I'll bolt.

I'm not ready to be someone's girlfriend. Or an alpha's omega.

Yet, this slow pace only seems to fan the flames between us. Every time he kisses me it's with more passion, more urgency, more heat. It's addictive. I want to be with him more and more. I'm becoming dependent.

A week passes and then another. And then he wants to show me the river. To take me out on a boat.

We walk from the centre of the city and, as we reach the outskirts, he tells me he needs to swing by his house to pick something up. I'm hesitant. We've only ever met on neutral territory. He's never come to my place, and I've never been to his. Stepping into his lair feels like another step forward in our relationship, nearing the point when he'll learn the truth and reject me.

"Just for a moment," he says, picking up on my uncertainty. "I need the key for the boathouse. You can wait in the hallway." He grins at me. I know he's humouring me, that I'm being absurd. A fussy, scared little omega.

"It's fine," I try to say in a breezy voice. "I'd like to see your house."

It's huge. A four-storey townhouse with a wide, polished door and a black-painted railing. I swing my head back to look up to the roof where a further set of windows nest among the tiles and two neat chimneys frame the building.

"Shit," I mutter. No student deserves to live in a place like this. "How can you afford—"

"My parents own it."

"Right," I say. The bankers.

The hallway is just as grand as the facade, with checked black-and-white tiles running over the floor and an old mirror resting against the wall. But it's clear four young men live here and not some posh family. Dirty pairs of trainers are littered along the wall, a kit bag with its contents spilling out rests at the bottom of the stairs, and the paintwork is scuffed.

He leads me along the hallway and I hear the heavy door slam behind us as the scents in the house creep into my nose. It smells masculine, like sweat and testosterone and something tangy underneath. I recognise Zane's scent but intermingled with the other three strong alpha scents.

Usually, smelling so many alpha scents together would be toe curling. The scents would curdle together, making the air rancid. But not these four. They compliment each other, combining to form something irresistible. My gland comes alive in my neck, scorching fiercely.

My hand feels hot in Zane's, and I want to turn around and walk straight out. Away from these scents into the fresh air. But Zane grips it and pulls me along. We're halfway down the hallway when the door at the end flings back and a man comes bounding through.

He stops when he sees us, and his gaze flicks between me and Zane.

"Hey," he says simply, stopping where he stands. He's smaller than Zane, but only by an inch, and he's just as broad. Unlike Zane's thick crop of black hair, his brown hair is shaven close to his skull, and his skin is lighter, a scattering of pale freckles running over the bridge of his nose and onto his cheekbones.

"Hey, Duncan." Zane tugs me forward, resting his other hand on the man's shoulder. "Rosie, this is my pack and crew mate, Duncan." Zane tilts his head in my direction. "Duncan, this is Rosie."

Duncan nods, his eyes not leaving my face, and I can feel the heat crawling up my neck. I search for resentment in his face, for jealousy, but I find none. Only curiosity.

Zane starts to ask his friend questions about their next practice session and Duncan nods, or shakes his head in response, his gaze continually flicking back to mine. I fidget from one foot to the other.

The scents of these two alphas combined is too much. It warms my body. I need to get away.

"Can I use the bathroom?" I ask.

Zane turns his head to look at me. Do I look flushed?

"Sure," he says. He points to a door further back down the hallway, and I hurry there, closing it behind me and leaning against the pane. I take two long inhales, but it's hopeless. The air is thick with their scents. Peering at my reflection in the mirror, I can see my cheeks glowing, the black of my pupils dominating my eyes.

I fill the small basin with cold water, the tap loud in the

55

confined space. When I twist it off, I can hear the voices of the two alphas talking lowly.

"This is the girl?" Duncan asks, and I notice his slight Scottish accent.

"This is the girl. What do you think?"

"Mate, what do I think?" He chuckles. "She's fucking adorable, and she smells like sex. Even over the blockers, I can smell it."

"Right?! The fucking restraint I've shown with this one, when all I want to do is bend her over and rut her senseless."

Despite the cool water I throw on my face, my skin burns. But I'm not sure if it's with embarrassment or anger. They shouldn't be talking about me like that, and yet it pleases the omega in me, stirs her. She wants to be bent over and rutted.

My body responds to the visual of Zane's strong hands gripping my hips, his solid body crashing against mine. A flush ascends through my whole body, and I shiver violently with desire. A pulse drums between my legs and I feel myself get wet, slick running into my underwear. The aroma fills the bathroom. There's no disguising it. They'll know.

Quickly, I flush the toilet and rush from the bathroom. Zane is waiting for me on the other side of the door.

"Alright?" he asks me.

His nostrils twitch.

I start to walk, but he grabs my wrist. His eyes are dark as night, his jaw set.

"Let me show you the rest of the house, Omega."

It's an order. One I don't want to refuse. I'm skittish and scared. But I also want this. My body's wanted this for weeks. I can no longer resist. So, I let him lead me up the wide staircase, knowing where we're going, understanding what this means, ignoring the rooms downstairs, and walking down another hallway to a room at the back of the house.

"My room," he tells me as he opens the door.

The room is large. Framed movie posters line the walls and there's a gaming desk set up in one corner, surrounded by piles of medical textbooks. A sofa and TV stand in another. Then there's the bed.

"You're wet, little Omega, so fucking wet. Let me taste."

His voice is almost a whine, and I'm not surprised. We are what we are after all, and we've been fighting against this need to take things further. Forcing ourselves to go slow.

I want this, I want him. Yet, I'm also afraid. Afraid he'll learn the truth about me and this will all come to a screeching halt.

I back up against the door, my hands behind my back, locking on the handle.

He watches me, and the lust in his eyes is overtaken by concern.

"Are you scared?" he asks me. "You know I would never hurt you. I'd never pressure you into doing something if you didn't want to. We can go find the key to the boathouse and go to the river instead if–"

"I'm broken," I confess. "This isn't going to work out how you think it will."

He steps closer, lifting my chin to look at him. "What do you mean?"

But I can't meet his eyes. They're too intense, and I'm already a mess for him.

"I can't come," I whisper, ashamed of the truth.

"And what does that mean?"

"You won't be able to make me orgasm," I whisper even

57

more quietly. This is it. I've been putting off this moment, holding back the truth, but now he knows.

He's silent. I hear the slight pant of our breaths and footsteps somewhere in this giant house. I can't look at him.

"You've never come?"

I want to turn around and bury my face against the door. I don't want him to discover the truth. To learn the truth, and discard me.

"Omega," he says more gently when I don't respond. "Are you telling me you've never come?" He strokes his thumb along my jawline.

"I ... I've never come with anyone else."

"But you've come? You can make yourself come?"

I squirm with embarrassment. "Yes."

"Talking about this makes you uncomfortable?" he asks.

I nod, my eyes flicking briefly to his. There's no amusement or disgust, just concern.

"You know, the thought of you pleasuring yourself is a huge turn on. You think I haven't fantasised about you doing that? That I haven't got myself off to the thought of you getting yourself off."

I shiver hard, and he lifts my chin higher, forcing my gaze back to his. I've come plenty of times imagining him. Every time we've been together, he's left me a needy ball of frustration. Frustration I've had to release or I'd combust.

"I said we'd take this slow, but I'm finding it fucking hard to wait."

"I don't want to wait," I gasp.

He smirks. "I'm going to make you come, Omega."

I know he thinks he will, but there's something wrong with me that can't be fixed.

"It isn't a challenge. We can still have fun if I don't," I tell him.

He can still knot me. God, I long to be knotted. Something I never gave much consideration to before has been occupying all my thoughts.

A crease forms over his brow. "I won't have fun if my omega doesn't come."

"Please don't make this—"

I don't finish my words because he kisses me then. A long, lingering kiss that has my whole body shaking.

I'm so wet now, I'm pretty sure my underwear is ruined. I've never been this wet before.

His arms wrap around me, and he walks us around to the bed, his mouth never leaving mine. My knees hit the edge of the bed and he lowers me down.

I stare up at the white ceiling, shadows moving across the surface. I'm so nervous, so scared this is going to go horribly wrong for me. But I can't fight the way I feel about this alpha any longer.

His fingers dig below the waist of my leggings, and he peels them down my legs, my knickers going with them, leaving my lower half completely bare.

"Shit," he mutters, parting my legs and gazing down at me, making me blush. "You're so wet, it's filthy."

I think he's going to touch me, but he doesn't. He shrugs off his shirt and I get my first look at how perfectly made he is. All bronze, tight-packed muscle. I shiver again and more slick gushes from me. It catches his attention, and he licks his lips.

He kisses me a second time, more hungrily, his tongue probing my mouth, his teeth nipping at my lips. His hands scrabble at my top, releasing the buttons, his fingers brushing

59

against the soft skin of my stomach as he does, until my blouse opens like a book.

I open my eyes when he pulls back from our kiss and see him gazing down at my breasts.

"Fuck, you are a tease. I didn't think you were wearing a bra, and I was right."

He reaches out and slowly cups my right breast, groaning as he does.

"You're wearing too many clothes," I tell him. But he doesn't answer. He's too absorbed by my breasts. His thumb brushes over my nipple, and it responds, puckering as electricity flows across my skin. He does it again, the rough pad of his thumb discovering the grooves of my creased areola.

"So soft," he mutters.

I am at his mercy. Frozen, not in terror, but in anticipation. I'm hanging on every breath. What will he do next? What reaction will he pull from my body?

"Close your eyes, Omega," he whispers, and swallowing my anticipation, I do.

"Why?" I ask him.

"So you're focusing completely on my touch. Can you feel it now?" He trails his fingertips down my throat, over my collarbone and up the curve of my breast to its peak.

"Y-y-yes," I say as my back arches up to meet his touch.

"And this?" He touches me again, but this time it's the warmth of his mouth as he kisses me gently on the neck, nuzzling under my ear. His hand ventures lower, running over my ribs and brushing against my stomach, down towards my hip bone. He strokes over this with his thumb, continuing to kiss my neck between whispered words. Words I hardly hear, just stolen syllables – good, girl, yes, mine.

The world is black beneath my eyelids, but colour spills across my vision regardless, sparked by the motion of his lips and his fingers. I float in this bliss, letting him worship me, not asking for anything in return.

I must be making a mess of his sheets. I must be scorching him.

His mouth travels down to my breast, and he kisses the tip of my nipple lightly before licking around it until it's wet and cool.

"Such pretty tits," he murmurs as he sucks my nipple into his mouth, and I groan so low it makes the mattress shake. "Ahhh, yeah, you like that. Like me sucking your tits." He kneads at it as he sucks harder, his teeth scraping against the sensitive skin.

The pulse between my legs grows stronger, and my whole body is electric and alive.

"I want to touch you now, Omega," he mumbles, his mouth still full of my tit. "Is that ok?"

"Hmmm."

"That isn't an answer. Use your words."

"Yes, yes, Zane."

"Alpha, call me Alpha when I'm about to kiss your pussy, OK?"

"Yes," I moan as his fingers trail up the inside of my thigh, edging deliciously close to where I want them. "Yes, Alpha."

He rewards me with a long hard suck of my breast, and then his mouth scoots down my body, kissing and licking me as he goes. His fingers stroke along the swollen lips of my sex, and his kisses halt above my pubic bone. He takes a deep inhale, groaning as he does, and then blowing it out slowly, warming everything between my legs with his breath.

"You smell so good. So fucking good. I want to soak my dick in your wet pussy, so badly, Omega. I want to taste you on my tongue."

I tense. I want him to. I want him to so badly. But then I'll disappoint him. I know I will. I won't be what he wants me to be. A good little omega who comes on his tongue and his fingers and his cock.

"Trust me, Rosie," he says, kissing at the seam of my lips with such tenderness I think I might cry. "If you want me to stop, tell me to stop. You want me to go harder, tell me to go harder. I'm willing to do whatever it takes to see you come."

His tongue prods between my folds, making contact with my clit. It's like an electric shock. I jolt, screaming out his name. It's never felt like that before. Just the simplest of touch, fleeting, and already it feels a million times better than anything that's come before.

"Hmmm," he hums against me and I buck. "You taste ..." He swipes his tongue through my folds, landing on my clit and then flicking away. I whimper, wanting him back on my nub. But his tongue explores me, sweeping back and forth, circling my hole and probing inside.

The feeling is overwhelming. He's not polite or cautious about this, he's loving my cunt with the whole of his mouth, and when his forefinger replaces the work of his tongue, brushing against a spot inside me that has ecstasy crashing over me, I can hardly breathe.

He returns to my clit, and I know as he circles it with skill that everything I've understood up to now was wrong. I'm not broken, I've just never been touched before. Not properly, not with the love and dedication he touches me now.

Chapter 9

I beg him. I beg him in a way I've never begged before. Oblivious to any shame or dignity. I want to come so badly, and I know with certainty he can make me. I grip handfuls of the cover so tightly my fingernails pinch my palms, and I bite down hard on my lip, squirming as he holds me down with the weight of his arm and continues his blissful torture. Long, full licks of my clit, playful strokes to my pussy. Tears run down my cheeks and hair sticks to my wet brow. Slick flows freely from me, and his hand must be drenched.

"I can feel it coming, Rosie. I can feel it against my tongue. The way this precious little nub of yours quivers with excitement every time I kiss it." He groans against me.

"Alpha," I pant, "Alpha."

"Now, sugar, now, I'm going to make you come. I want you to scream. Scream so every other alpha in this house can hear you. Scream my name."

And then he flicks me hard with his tongue, hard and fast, and my world goes blinding white as an orgasm rips from my core and ricochets across my body.

"Yes," I scream, obeying his order. "Yes, yes, yes! Alpha! Zane!"

I don't know how long I hang there suspended in ecstasy,

aware of nothing but the pleasure carouseling around my body, my ears humming and my mind blank. But gradually, gradually, he lowers me back down to earth and I open my eyes to find myself lying, sweaty and dishevelled, on his bed.

He's undone me completely and utterly.

With one last lingering kiss to my pussy, he lifts his head and I see how his mouth and his chin glisten with a mixture of my slick and his spit. He swipes his arm across his face and flops down on the bed beside me.

"There's nothing wrong with you, sugar. You're perfect."

I have no breath left to speak. I simply stare up at his beautiful face in wonder. Finally, I roll onto my side, my body still light and boneless. A wide grin lies spread across his face. He's obviously pleased with himself, which, considering what's just happened, is fair enough.

I skate my palm across his sculptured form, loving how warm he feels and the strength that lies beneath his skin.

"You're still wearing too many clothes," I tell him as I run my fingers down to the waist of his joggers, brushing over the happy trail of fuzz on his lower abdomen.

"Then do something about it, Omega."

I scrabble up onto my knees and he lies against the head-board, hooking his hands behind his head and watching as I tug down his trousers and his boxers. My eyes widen as his stiff cock springs free. It is certainly big, like the rest of him. Extra large and perfectly formed. A thick vein runs its length, and it curves at an angle that tells me he'll be hitting all the right spots. The head glistens with precome and I bend down to lick it from him with my tongue. It jerks against my mouth, and I curl my hand around his base, noting how my fingers are unable to meet. He will stretch me wide open with this cock.

He is hot in my hand and rock hard. Gripping him, I run my fist down his length.

"I like seeing my dick in your little hand, Omega." I continue my action and more precome dribbles from his head. He groans. "I'd like it even better in your mouth."

I swallow. I've never been any good at this and I don't want to disappoint him after the head he's just given me. But I want his cock in my mouth. I want to taste him as badly as he wanted to taste me. I want to know the flavour of his come. Will it taste as good as his scent?

I dip my head down to meet him, and immediately he buries his hands in my hair, guiding my head closer. Opening my mouth, I take him inside, pressing my lips around his girth and letting him rest flat against my tongue. The taste is dense and salty and I think of the water, of the sea, of plunging into its depths.

"Beautiful," he mutters, groaning as I swivel my tongue around his swollen head. More of him leaks into my mouth, but it isn't enough. I want to drown in his come. I want to choke on it. I've never felt so wanton before.

I start to suck on him, my mouth matching the pace of my fist, and his hold of my hair grows tighter, his moans louder. I kneel between his thick thighs, and gaze up at him. He stares straight back, eyes locked on me, pleasure clear on his face. I suck harder, take him further into my mouth, loving how that drives a purr from his chest. Spit trickles down my chin, and wet sloppy noises fill the bedroom, but I don't stop, not even when he hits the back of my throat and I gag.

"Fuck, Omega! Fuck!" He bucks his hips beneath me and his cock pulses against my tongue. I know he's close, so I give him one long, vigorous suck, savouring how good he feels in my mouth, and with a deep growl, he gushes down my throat. Desperately, I try to gulp him down, but some spills over my lips and down my chin anyway.

"Drink it down, Omega, drink it down." He takes my hands and guides them down to the base of his cock, squeezing our hands around his knot as he expands. I gasp as I realise the pure size of it.

I slide my mouth off his cock with a pop.

"Don't let go," he commands, flinging his head back and closing his eyes, and so I've no choice but to let his come roll down my chin and drip onto my chest.

The room is quiet again except for our panting breaths. I can hear a door close somewhere in the house and the faint murmur of music.

"How many of you live here?" I ask, snuggling up beside his warm body.

"There's four of us in our pack, four of us in this house. Me, Duncan, Ollie and Seb."

"It's enormous for four people."

"We're pretty enormous for four people." I can't argue with that. "Besides, even in a pack, alphas need their space, their patch of territory. We each have our own room and then there are some communal areas too, like the gym and the TV room."

"You have a gym?"

"It's just a couple of rowing machines and some weights really, but it's good to train together."

Gently, he releases my hands from his deflating cock and pulls the covers up over our bodies.

"Now I've got you into my bed, I'm keeping you here," he tells me. "The river can wait."

I give him a little pretend look of disappointment, but really

I'm glad. I want to stay tangled in his bed, floating in the intensity of his scent, especially when he starts to kiss me all over again.

* * *

We stay in his bed for the entire afternoon, kissing and fooling around. He fingers me and brings me to orgasm a second time and I beg him to have me, but he says he wants to take his time with me, to savour the moment.

"I'm so wet and so needy," I whine against his mouth, but he remains resolute.

As the light begins to fade outside his window and shadows creep across the room, he rolls away from me and swings his legs to sit on the edge of the bed.

"It's coming up to dinner time," he tells me. "The pack will be eating together in the kitchen. Will you come and meet them?"

I shake my head. "I reek of slick and come. I don't think it's a good idea."

"Yeah, you're probably right. You smell even better than usual." He inhales and grins. "But I do want you to meet them, Rosie. It's important to me."

I swallow. It's hard to say no to him.

"I'm not ready yet." We're meant to be taking this slow, keeping this casual. Meeting his pack seems like a step towards a more serious relationship.

He doesn't argue, despite the look of disappointment that passes across his face. "I'll bring us something to eat up here." He tugs on some joggers and disappears out of the room, shutting the door behind him.

I wrap the sheet around my body and wander around his room. Across the top of his chest of drawers, toiletries lie scattered, and I pick up each one, sniffing the contents and reading the labels. I open the drawers and glide my hand over the layer of clothes housed in each one. They are all soft and expensively cut, and I wonder if these alphas have someone who does their laundry. Next, I examine the movie posters. The Godfather and Scarface, Alien and Pulp Fiction.

I'm just making my way over to his desk, when the door opens, and he walks in with two bowls of pasta.

"They're disappointed not to meet you," he says as we settle on the couch together.

We eat in silence, and when he's done, he sits back and watches me finish mine.

"I'm not trying to pressure you into anything, Rosie. You know that. But they are my family and if we're dating, I want them to get to know you."

"We're dating?" I ask him, raising my eyebrows as I chew.

"By my count, this is our fifth date and we're sleeping together, aren't we?"

"We haven't slept together yet," I remind him.

"Well," he says, taking the plate from my lap and placing it on a side table, "I'm about to change that."

"You are, are you?" I arch my eyebrow higher.

"Yes." Before I can argue back, he's scooped me into his arms and maneuvered me into his lap. My gland tingles madly in my neck, my body already buzzing with the thought of what is about to come next. I straddle his lap, my knees resting on the seat of the couch. "Are you on contraception?"

I nod.

"It may be uncomfortable the first time."

"I'm not a virgin, Zane."

"I know … but …" He grins up at me, his hands cradling either side of my ribs. "I'm not being boastful or anything, but have you ever been with a guy as big as me?"

"How would you know you're big? You go around comparing dick sizes?"

"I live in a pack, Rosie."

I pinch his bicep. "I don't want to inflate your ego."

"So that's a no then?" His grin widens, and he creeps his hands up my spine, tracing his fingers over my sensitive gland. I giggle and lock my arms around his neck, lowering my head for a kiss. He wraps one arm around my waist and presses me down, my thighs spreading as he does and his cock prodding at my entrance. I close my eyes, my heart thumping in my chest.

We're going to do this. Finally.

He holds me flush against his warm chest. "Are you sure, Omega?"

"Yes, Alpha," I whisper, and he pushes me down onto his waiting cock.

The stretch has me wincing, but he grinds me down slowly, taking his time, waiting while I relax around him. Gradually, gradually, I take more and more of him. I hang on to his shoulders, steadying myself, my nails digging into his flesh.

When I can't take anymore, he strokes at my gland and kisses a trail down to my breast, sucking and nibbling on each nipple in turn. My body responds, opening for him further, and I gasp at the sheer size of him.

I'm anchored to him now. Filled to my brim. I have no more to give, nowhere else for him to go.

He groans, lifting his mouth to my ear.

"Good girl." He glances down at his lap, and my own gaze

69

follows. We both stare at where we are joined. "Shit. Shit. I need you to move, Omega. To bounce on my dick. Can you do that?" I whimper. I don't think I can. The stretch is so wide. "Try for me, sugar."

He lifts me a little, allowing me to slide along his cock. I realise how good that tiny bit of friction feels, how much better it will feel if that friction is increased. I lift up further on my knees, his cock dragging against my walls and that special spot as he slips further from me. When only his head remains inside, I slam back down and we both grunt in unison.

"Fuck, yes," he says, lifting me up and pounding me down. Despite the size of him, we move easily, my slick lubricating our movements. Soon I'm riding him with ease, my tits bouncing in front of his face. But although I'm the one on top, he's the one dictating the pace and the depth, his strong arm guiding my body up and down his cock.

I guess he's got the measure of me. He knows that the weight of his big alpha body would have been overwhelming, suffocating. This way I have the pretence of being in control, even if secretly I'm happy to give myself over to him, to let him use me as he wants.

Soon I'm faltering, especially when he brings his hand from my neck to brush against my clit and won't allow me to lessen my pace, forcing the sensation to build in my body until I'm crashing straight through into ecstasy. Even then, he keeps me moving along his cock as my body jolts in convulsions of pleasure, until he follows me there, growling low and coming inside me.

His growl deepens as he holds me down firm on his cock and his knot expands at my entrance. Light streaks across my vision and I bite down hard on my lip, my nails sinking further into his shoulder. I wriggle, trying to squirm away, but he won't let me go, forcing me to take his knot and succumb to the pleasure that follows immediately after as he locks into me. I come, harder than I ever have, so hard for a moment I lose myself completely, and then I flop breathless and overcome with emotion against him. He wraps me in his embrace, his hands stroking every inch of my body, shushing me gently as I sob against his shoulder.

It's too much. All this is too much and I no longer know myself.

Chapter 10

After that, we're crazy about each other. Every evening, when lectures and training are over, he comes to my room and we fuck until the early hours of the morning. My body is raw and sore, bruises litter my waist and my hips, and love bites on my neck and my shoulders.

I can't get enough of him and the way he makes me feel. I don't care that I'm tired, that I struggle to keep my eyes open in my classes. My mind and my body are obsessed. It's what I feared would happen and yet, now I'm here, I find I don't care.

After two weeks of this routine, I receive a note from the girl in the room next to mine pleading with us to shut the fuck up so she can get some sleep.

Zane reads the note over my shoulder, his hand tight around my waist. He chuckles.

"What?" I ask, cringing in embarrassment.

"I don't think you could be quiet even if you tried."

I give him a nudge with my elbow. "I can't help it."

"Time for you to come back to my house. Are you ready now?" He kisses my shoulder lightly. "I don't like being away from my pack so much."

I reach behind me and stroke my fingers through his hair. "I know." He's constantly on the phone to them, messaging or chatting, despite seeing them once or twice a day for training. It's clear to me now how knitted together they are.

"It'll only be Duncan there tonight. Seb and Oliver are out." He kisses me again. "I'm not willing to spend a night away from you, Rosie."

I bend my head forward as his mouth moves toward my gland, and he swipes his tongue over it, making the tissue-thin skin quiver.

"I'll come," I murmur, closing my eyes.

"Good," he murmurs. "My bed smelt so good after the last time you were there." He steps around to face me and lifts my chin. "I'll see you later, sugar."

I remember the scents in his house. How overpowering they were. How they made my gland tingle. And then I think of that conversation I overheard between Zane and Duncan about how it had made me wet.

Going back to his house feels somehow dangerous.

I try not to think about it for the rest of the day, but I find my eyes glazing over as I read passages from textbooks in the library and nearly miss my laptop buzzing in front of me. I answer the call and the screen fills with the faces of my sisters.

"Hang on," I hiss, snatching the laptop up into my arms and trotting outside. I find a quiet patch of grass behind the library and settle down with the computer resting on my crossed legs.

The scent of tulips weaves in the breeze, and the remains of blossom hangs in the branches above my head and scatters across the lawn like confetti.

"Hi," I wave at them, and they all grin, waving back at me. Little Poppy the youngest, the twins Lily and Clover, and Daisy, the eldest. "How are you all? I miss you all."

As I say the words, I feel the truth of it right down in my

gut. How much easier it would have been to stay at home and attend the omega college like my mum wanted. To stay with them. None of those arguments. None of the heartache. Just their easy conversation and their smiles.

But then I'd never have met Zane. I wouldn't be experiencing what I am right now. Sex and passion. I feel like a new person. The real me.

They all start talking at once, Lily and Clover squabbling to try to silence each other and Poppy speaking over them both regardless. My eyes flit around the screen from one sister to the next, trying to keep up with their pieces of news and cooing and nodding at the things they have to tell me.

Poppy presents a new book, which she swiftly flicks her way through, reading me the words; Lily and Clover want to relate all the gossip from their dance club; and Daisy has a string of questions about her science homework.

Finally, they all run out of steam and with kisses and more waves, the youngest three skip off, leaving just me and Daisy. I help her through her homework, and then she obviously has something else she wants to talk to me about.

"Are you OK?" I ask her. She's only a couple of years younger than me. She'll be taking her exams next year and making her own decisions about life. I wonder what she'll choose and if she'll have the strength to resist my mum's demands.

Looking at her on the computer screen is like peering at a slightly distorted reflection of myself. Our eyes are round, although hers are a shade lighter. Her face stretches a little longer and her nose forms more of a cute button than mine. But we share the same heart-shaped lips and the same creamy pink complexion. She also shares my love of learning, curious about everything, and I hope she'll choose to do more than be some alpha's omega.

Daisy glances over her shoulder, then leans in closer towards the screen, her voice a whisper when she speaks, "I think I'm going to get my first heat soon. I've been having a load of pre-heat symptoms."

"Oh," I say, the heat rising to my cheeks. "Oh, that's ... Have you told Mum?" Daisy bites her lip, her hands wringing in her lap, and nods. My mum will be freaking out and putting the house on lockdown.

"Yes, Mum's being really lovely about it actually." Daisy giggles when she spots my surprised expression. "Like I said, it's coming on slowly, so we've had some time to prepare. Mum took me to the doctor and they confirmed it, she thinks it'll be here soon." I can imagine our family doctor prodding and poking my poor little sister, just like she'd done to me. All those tests, all those searches for explanations that never came. I shudder at the thought, but Daisy doesn't seem to notice. "Mum took me out shopping to find stuff for my nest and we set up my room real nice."

My cheeks burn more fiercely, and I swallow down a hard lump in my throat.

My sister twists a piece of caramel hair, the same shade as mine, around her finger. "What is it like, Rosie?" she asks me, her eyes flicking up to meet my gaze. "I guess I was younger when you had your first one so I never even noticed that it happened and we never talked about it." My sister's face blushes the colour mine must be.

"Oh ..." I fidget on my seat, a lump forming in my throat, preventing the words from coming. "You know ..."

"Pretty awful, huh?" She sighs, her shoulders slumping. "Mum got me a toy, which she says will help."

"You're not going to find an alpha?" Daisy's eyes widen in horror making me hate my mum for all the lies she's told us. For telling us casual sex with alphas would ruin our reputations, would end all our chances of finding a nice, respectable mate. "It might be better," I tell her. I don't want my little sister to suffer when everyone knows being with an alpha can make the whole horrible situation exquisite.

"Sure," Daisy smiles, "But Mum and Dad would never go for that. Anyway, I'm kind of pleased that I'm getting my first one soon. Then it's out of the way, sort of thing."

I hum my agreement. "Maybe talk to Mum about an alpha, Daisy," I say, knowing in my heart there is no chance my mum will agree to it.

"Maybe." She tilts her head to one side. "That's Mum calling us for dinner." She meets my eye. "I never got to hear about your news."

"It's OK. Go enjoy home-cooked food while you can. I'm living off baked beans and pot noodles here." Not strictly true. Zane's been taking me out to eat a lot.

"Yuck." Daisy pulls a face. "Come back soon, then. Come visit us. We miss you. And we can fatten you up."

"I'll be home for the holidays. It's not that long."

"It is." Daisy slumps her shoulders for dramatic effect. "It's not the same without you here."

"I bet there are fewer rows."

Daisy shakes her head.

"Oh, come on," I say. My mum and I spent the Christmas and the Easter holidays squabbling, her constant digs and off-hand comments driving me up the wall. I guess she thinks if she chips away long enough, I'll give in and be the good omega daughter she wants. Bonded and married.

"It's summer soon. We'll go to the beach loads. Keep you out of Mum's way." I smile at her. "Love you, Rosie," she says, blowing me a big kiss. I return it and then we wave and hang up.

I lean back against the trunk of the tree. That sensation of missing them has gnawed larger in my stomach. I feel hollow, empty.

My little sister is going into heat. A tear trickles down my cheek. What should I feel for her? Happiness? Concern? Relief?

So why do I feel sadness for myself?

Chapter 11

Zane waits for me outside my lecture hall later that day, dressed in shorts and a t-shirt, both splashed with water, his kit bag hanging off his shoulder.

"Did you come straight from the river?"

He sweeps his damp hair from his face. "Yes."

"You're so wet."

"It's hot out there today." He throws his bag to the ground and reaches for my hips, walking me towards him. "You don't mind me all hot and sweaty?"

I sigh. "You smell amazing, you know you do."

He smiles to himself and then leans down to kiss me, right there on the pavement with people weaving around us. My cheeks warm, but it's not from embarrassment. Everybody can see him kissing me and somehow that heats my blood. There are plenty of girls who would love to be in my place. But it's me locked in his embrace, my mouth he's plundering. I want them to all know I'm his, for now anyway.

When he breaks the kiss, he doesn't let go of me. "I have two confessions to make," he says, resting his forehead against mine.

"Oh?"

"I'm here to escort you to my place. I'm not giving you the

chance to back out."

"OK." I nod.

"And I got something for you?" He plunges his left hand into his pocket and pulls out his fist. He lifts it between us and opens his hand.

A fine gold chain trails across his palm and in its centre hangs two tiny oars crossed over one another.

I touch them with my forefinger. "It's so pretty."

"I told you I want to spoil you."

"Are you sure that's all this is?"

He smirks a little as he fastens the chain around my neck and allows the oar charm to drop over my chest.

"People know about you now, Rosie. They know you're an omega. You're going to have other alphas sniffing around. So, yeah, maybe I want them to know you're mine."

I swallow as I finger the necklace. I don't know how to feel. Things are moving so quickly between us. I'm being swept along in his current. But instead of feeling like I'm drowning, I'm floating, suspended. I'm happy to be carried away.

We walk back to his, stopping on the way to pick up chicken and salad, which we eat at the huge communal table in his giant kitchen. The house is empty, and when we're done, he leads me immediately to his bedroom, taking me on my hands and knees on the floor.

"You wanna watch a movie?" he asks afterwards.

The TV room is more like a mini cinema. The room is windowless and black, and a screen dominates an entire wall. A few large sofas are positioned around the room, and we settle down on one together, Zane wrapping us up in a blanket.

The opening credits have just finished, when the door at the back of the room opens and Duncan strolls in.

"What you watching?" he asks, sitting down on a sofa next to ours, a can of lager in his hand.

"A Marvel movie. Rosie's never seen them."

"You never saw them?" He cracks open the pull on his can, capturing the emerging foam with his mouth.

"It's always an endless loop of Disney princess movies back home." He looks at me quizzically. "I've got four little sisters."

"Ahhh." He nods, then leans back on the sofa. "Thor is the best."

His scent curls into my nose. It's more earthy than Zane's, reminding me of wide open spaces and freshly cut grass. I try not to notice how well the two alpha's scents blend together, how they make my gland tingle.

Perhaps Zane notices though, because his fingers venture under the hem of my top, skating across my stomach, stroking my skin and creeping higher and higher until his hand slips under my bra and cups my breast. I stifle a moan as he rolls my nipple.

It's dark in this room apart from the light from the movie. I don't think Duncan can see what we're up to, but I can make out the outline of his face and the glint of his eyes.

My nipples harden under Zane's attention and he leans down to kiss me. I push him away.

"We're not alone," I remind him in a whisper.

"I don't think Duncan cares if we're fooling around," he replies in a voice that's far too loud. Duncan turns and looks our way and his alpha eyes find mine.

"You think I didn't hear you the other night. The whole street heard you the other night."

"She sounds good when she comes, doesn't she?"

Duncan's gaze locks with mine. "She sounds delicious. She

had us all hard as stone." Heat crawls across my skin and slick trickles from my cunt. "She smells like she needs to be fucked," he adds.

"She always needs to be fucked. This omega is always wet."

Zane squeezes my tit and a moan escapes my mouth. I shouldn't like the way they're talking about me, these dirty things they're saying, but I do like it. My whole body is on fire, my heart pounding.

"You should see her when she comes. She looks even better than she sounds."

Duncan slides his tongue along his bottom lip. "I'd like that."

Zane kisses me before I can respond; a deep, penetrating kiss. It overwhelms me. I'm lost in the feeling and the dark of this room. His hands scrabble at my skirt. He whispers in my ear, "Can I show him, Omega? Can I show him how beautiful you are?"

"Yes." The word slips from my mouth. I want Zane to make me come. And I want Duncan to watch. It's wrong, perverted. But I want it.

I've been thinking about their words out there in the hallway, thinking about the two of them together, far more often than I should.

Zane travels down my body, taking my underwear with him.

On screen, the Avengers engage in battle, booms and rattles making the room vibrate as Zane presses his mouth to my sex and my cries are drowned out.

I close my eyes too ashamed to look at Duncan, but knowing his murky blue eyes are locked on me.

Zane knows my body intimately now, every inch of it. He knows how to force a quick orgasm from my core or how to string it out and build it up slowly. Tonight, he goes for something in between, swirling his tongue around my clit in long, firm strokes.

"What does she taste like?" Duncan growls.

"Like honey and vanilla ice cream."

I huff. I taste nothing like that.

Zane flicks me hard in punishment and I buck, crying out. Both alphas purr their encouragement and the sound travels deep to my core.

"Does that feel good, little Omega?" Duncan asks, his voice hoarse.

"Yes, Alpha," I mutter, then realise my mistake. He's not my alpha, Zane is. But it doesn't seem to aggravate Zane. In fact, he rewards me with another flick that has me almost tumbling over.

"Please, Alpha," I beg, my hands tugging at his hair.

"Let her come, Zane. I want to see."

I open my eyes and find myself drowning in Duncan's fiery glare. I can't look away. Not even when my body shakes and my orgasm crashes over me and sweeps me away.

I call out Zane's name, but it's Duncan's gaze I meet.

I fall quickly and Zane gathers me up in his arms, bundling me upstairs to his room. I cling to him, burying my face in his neck and taking gasps of his scent. In his room, he kicks the door closed behind us and sits me on the edge of his bed, parting my thighs and standing between them. He fumbles with his fly, tugging himself free, and the next moment he's plunging inside me. Together we groan.

"You were so fucking beautiful down there, sugar. It took every single bit of self-control I had not to fuck you in front of him." I whimper, visions of Duncan watching me getting fucked flashing through my mind.

Zane thrusts inside me, grabbing my backside and pulling me firmly towards him. I roll back onto the bed, shifting his angle, allowing him to lift me higher onto his cock. He fucks me hard and part of it, I think, is to remind me I'm his. To reassert I belong to him.

* * *

At some point early in the morning, he stirs me to say he's heading off to train. I kiss him, pleading for him to come back to bed, and then I fall back to sleep. When I wake again, it's late morning. Sunshine streams through the window. I lie out flat in Zane's giant bed, listening. The house is silent. They've all gone down to the river and I know they'll be there for most of the day. I shrug on one of Zane's t-shirts and pad down to the kitchen. The remnants of the alphas' breakfasts lie strewn across the table and the counters. It seems strange to be in their home alone, an intruder. As much as this thing between Zane and I is growing, his true family, loyalty and love lies with them.

I shake some cornflakes into a clean bowl and pour on cold milk from the fridge. Then I sit at the middle of the table examining the discarded plates around me. Their combined scent lingers in this room and I'm not sure if I'm betraying Zane when I take long inhales of it, driving my gland to buzz in my neck.

Would he care? He was the one who instigated the events of last night. He wanted his pack mate to watch me. My cheeks burn with the memory, but at the same time, a pulse stirs between my legs.

I know they have girls here. Orgies at this house are the thing of urban legend, according to Sophia. It's one of the reasons I turned their invitation down in the first place.

But things are different. I'm different now. I was so afraid of what being with an alpha would mean, fearful of all the things I would lose, that I never considered the things I would gain.

Last night, I let another alpha watch as my alpha made me come with his mouth. The very thought of it would have been outrageous to me only weeks ago. Now I'm left wondering if I want to take things further.

I fiddle with the charm hanging around my neck. I knew it was dangerous to come back to this house. The scents, the alphas. It's all too tempting.

After I've showered and dressed, I go to meet Sophia for lunch. She's been bugging me, moaning that she hasn't seen me, even though we've been in lectures together every day.

We meet in town and buy sandwiches before walking out to the park and lying out in the sunshine.

I yawn and stretch on the grass and Sophia rolls her head towards me and grins.

"What?" I ask her.

"Feeling tired, Rosie?"

"Hmmm," I say noncommittally.

She laughs. "You've gone from 'I don't want anything to do with relationships' to being permanently stuck to that boy's side."

"It's the early days. You know what it's like in the early days."

Sophia wiggles her eyebrows. "Oh, I know. But you can tell me the details." She rolls on to her side and tucks her hands under her cheek. "It's good, right?"

I gaze up at the blue sky and the hazy clouds that skim across the sun. "I like him far too much."

"That's good, though, right?"

"I don't know. It's all moving so quickly."

"I'm so pleased for you, Rosie. Even if you have completely abandoned me."

"I haven't abandoned you. I'm here now."

"And where's the lover boy?"

"On the river training with his pack."

"That is something I'd like to see. They are all so fine."

"I've only met Duncan."

"Really? Haven't you met the rest of his pack yet? Is he trying to keep you to himself?"

"No, it's nothing like that. He wants me to meet them, but it's a little intimidating."

"Oh," she says, shuffling closer to me. "It's just that I heard ..."

Her gaze flicks over my face.

"What did you hear?"

"That they used to have an omega."

That doesn't sound like news to me. We know they invite girls around for sex. "I know, Sophia, did you forget about that invitation?"

"No, not like that. I mean, a pack omega – she was part of the pack. Apparently, she lived with them and everything."

I turn my head and stare straight at Sophia. "What?"

"She was theirs. All of theirs. They shared her."

My stomach sloshes and acid rises up into my throat. I swallow it down and try to modulate my voice. "It happens," I tell her. "Omegas are rare these days. And you hear of alphas forming packs with one omega."

"Lucky omega," Sophia mutters.

A pack omega. A girl who belonged to the pack. Who was she?

And why do I care? Why does the nausea churn in my stomach just imagining her?

Am I jealous? Why? That's not what I want.

Then I think of the fire in Duncan's eyes, the intensity of his scent, the danger in his voice. And I shiver.

Chapter 12

Zane calls me later that day, wanting me back at his house that evening. But I make excuses. I'm confused and I can't get a handle on my feelings. This mixture of shame and desire, jealousy and fear, spinning inside me and making me sick.

But he's there outside my dormitory door that evening.

"How long have you been waiting there?" I ask as I unlock the door.

"An hour," he replies. "You know, you could just give me a key to your room."

"And have you snooping through my stuff while I'm not here, no thanks."

"Now I'm intrigued," he says, swinging his gaze around my room as he steps inside. There isn't a lot here, just a few pictures of me and my sisters. "What do you have hidden away?"

"Only a dead body or two and some voodoo dolls of my enemies."

I drop on the edge of the bed and he comes to sit next to me. For once, we're quiet.

"Are you going to tell me what's going on?" he asks, taking my hands in his.

"What do you mean?"

"Not wanting to come to my house tonight." His body seems tense next to mine and he pauses as if he's searching for words. "Is it because of last night? What happened with Duncan?"

My body responds in a confused manner. My face flushes with embarrassment, but my gland buzzes with arousal. Last night was hot and erotic. I never knew being watched like that could turn me on so much. And yet, what does that say about me?

"I didn't mean to push you. I got carried away …" Zane continues.

"You didn't push me. I wanted it." I chew my lip, my stomach churns. "I'm confused."

He guides my chin around so that I'm looking into his eyes. "What's confusing, sugar?"

"How I'm feeling."

"You wanted to do it?"

"Yes."

"But now you regret it? You didn't enjoy it?" His body's still tense, his eyes locked on mine. He's trying so hard to understand me.

"I did enjoy it," I whisper, finding it hard to admit the words out loud.

"There's nothing to be ashamed about, you know that, don't you?"

I laugh bitterly. "I wish I could believe that. But when you grow up being told exactly how a good omega ought to behave, it's hard to banish those ideas from your head. What we did last night was–"

"You are a good little omega, Rosie," he says, his voice deepening. "A very good omega. Do you know how proud

I was to show you off like that? To have him watch you come on my tongue? It was one of the fucking greatest experiences of my life." I shiver hard and he pulls me into his lap. "So now what?" he asks. "I can keep coming to this poky room of yours, or we can go back to my place. The decision is yours."

"If we go back ..."

"If we go back ..."

"It could happen again."

"Would you like that?"

"Yes," I breathe.

I pack an overnight bag while he pokes around my drawers.

"You and your sisters all look so alike," he says, examining the picture in the frame I have by my bed. "Am I going to get to meet them?"

I crinkle up my nose. "I don't know. If my mum finds out about you, she'll have our wedding plans sorted in less than a week."

Zane snorts.

"I'm serious," I say. "I think it's best to keep it on the low-key from my family for the time being. Honestly, I don't need the additional hassle this will cause with my mum."

"You just made it sound like she'd be pleased."

"She will be, but then ..."

He nods. "There's no rush."

We catch a taxi to his pack house.

"Want to watch another movie?" he asks me as I place my bag on his bed. I nod and he rests his forehead against mine, his alpha eyes bottomless up close. "Are you sure?"

"Yes Alpha," I say, and then we're walking back down the stairs, my head a little dizzy. He cooks us a big bowl of popcorn, then we snuggle up on the sofa in the TV room and he lines up

89

another Marvel movie.

As the movie starts, I wait with anxious breath to see if any of the other alphas in the pack will join us this time. They don't, and I relax into Zane as the movie progresses.

Perhaps last night was a one time thing after all. And now, the battle in my head can stop.

Soon, Zane is kissing down my neck and my hands are roaming over the contours of his chest. Our breaths become more ragged and I can feel the heavy thump of his heart and his hardness pressing into my thigh. He drags his teeth down the tendons of my throat as his hands massage my breasts. I'm so lost to it, I barely hear the door open and Duncan flop down on the sofa next to us.

I open my eyes and find him staring straight at me, his eyes as fierce as they were last night. He's dressed in grey sweatpants and a black T-shirt, and his feet are bare. Just seeing him again has my gland tingling and my stomach fluttering with nerves.

None of us say a word. I don't push Zane away as he slides my top up, exposing my tits, and begins to nibble on my nipples. My eyes remain on Duncan. He leans back on the sofa, his legs planted wide, and his gaze falls to my chest as he slips a hand into the crotch of his pants.

I whimper a little knowing what he's doing as Zane shifts down my body, his head soon between my legs.

It's just like before. I lie there on show as Zane pleasures me. Only this time, Duncan does more than just watch. I can see his hand working inside his trousers, his jaw tensing and releasing with pleasure. For a moment, the sound of the movie dies down and I can hear the rustle of fabric and Zane's wet mouth on my sex.

I don't know why I find this such a turn on but I do. I like him watching us together. I like that it turns him on. That he's sitting there wanking while Zane gets me off. It's dirty and filthy and I want more.

Zane thrusts two fingers inside me as he flicks his tongue backward and forward over my clit until I can hardly bear the combined sensation. It's too good. Too much.

My eyes fall shut as I squirm in ecstasy and when I open them again, Duncan is right there. His face hovering above mine.

I look straight up into those murky eyes and pleasure cascades through my body as he bends closer. His breath is warm on my face, his scent engulfing my senses. He presses his mouth against mine, swallowing my breath and my moans of pleasure. He kisses me, his tongue plunging deep inside my mouth as Zane ravishes between my legs with his lips and his fingers.

And then Duncan's hands are on my breasts, squeezing them roughly between his strong fingers as he kisses me mercilessly.

I can't breathe. Can't think. My mind is blank. My lungs sting with the lack of air.

And then I come, bucking and arching beneath the two alphas as they hold me down and continue to work my body. They don't let me fall. I've barely caught breath when another orgasm rips through my body, and then Zane is scooping me up in his arms like he did the other night and carrying me away.

I screw up my eyes, too frightened to meet Duncan's gaze. Too confused.

Having him watch me was one thing, having him pleasure me too? It made me feel powerful and desirable.

I shouldn't have liked it. Surely, it isn't normal. But I did like it. I liked it a lot.

"It's OK," Zane whispers as he lifts me up the stairs. "You did so well. You were so precious for both of us. You don't mind that he kissed you?"

"No," I admit.

"You liked it?" he whispers into my ear, nuzzling against my neck.

"Yes."

He lays me down on the bed and I watch as he strips out of his clothes and stands there naked, his cock stiff for me. I expect him to climb into the bed, but he doesn't. He twists the chair at his desk around to face me and sits down. Then he pats his lap.

"Come here, Omega," he commands.

And I saunter over, shedding my top as I do. I go to climb onto his waiting thighs, but he turns me around so my back faces him.

"No, this way, Omega," he says and lifts me onto his lap, sliding me backwards until his cock nudges against my backside. I shuffle against him, letting him find my pussy and thrust inside. His arm glides around me, cradling my chest as he cups my breast, and with his other hand he parts my thighs and fondles my clit.

We've never done it this way before, but instantly I see how it hits all the right spots and I grind my backside against him in languid circles, making him groan.

"That's it, like that," he tells me. "Ride me, Omega."

I work him like he wants and, as I do, I hear the soft pads of footsteps on the stair and along the corridor and I know where this is leading. I could stop this right now if I wanted to. But I don't. I want this.

I'm facing the entrance, nothing to shield me as the door creaks open. I'm nude, pinned on my alpha's cock, grinding against it for anyone to see.

Zane's arm around me grows tighter, holding me in place so I can't run away.

But there's no need. I know who the intruder is, hovering in the doorway.

"Come in," I tell him, and Duncan steps inside the bedroom, closing the door quietly behind him. I meet his gaze briefly, then fling back my head in ecstasy, arching my back to intensify the angle of Zane inside me, and I ride him harder, bouncing on his lap.

"Tell her," Zane says to his pack mate.

"You look incredible, Rosie." Duncan's voice sounds strangled, tortured. "Like a fucking goddess."

"Help me then," Zane continues. "Help me worship this goddess. Do you want that, Omega? Do you want this other alpha to touch you?"

"Yes," I beg, "yes, please, Alphas."

Duncan growls low and stalks towards us, halting in front of us and dropping to his knees. My body shakes in Zane's arms as I wait to see what Duncan will do. His eyes glint with lust and wickedness, and I shake harder, hardly able to keep up my rhythm on Zane's cock.

Duncan's face remains passive as he lifts his hand to my face. Stroking my chin with his fingers, he parts my lips with his thumb and thrusts it into my mouth.

"Suck," he says, and I do, giving the coarse pad a little nip.

He doesn't react, simply releases his hand from my face and then reaches between my parted thighs. Immediately Zane removes his hand, bringing it up to curl gently around my throat as Duncan swims his thumb through my slick folds and discovers my clit.

I jerk when he does. While Zane's fingers there had been good, he could give me only the stuttering attention of a man lost in the throes of his own pleasure. Duncan gives me his whole care and his full concentration. He skims around my clit as I ride Zane, my tits bouncing close to Duncan's face as Zane tweaks one nipple and grips my throat.

If anyone saw us now, they'd think we were perverted and dirty. I can't tell anyone about this. And anyway, I like that it's private, that something is happening between the three of us that no one else will fathom.

They're both whispering to me now, garbled words of praise and worship, but I don't hear a word. I'm riding high, wondering how I ever found one pair of hands on my body, one set of lips, enough.

"Is she tight?" I catch Duncan asking his friend, as my legs shake harder and my core clenches around Zane's dick.

"Tight but wet, always so wet."

I come. For the third time I come, with Zane's cock in my pussy, Duncan's fingers on my clit, Zane's hands on my tits, and Duncan's mouth on my stomach.

"Good girl," Zane moans as he comes straight after me, hot spend filling my pussy. Duncan lifts his eyes to watch my face as Zane's knot locks into me and pain and pleasure pass over my features.

"Fuck," he mutters, "fuck, he knotted your tight little pussy. And you took it, like a good omega should."

I collapse against Zane, panting as, carefully, he carries me over to the bed.

Duncan remains on his knees on the floor.

"Alpha," I call to him, inviting him to join us, and Zane purrs his approval. We both snuggle under the covers as Duncan stands and sheds his clothes.

I can't help a little gasp when I see him naked. He's fairer than Zane and the hair that covers his chest and trails down to his cock has an almost red glint to it. But he's just as big, his body sculpted like Zane's and his cock hanging heavy between his thighs.

"It seems you're not the only one who's big in this pack," I whisper to Zane.

"Trust me," he says, "it's one thing we all have in common."

Somewhat cautiously, Duncan approaches the bed. "Are you sure about this, Rosie?"

"Get in, Duncan," Zane tells him. "She likes to cuddle after sex." I blush a little. Zane seems to know me better than myself.

The other alpha climbs into the bed and scoots up close to me. His body is warm like Zane's and lying pinned between the two of them, still knotted to Zane's cock, feels safe and comforting. I rest my head on Duncan's shoulder and he kisses the crown of my head affectionately, brushing the hair from my face.

"Are you sure you're OK, Omega?" he asks. "With what just happened, I mean."

"We'd never want you to do something you were uncomfortable with," Zane adds. "We'd never force you to–"

"I know," I say, confident that it's the truth. While I know they have the alpha instinct to rut and knot me, to have me submit to their will, I also know they harbour instincts to protect and to care for me too. If I ever said no to them, they'd respect it.

95

"How did you all meet?" I ask as our breathing falls into sync and I rise and fall on Duncan's chest in time to the press of Zane's expanding chest behind me.

Duncan looks at Zane and then answers my question. "There were a lot of trials and training to earn our spot on the boat. We spent weeks together while we competed for our places. It was clear there was something between us. We clicked. We were already talking about forming our pack when they picked us for the team. I think it was inevitable. A group of four guys who work so well together, that are so in tune with one another, would always make the strongest team."

"None of us have siblings. These guys are my brothers. In fact, it's more than that, the bond is stronger," Zane adds.

"Is it like a bond between an alpha and an omega?" I ask. The bond once activated is there for life, binding two people together irreversibly.

"I think it's similar," Zane says. "I believe I was fated to find my brothers and we'll be together until the end of our days."

Duncan nods and I suddenly feel like an intruder, trespassing onto something special and sacred. Something, however, that they've invited me into.

"And has there ever been an omega in your pack?"

Duncan's eyes flick down to mine and Zane stiffens behind me.

"Aye," Duncan says simply.

"Oh."

Zane nuzzles against my gland as Duncan adds, "For about a year. It didn't work out and she went her own way."

"How long ago did she leave?"

"Six months."

"Oh." I say again. It seems so recent, but then I remember

that this pack is a relatively new one. "How long has the pack been together?"

"Coming up two years," Zane mutters against my gland. I've been seeing Zane for a month and we've somehow avoided talking in detail about his pack. I've been in denial, trying to push it from my mind. I've fooled myself into thinking it could just be me and Zane. But it never could. This is a man who is prepared to share everything with his pack. His home, his life, his omega.

"Tell me about the others," I say, feeling brave enough to face this lying between them.

"There's Ollie and Seb. Ollie's an undergrad like us. Seb's older. He's doing his PhD," Zane says.

"And were you all rowing before you came to this college?"

"Yeah, being a rower is a huge advantage to getting into one of the top colleges." I nod, that much I know. "Our schools had us rowing as soon as we could pick up an oar."

"Except Seb," Duncan adds, "he didn't start rowing until he got to college."

"So which one of you is in charge out there on the water?"

I feel Duncan shake his head on the pillow above me. "It doesn't work like that. No one person's in charge. We work together, as one, as a pack."

"We all have our role." Zane points above our heads. "Ollie is our most technically proficient rower, so he sits at the stern."

"Stern?"

"Back of the boat. He's our stroke. He sets our pace. Then it's our power engines in the middle, Seb and Duncan. And then I'm at the bow, steering."

"It sounds complicated."

I want to ask them more, but sandwiched securely between

the two alphas, I soon drift away into sleep, my body still buzzing.

It's dark when I'm woken by the sensation of a wet mouth nuzzling my throat and hands roaming between my legs and over my breasts.

"Omega," Zane growls in my ear. His hard cock prods against my backside and I wriggle against him, making him groan. "Are you awake?" he asks.

"I am now," I giggle, realising there's still another body in the bed with us, and there are two pairs of hands roaming me. My body responds, stirring into life immediately. I find Zane's mouth and kiss him, but my hands glide through the covers and wrap around Duncan's stiffness.

"We want to fuck you, Omega," Zane whispers. "You smell so good in this bed, it's hard to sleep."

"You're a tempting wee dish," Duncan adds.

"I want to be fucked," I admit, squeezing Duncan and rubbing my fist down his shaft. I smell the arousal of both alphas. It's intoxicating.

Zane flips off the covers and drags me up onto my hands and knees, his grip tight on my hips. In the dim light, I can make out Duncan observing us, his eyes locked to my backside as Zane thrusts his way inside. I'm jolted forward by the force and Zane has to pull me back up onto my hands.

"You want him too?" Zane grunts, pounding me hard so that the breath is knocked from my lungs.

I stare up into Duncan's eyes, full of lust, full of desire, and then my gaze drops down to his groin. His cock is hard and even bigger than it looked hours earlier.

I've been imagining this. Desires have seeped into my mind unbidden. Stirred me up. Images of them both ... with me.

Do I act on those desires? And if I do, will there be any turning back?

Duncan's cock jerks under my scrutiny and a drop of pre-come beads on the tip. I want to taste it.

"Yes, Alpha. I want you both."

Duncan scrambles up onto his knees. He palms at his cock and I'm sure my eyes are wide. He draws closer, the head bobbing in front of my face.

"Omega—"

"I want it," I tell him. "I want you in my mouth."

Zane's fingers dig into my flesh and he pounds harder as Duncan lets out a groan and guides his cock carefully between my waiting lips.

I'm so eager to taste him, to know his flavour, that I suck him immediately and he wraps his fingers around the back of my skull. I'm held in place by Zane, so I can't move my mouth up and down his shaft as I want to. All I can do is suckle at him as he begins to work his hips with steady shallow thrusts into my mouth.

"Fuck, that looks good, Duncan," Zane says from behind me. "Omega, you look so beautiful with your mouth stuffed full of his cock."

I see Duncan's eyes lift from me and meet Zane's as they both fuck me and I'm sure I can feel something in the air. Something crackling and alive.

Zane's work soon has me moaning around Duncan's cock, and the second alpha's movements become fiercer. He lunges deeper, hitting the back of my throat. I take it, I take them both. I'm far gone on my own pleasure, and so my throat relaxes, letting him penetrate deep. I can hardly breathe, but the asphyxiation only seems to heighten my pleasure, making everything more intense and all-consuming.

Soon, I'm howling as I come, my arms and legs jelly. I'm suspended only by the alpha in my mouth and the alpha in my pussy. I convulse and jolt as I succumb to the pleasure of my orgasm and both men continue their relentless rhythm. Driving in and out of me, showing no mercy.

Zane is the first to spill. His thrusts faltering, his hands holding me tight to his dick as his hot spend floods into me. And then Duncan follows, his fingers pinching my scalp as his come flows into my mouth. He tastes different to Zane, but just as good, and I try my best to gulp him down, the liquid warming my throat and my chest.

"Shit, knot her, Zane. Knot our wee omega."

Our omega. I look up at Duncan. His hands are locked around the base of his cock now, holding his own expanding knot as his cock throbs in my mouth. But he's watching his pack mate again, not me.

Did he mean that? *Our* omega? Do I belong to both of them now?

I hardly know Duncan, and yet I'm not frightened by the idea anymore. Now I've experienced what it's like to be with both of them, the idea of having them both appeals to something deep and dormant inside me.

I want this.

I want this more than ever.

Chapter 13

Noises in the house wake me the next morning – the slam of doors, the groan of pipes and the stomp of footsteps. But both my alphas lie beside me, the low rasp of their breaths audible as they sleep. I lie sandwiched between, examining both their peaceful faces. They look content, satisfied, and pride swells in my belly knowing I am responsible.

As I watch him, Duncan's auburn eyelashes flicker and his eyes flutter open. His vacant gaze meets mine, and for a moment I'm stunned by the murky blue of his irises. A shy smile spreads across his face.

"Good morning, wee yin," he says, reaching out to stroke my cheek.

"Wee yin?" I ask.

"Little one. Have you been awake long?"

"No," I whisper.

His thumb glides to my mouth and he traces my bottom lip. "How do you feel?"

"Sticky," I confess.

He chuckles. "That sounds very satisfactory." He leans closer and presses a firm kiss to my waiting mouth, pulling away all too soon to add, "but we'd better get you showered."

We slide quietly from the bed so as not to disturb Zane, and Duncan wraps me in a gown hanging on the back of the door and leads me to the bathroom.

Even the bathroom in this house is larger than my dormitory room and looks as if it too was designed for communal use. Two sinks line up under a square mirror and both the bathtub and the shower cubicle could hold several people. The walls and floor are decorated with black-and-white tiles and the Victorian style taps are a rusty gold. Crisp white towels hang waiting over a reclaimed radiator and a fluffy bath mat lies on the floor. It's more than inviting.

Duncan turns the shower taps, keeping his hand under the flow while he tests the temperature.

I perch on the closed toilet and wait.

He peers over at me. "You want to ask me something?"

"I want to ask you lots of things."

He nods. "Go ahead."

"What are you studying?"

"Engineering. And you're studying physics?"

"Yes." I hold my chin up defiantly.

"Smart girl," he says, adjusting the taps, "I like smart girls. We all do."

"Why engineering?" I ask him.

"It's a family tradition. My grandfather started an engineering firm years ago and my father runs it now."

"You're going to work for him?"

He beckons me over and I stand, letting the gown fall to the floor and enjoying the glint that flashes in his eyes.

"That's the plan."

I take his offered hand and he pulls me under the waiting water. The shower head is as big as everything else in this house and so the water falls over us both, warm and powerful.

"Is that what you want?"

"Aye. I mean, if I got the chance, I'd want to row professionally. To go to the Olympics. That's what we're all working our arses off for."

I whistle. "The Olympics?" I had no idea they had such ambitions.

He grins. "It's what we're aiming for, but it's not like I hate engineering. I'm not being forced into it. It's a family passion. I've been taking apart toy trains and rebuilding them since I was a kid."

He selects a bottle from the shelf and squirts body wash into his palm. Then he squats down and washes between my legs, scrubbing away the dried slick and come. His hands on my skin feel heavenly, especially when he strokes between my legs.

"You have a beautiful cunt, wee yin. Zane's been bragging to us all about how beautiful it is. I thought he was exaggerating."

"I think you're exaggerating."

"I'm not."

I see his cock stiffening and a shiver of desire runs through me. He lifts his eyes to mine and he must find the confirmation he wants because he stands and walks me back against the cool tiles and kisses me. Water runs over our heads and down our faces, making our kiss wet and slippery, and I gasp for air. His hands glide up my body cupping my breasts and squeezing, causing me to moan into his mouth.

"Omega?" he asks.

"Yes," I answer, pushing my hips into his. He doesn't need any more invitation than that. His hands hook under my backside and he lifts me up against the tiles, thrusting inside me in one swift action. He sinks all the way inside, a long strangled groan building in his throat. A moan that tells me he's been wanting this for some time.

The stretch inside is as wide as when Zane has me, but I'm growing accustomed to the stretch now, my cunt adapting, accommodating the size of these men.

He stands there panting, buried inside me, his forehead resting against the wall and the water running down our bodies. I hook my legs around his waist and dig my heels into his arse.

He growls at me. "Impatient wee thing," he mutters, his Scottish accent thicker than ever. He squeezes the tops of my thighs and starts to rut into me, powerful thrusts that have my spine and my skull crashing against the tiles and the water splashing between our bodies.

It seems crazy to me now, how difficult it used to be to come, how awkward an encounter like this would have seemed. But these two men are experienced, built for fucking, designed for rutting. Their bodies seem crafted for my pleasure entirely. Or perhaps it is the situation itself. The fact they both have me so turned on, so tightly wound, so damn wet, that the orgasm comes easily. I'm a mess in Duncan's arms in no time at all, begging him to pump me full of himself, to knot me hard.

But the alpha has other ideas. He seems to want to make this last. He's in no hurry. He continues to fuck me as the water turns tepid and then cooler and only comes when ice-cold water falls on both our heads. I gasp under the sting of it, combined with the stretch of his knot, and then he walks us out and wraps us in the large warm towels.

I shiver a little and he rubs the towel over my skin, warming me up.

"I'm not sure we got any cleaner," I tease, as I sit in his lap, locked to him by his knot.

"I think it was more fun getting you dirty again," he purrs.

"Will Zane mind?" I ask him, not quite able to meet his eyes, tracing my fingers along his shoulders instead.

"No," is all he says to that and I hope he's right. "It's about time you met the rest of the pack, though, Rosie," he adds softly.

"I know."

"Are you scared?"

Am I? I'm not sure. It's hard to remember now why I was so reluctant to meet Zane's pack, what kept me away. Yes, it was fear, but also shame and uncertainty. Perhaps I always knew deep inside I wanted to be owned by more than one man and perhaps that had always sickened and terrified me.

"My mum and my aunts are all omegas. They were all mated, pregnant and married by my age. I've never wanted that. I want to be someone and go somewhere. I don't want an alpha telling me what to do."

"Zane would never do that. And neither would I. We know what it's like to live differently, the battles you have to fight with the people you love to make them see it's right."

"You mean your parents?"

"Aye, my parents would like me settled down with an omega. None of our parents were happy we formed a pack. Apart from Seb's mum. She thinks the sun shines out of his arse. But, anyway, now we're in with a shot at the Olympics, they're all coming around to the idea."

He asks me more questions about my family as we wait for his knot to deflate and I tell him about my sisters, about how I've always wanted to show them that an omega can be more than her body and her desires.

"I told you, we like smart girls," Duncan says, lifting me

105

from his lap as his knot retreats. "We all work hard in this pack and we expect our omega to as well."

I don't know what he means by that, but I follow him out of the bathroom and back into Zane's room. Zane is sitting up in bed, scrolling through his phone, one hand tucked behind his head.

He grins when we enter the room hand in hand.

"Did you fuck?" he asks us. Duncan nods and Zane's green eyes find mine. "Come here, sugar." His tone is light, but there's authority there too and I drop Duncan's hand and climb into the bed. Zane drags me onto his lap and stares into my eyes. "Was it good?"

"Yes," I whisper, my heart pounding in my ears and Zane's scent strong in my throat.

"Did you come?"

"Of course, she came," Duncan growls, flopping down on the bed.

"See," Zane tells me, "there's nothing wrong with you."

"I know," I whisper. Not believing him. I haven't told him everything. I haven't told him the whole truth.

"You are perfect." His hands stroke up my back and over my gland and Duncan reaches down to kiss my shoulder.

"Do you mind?" I ask Zane. "That I slept with him … we didn't talk it through."

"Do you want him?"

I nod.

"Do you still want me?"

I nod my head with vigour. "Zane, I want you both."

A smile spreads across his face and his eyes soften. "When you said it last night, I didn't know if it was just in the heat of the moment."

"No, I meant it," I say, swallowing hard. I turn to look at Duncan.

"We've done this before, Rosie," the other alpha says. "Been in a relationship with one girl. It's not new to us. We like sharing. We like to see others pleasuring our girl. But I know this is new to you and if it isn't what you want—"

"It is ... it is what I want." I think of last night, of both alphas having their wicked way with me, and my whole body burns with fire. I want them both. I want to be loved by them both.

"She's getting wet again," Duncan chuckles.

Zane bops me on the nose. "Fucking greedy little thing." I feel him stiffen beneath me. "My turn next."

"Don't you have training?" I ask him, grinding against him as Duncan nuzzles my neck.

"Not until later. We have the whole day to play."

* * *

We spend the day in bed together, the alphas taking it in turns to fuck me. Sometimes the other simply watches, sometimes joins in, having me rub or suck his cock. By nightfall, I'm thoroughly exhausted but satisfied.

They bring me dinner in Zane's room. For all the talk of meeting the rest of the pack, it seems they are keen to keep me to themselves today, but the topic crops up again as we eat.

"It's pack lunch tomorrow. Your chance to meet Oliver and Seb," Zane tells me.

"I can't. I'm sorry." I swing my gaze between the two of them. "I have a shift at the museum and work I need to hand in."

"What time's your shift?" Duncan asks.

"Eleven."

"OK, well, come watch us train in the morning. You can meet them then."

I twist stands of spaghetti around my fork and nod. "OK."

"They're going to love you, Rosie," Zane reassures me.

But I'm still nervous. This relationship between the three of us is brand new and shiny and precious. What if the others don't like me? What would that mean for me and Zane and Duncan?

When our plates are empty, their hands and mouths are back on me.

"I thought you had training?" I protest.

"We're skipping it," Zane mutters against my breast.

"Won't you get in trouble?"

"Yep," he nips at my nipple making me squeak. "But it's just a workout in the gym and you've been working us hard all day."

"Sounds like I need to work you some more, for the sake of your training," I say, resting my hands on his shoulder.

His eyes flick up to mine with a growl and before I know it I'm being flipped onto my back.

* * *

The alarm goes off at some ungodly hour when the light is still new and the birds outside are chirping with excitement.

I groan, throwing my arm over my face.

"Come on, sugar," Zane says, throwing back the cover, grabbing an ankle and dragging me to the edge of the bed. "We've got to be down at the river in thirty and you need to shower if we don't want every alpha in this city coming to sniff you out."

I flop back against the mattress. "It's so early, let me sleep."

"Nope!" He tugs me to my feet and gives my arse a slap. "Get moving."

I pout at both the alphas and they chuckle.

"Fuck, get dressed, Omega, or we won't be responsible for our actions," Duncan says.

I do as I'm told, rinsing quickly under the shower before I dress. Zane examines me in my cutoffs and tank and yanks one of his hoodies over my head.

"It'll be cold down at the river this early," he tells me.

"How early is it exactly?" I ask.

"Five thirty. We have to be there for six. Come on, we have to get moving."

We walk down to the kitchen where Duncan has buttered toast waiting for each of us. I nibble on my piece as they lead me into the back garden and wheel bicycles out of the shed.

"We're cycling?" I ask.

"Yes, it's the quickest way," Zane says.

"Is there a bike for me?"

He shakes his head, a wicked grin spreading across his face.

"Oh god, what?" He climbs onto his bike and motions to the handlebars. "Is it safe?"

"I won't let you fall. Come on, we're going to be late and we're in enough shit after yesterday."

I roll my eyes and fold my toast in half, slipping it inside the pocket of the hoodie. Then I turn, grip the handlebars and haul my bottom up to rest on the bar.

"Lean into me, Rosie," Zane instructs and, as I do, his arms cage around me.

At first, we wobble as he weaves us down the garden path

109

and out the back gate, but once we're on the lane and moving fast, the ride is smooth if a little harsh against my backside. A backside that's a tad sore from yesterday's exertions.

The lane takes us around the back gardens of the large town houses and then out into the countryside, fences and trimmed bushes giving way to untamed trees and fields. The birds continue their song as we pass under the boughs of trees dressed in full leaf and down towards the river glinting in the distance.

Zane hums as he cycles and occasionally peppers me with kisses, the bike swerving every time he does and causing me to scream.

"Have some faith, will you? I'm not going to let us crash," he says.

"Just keep your eyes on the path," I tell him and he huffs, pedalling hard to catch up with Duncan. We follow him through a gate and onto a path leading into thick water rushes that sway as high as our heads, and then the river bank comes into sight lined with boathouses. Some are worn, paint peeling, doors hanging from their hinges. Others are large and newly varnished with impressive balconies overlooking the water.

Zane follows the path along the river and slows up as we come to the largest of the boathouses. The wide double doors are pulled back to show a lower room full of boats and oars of every size.

He slows the bike and then holds it steady as I slide off the handlebars, my feet landing on grass damp with dew, a slight morning haze skimming above the water. As he wheels the bike up to the house, two men appear, balancing a long, polished boat between their shoulders.

"Morning," Zane calls as we step aside to let them pass on

the path. The man at the front holds up a hand in salute and the other grunts. I can't see their faces, but their builds are as big as Zane and Duncan's and their scents familiar. It's their other pack mates.

I twist to watch them continue down to the water and lower the boat to rest on the surface.

Zane locks his bike against a stand and takes my hand.

"Come on, let me introduce you."

I squeeze his hand and take a deep inhale, suddenly nervous again. Then I run my fingers through my hair, sure it must be a tangle around my head.

The man at the front of the boat stands first and, catching sight of us approaching, smiles. He's breathtakingly beautiful, all chiselled cheekbones, full lips, and thick golden hair that brushes his shoulders. His eyes, I see as we draw closer, are a honey brown colour and his skin a similar tone. He looks like a muse you'd find in a painting, draped in robes with flowers twined in his hair. But as beautiful as he is, there is something distinctly masculine about him too. His shoulders powerful, his arms strong and his scent predatory. A mixture of leather and blood orange.

He beams straight at me, those honey eyes dancing over my face.

"Ollie, this is Rosie," Zane tells him.

"Rosie," Ollie purrs, holding out his hand to me. "You're the one who's been capturing all Zane's attention."

I let him take my hand and he wraps it between both of his, his hold warm.

"Duncan's too, actually," Zane says, and I try hard not to blush as the alpha's lips twitch.

As if summoned by his name, Duncan arrives at my side and

111

drapes an arm casually around my shoulder.

"She's come to watch us practise," Duncan tells Oliver.

"They dragged you out of bed early, did they? I was wondering if you guys would show up at all." He drops my hand and winks at me. "Hope to be seeing more of you, Rosie."

And my stomach swoops.

He marches back up towards the boathouse, followed closely behind by the fourth pack mate. He couldn't be more different from Ollie. His hair is jet black and his chin stubbled, his eyes a dark brown and his brow heavy. He's older than the others and the tallest by several inches, with the strongest build. He wears a sleeveless top and over his arms trace a tangle of dark inks.

"Seb," Zane says, reaching up to slap him on the shoulder, "this is Rosie."

The alpha swings his gaze around to meet mine, and he glares at me with such ferocity I find myself wanting to drop my eyes to the ground. But they're hypnotic too, dark and swirling. And his scent ... his scent crackles on my tongue and my gland hums.

He holds me in his stare for no more than a heartbeat. Then, saying not a word, he stomps past us towards the boathouse.

"Someone got up on the wrong side of the bed," Zane mutters, scrubbing his hand over his head.

"He didn't seem very pleased to meet me," I say, and I bite down on my lip to stop it from trembling, goosebumps running up my arms.

It feels as if someone just shoved me hard and tried to knock me off my feet.

I rub at my forehead.

Why should I care if their housemate doesn't like me? He

doesn't even know me.

And yet, I've been riding high these last two days with Zane and Duncan. This is a punch to the gut.

"He's not a morning person," Duncan reassures me, rubbing a circle over my back. "Come sit down here, Rosie. We've got to get set up before we head out onto the water."

He takes me to a bench that rests next to the water and I watch them carry down the oars from the house and fiddle with the seats in the boat. When they're satisfied, they climb into the boat one at a time, the shell wobbling on the surface and sending ripples soaring across the river. On the other side of the river, a family of ducks emerge from the grass and sink into the water. Spying me, they swim over, quacking at me. I tear up the remains of my toast and toss it into the water. The ducks peck up the crumbs eagerly.

Finally, each alpha sits in position; Zane at the front, followed by Duncan and Seb, and then Ollie bringing up the rear. Each one grabs his oar, and they push themselves away from the bank. For a moment they are suspended, their reflections vivid beside them so that there are eight alphas, not four, out on the river. Then Ollie gives a low rumble of a signal and together as one, they dip the blades of their oars low in the water and drag them through, gliding forward on their seats as they do. They are perfectly synced, choreographed dancers moving as a single entity, a pack, mirroring each other's actions exactly. If I ever doubted how close this pack was, I don't now. The bond between them is as clear as their reflections.

I stand, hypnotised by the alluring scene, the slosh of the water, the glide of the boat, the grace of their bodies. They skate by me on the river and three pairs of alpha eyes turn to watch me as they pass. Not the fourth pair, though. Those eyes stare resolutely ahead.

Chapter 14

After I finish my shift at the museum and my assignment in the library, I return to my room. An unease has occupied my body, lurked low in my belly, since the river. Seb's reaction to me knocked me off centre. I need space tonight to think and let my body recover. So, I'm annoyed when I hear that knock on my door. I told Zane I needed some time alone.

Except, when I draw back the door, there are two women standing there, not a man. Two omegas, I can tell by their fragrant scents. Scents they obviously aren't trying to hide under blockers.

"Rosie?" one asks me with a smile. She's small and curvy, with blonde hair that falls in waves around her face.

"Yes," I say in confusion.

"Hi, I'm Paris and this is Francesca." She points to her friend, who is slightly taller with chestnut hair and large brown eyes. She wiggles her fingers at me.

"Hi," I say.

"We're so sorry we didn't come and introduce ourselves sooner, but we only just heard about you."

"Heard about me?" I stare at them in confusion.

"You're an omega?" Paris asks slowly, as if I'm dumb.

I shuffle from one foot to the other. There's no point denying it. Most of the college must know by now. But it seems blunt to be asked like that. "Yes, I am."

"We're from OmegaSoc." Paris grins. "I'm the chair and Francesca is the secretary."

"Oh, I'm not really …"

"We always make it our business to come and introduce ourselves to all the new omegas, make sure you have everything you need and are safe and settled."

"Thanks, I'm absolutely fine–"

"We also arrange events for us omegas; talks from medics on the latest treatments," she leans in, "joint 'do's with the Alpha Society."

"The Alpha Society?!"

She obviously thinks I'm interested in that because she nods with enthusiasm. "Yes, we can introduce you to all the most eligible alphas. We have dances and speed dating events," she drops her voice, "and we have a special, safe way of finding an alpha for a heat if you need one."

I swallow, my cheeks heating. "I don't …" I look up at the two perfectly made-up girls in their neat Chanel jackets and matching skirts. "It's kind of you to come, but I'm not really interested in joining any societies. And I'm already seeing someone." Not one someone, two, but they don't need to know that.

They both frown.

"Zane Amir?"

"Yes," I answer, not surprised they've heard.

The two girls glance at each other and then back at me. Paris reaches out and rests her hand on my shoulder. "Just a friendly word of warning to be careful with that one."

My body freezes, my jaw tightens. "Why?"

"Let's just say, he and his pack are known for being into some ..." She coughs and looks to Francesca for help.

"Shady shit," the other girl says bluntly.

"Oh," I say, trying not to laugh. Does that include spit roasting omegas? In which case, their warnings come a little late. "Thanks for the advice. I'll be careful, and if I need any help, I'll be sure to look you up." I start to close the door.

"And come to one of our events," Paris says, shoving a very pink pamphlet at me. "There aren't many of us at this college, and we need to look after each other."

She's right. There aren't. There are so few of us to begin with and most of us are snapped up by alphas, bonded and mated, before we get a chance to make it to college. Especially omegas like me without the financial resources that protect omegas like Paris and Francesca.

I pause. "How many are there?"

"About twenty," Francesca says, examining her nails.

"And the alphas?"

Francesca glances up. "Probably several hundred."

"Shit," I mumble.

A smirk plays across Francesca's face. "Yeah, there's plenty of choice. No need to get tied down to the first one you come across." She raises a knowing eyebrow.

"Call us," Paris adds, and then they leave.

* * *

I oversleep the next morning. I suppose my exhausted body needed to catch up on rest. So, I'm dashing down the stairs two at a time when I spot Zane waiting for me by the door.

He taps his watch with a grin. "You're late."

"I know," I mumble, grappling with the door and dashing past him. He halts me with a firm hand on my shoulder, and kisses me on the lips, before taking my bag from my shoulder and slinging it on to his.

"You're going to be late too if you walk with me."

He shrugs. "My lecture hall is right around the corner from yours and I can just sneak in the back."

We walk quickly along the pavements, our joined hands swinging between us.

"We missed you last night," he says.

"I missed you too."

"Then you're coming round tonight, right?"

I should probably catch up on more sleep, see some of my friends and generally be a hell of a lot more independent than I am being, but his scent has my skin humming and the allure of being in bed with both my alphas is far too strong for me to resist. I realise I am much weaker willed than I ever believed.

I nod with a sigh.

"Why the sigh?" he asks.

"I'm not sure it's healthy to be together all the time."

"Why?" he asks simply. "Are we making you unhappy?"

"No." Quite the opposite. I don't think I've ever felt this happy before, or this loved.

"Then why's it a problem?"

"We're young, and these things never end well, do they? If I let you consume my life completely, what will be left when you're gone?"

He's quiet and I can tell he's thinking as his thumb slides over the back of my hand. It rained overnight. The paving stones are a dark grey and sodden with water, and the leaves

118

on the trees overhead are wet. Droplets fall occasionally, streaking towards the ground. One lands on his shoulder and, from the corner of my eye, I see it sink into the cotton fabric of his shirt.

He exhales a long breath. "I think we never know what the future is going to bring. We have to work hard, prepare the best we can. We shouldn't stop ourselves from doing what we enjoy now for fear of what might come. Maybe you'll snap my heart right in two, Rosie, but I believe you're worth the risk."

He stops us and swings me around for another lingering kiss, one that will make us even later for our lectures. When he pulls away, I realise we're already at the hall. He hands me my bag.

"What about Seb?" I ask him. The alpha's sullen reaction towards me yesterday has me rattled. Maybe it is just that omega-need to always be liked, to always please an alpha.

"You just caught him at a bad moment. Seriously, don't worry about it, Rosie."

I nod. Why is it bothering me so much? Is it because for a moment I looked at that pack out there on the water and saw something I wanted, somewhere I wanted to belong?

I curl my hair behind my ear. Fantasies. I could never be a pack omega. My parents wouldn't approve. Society would look down on me. I'd never fulfil those dreams I have of studying the stars.

Besides, Seb obviously has no interest in me.

"You're sure?" I ask Zane.

"Absolutely. Come round tonight, alright?"

And I can't resist. I'm in Zane's bed again that night, lying on my side, pinned between my alphas. Duncan fucks me lazily from behind, his pace considered as I kiss Zane, my arms around his neck and his fingers at my clit. Duncan's hands rest on my hips, but his thumbs stray over the globes of my arse. I've discovered he has a love of my backside, squeezing and pinching it whenever he can.

"I'm going to come," I say into Zane's mouth, and Duncan's thrusts become harder, his thumbs skating over my arse and Zane's fingers flicking me harder. I buck between them wildly as I come and as I do, the pad of Duncan's thumb knocks against my anus and enters just a fraction.

I gasp, pleasure crashing through me.

Unexpected but welcome.

Chapter 15

The next day, I don't have any lectures until the afternoon, so I stay in bed and wait for the boys to return from training. The front door whacks open just after eight, and the house fills with their animated voices as they discuss the morning's training session. Their heavy footsteps pound the staircase, and then I hear the blast of the shower, their voices audible above the water.

Lying back against the pillow, I imagine all four of the pack in there together, hard naked bodies pressed up against one another as they soap each other's bodies.

Shit! My imagination. It's taken a warped twist since I've started hanging out with these boys. Ideas I've never entertained before, possibilities, fantasies, creeping into my mind. My skin grows hot thinking about them, thinking about what it would be like to pad along the hallway now and slip in between their towering bodies.

Maybe I'd be brave enough to try it, if it weren't for Seb. I suspect he'd push me straight out of the bathroom and bolt the door. I'm not pack, I don't belong in those intimate moments they share. And why does that sadden me? I've never wanted to belong to an alpha, let alone four. I relish my independence, my freedom. Being caught up with four men would crush that entirely.

I'm still lost in my thoughts when Duncan and Zane come barging through the door, towels tied around both their waists, their torsos gleaming with water.

"Ahhh, you're still here," Duncan says, diving straight into the bed and snuggling up to me.

"Hey, you're all wet!" I protest.

"And so are you." He grins, sniffing. "What are you still doing here, Rosie? Not cutting class?"

"Nope. I don't have any lectures this morning. I was going to lie in and then sneak around your house when you're all out."

Zane peers down at me as he pulls on his briefs. He looks torn. "I wanna stay, but it's dissections and they're my favourite." He yanks his jeans up his legs.

I laugh. "Are you telling me dissecting dead bodies is more enjoyable than rutting me, Alpha?"

"It's a toss up," he says with a cheeky grin.

"I don't have class until after lunch," Duncan tells me, nuzzling into my neck.

"Ahhh shit," Zane says, his fingers hovering at his half-buttoned fly. "Don't make this harder than it is."

"Are you going to do wicked things to me?" I ask Duncan. "While Zane's away."

"Too fucking right, wee yin. I'm going to take advantage of having you to myself." He rolls me towards him, his hands slithering down my side.

"You two are cruel," Zane mutters, turning his back on us as he continues to dress.

I let out a few exaggerated sighs as Duncan nibbles on my throat, just to torture Zane a little more. He tugs his sweatshirt over his head and stomps from the room.

"Goodbye, enjoy shagging while I'm out learning how to save people's lives."

He slams the door and Duncan and I burst out laughing.

"He doesn't like being left out, does he?" I say, climbing on top of Duncan and straddling him.

Reaching up, he traces the circles of my nipples. "Actually, he's pretty good at sharing. We all are." His eyes flick up to mine. "But it's more than that. Being in a pack is about wanting each other to be happy, about making sure that happens for each other, looking out for each other."

"That sounds nice," I say wistfully.

"You don't have anyone to look out for you, wee yin?"

"Sophia, I guess. And my sisters, but they're still young. I mostly look out for them. And my mum," I groan, "she thinks she's looking out for me but ..."

He tugs me down so I'm lying flat against his chest. "But what?"

"It sometimes feels like she's looking out more for herself. She's more worried about her reputation than my happiness. In her ideal world, I'd be mated to an alpha and out of her hair."

"You're not exactly in her hair now. You're doing your own thing here at college."

"That's not how she sees it. She thinks I'm a walking disaster. That I'm going to land myself in trouble." I rest my ear against the alpha thud of his heart. So powerful. "Maybe she's right."

"She isn't," he says. Then he rolls me off his body and I squeal. "Come on, let's go to my room."

"Your room?" The dark mood that hovers over my head with

123

that last confession, lifts. "Yes please." I scurry from the bed, bouncing on my toes as I grin up at the alpha.

"Steady on." He chuckles. "It's not that exciting."

"But maybe it'll give me more of an insight into you. I said I wanted to nose around the house."

"Come on then, you snoop." He drapes a dressing gown over my shoulder and ties the towel back around his waist. I skip by his side as he leads me to the room next to Zane's and I realise that he really must have heard everything between me and Zane. The walls in this old house are paper-thin.

As we step inside, I let go of his hand and start to explore. The layout is a mirror image of Zane's. The window and the old fireplace are identical and the big bed and desk are set up in the same manner. But the decor is different. Across his desk are huge A3 pieces of paper with pencil sketchings. I step in closer to take a look. Complex diagrams of engines and machinery scrawl across the pages.

"Is this your college work?"

"Aye" he tells me. "Some of it, some is just stuff I'm fiddling with."

I turn my head to smile at him and catch sight of the shelves running along the walls and across the top of the fireplace. Carefully positioned on top sit models – the kind you painstakingly build and paint yourself.

"Oh my god." I stroll up to him and fling my arms around his neck. "I think you're an even bigger geek than I am. Do you build all those yourself?"

"Aye. It helps relax me."

"You find it hard to relax?"

"It's an alpha thing." He shrugs one shoulder, his hands coming to rest on my arse. "All this pent-up energy, burning away at you the whole time." He squeezes my cheeks in his palms. "You know what else helps with that, wee yin?"

"I think I can guess."

"I want my bed smelling like you," he tells me. "I want you coming all over my sheets."

I nod my head slowly, pretending to consider his request. "Yeah, I think I can do that."

"Aye, you can," he says, sliding the robe off my shoulders. His hands return immediately to my arse, and he kneads at it as he sweeps his tongue down my throat.

"You're an arse guy," I say.

His head snaps up. "What does that mean?" My cheeks redden.

"I mean, some guys like tits, some like legs and some like butts."

"You have a very ripe, very squeezable arse, Omega." And he gives it a fierce pinch to show me what he means.

"I'm pretty partial to an arse myself," I say, reaching down, untying the towel and groping his arse cheeks. They're much firmer than my own, lined with muscle.

I guess I'm becoming more confident with these alphas. More willing to take the lead. To show them what I want.

"Yours is far superior," he tells me firmly. "Sometimes I want to take a giant bite out of your bloody bottom. The way it jiggles with just the perfect amount of wobble."

"OK," I say, meeting those ocean eyes.

His eyebrow twitches. He stares at me. "OK what?" he asks slowly.

"You can bite my arse," I tell him innocently.

He groans and runs a hand over his shorn head. "Don't tease me like that, wee yin."

"I'm not teasing. I'm serious." I think of that stray thumb against my ring the night before. Of how unexpectedly good that had felt. How I want to know if other stuff would feel just as good.

In a moment, he has me face down and bent over the side of the bed, and he is kneeling between my open legs. He glides the back of his fingers up and down my legs, and slick trickles onto my thighs. Leaning in, he licks it away with his tongue and his hands reach my rump, kneading and massaging. I lean into his touch. It feels good, but it's not where I want it. Everything between my legs pulses, and that's where I need his fingers and his mouth.

As if he knows what I'm thinking, his thumb strays to my clit and fondles it. I moan, undulating my hips to increase the pressure of his touch, and without warning he nips at my cheek.

I squeal, jerking away, his thumb gliding against my wet clit as I do. Electricity sparks through my body and I come as he continues to circle my nub.

Gently, he presses a kiss to the spot he just bit. "OK?" he asks, rubbing his stubbled cheek over my backside. Then he kisses the base of my spine, his chin nudging between my cheeks. I gasp at how intimate that feels.

He kisses a little lower, his thumb continuing to flick against my clit, keeping me in a state of heightened sensation.

"Want me to go lower?" he whispers, his breath warm against my skin.

This wasn't what I had in mind, but now I'm curious. I want him lower.

"Yes, lower, Alpha."

I hear him shift on his knees behind me, and carefully he

spreads my cheeks open with his free hand.

"Tell me to stop if you don't like it."

"I will." My body is putty after my first orgasm, primed for another and another, and so I don't tense as his lips drop lower, nuzzling between my cheeks, finding the crease of my backside. All my focus trains on his lips, prized for the next kiss, lower still and then lower again until they press against my hole.

It's so incredibly intimate and I sigh, tripping over again, my hips bucking, and my hole bucking against his mouth.

"Aye, you like that, wee yin?" he whispers, his hot breath sweeping against that sensitive part of me.

"Y-y-yes," I gasp. "Don't stop."

His lips press more firmly and then I feel the wet glide of his tongue sweeping over my hole.

That action shouldn't feel so insanely good, but it does, the sensation at my clit and at my arse overwhelming.

He continues to torture me sweetly with long firm sweeps of his tongue, as if he's enjoying the most delicious ice cream and not my backside; his tongue sometimes rigid, sometimes soft.

I'm not ashamed, not embarrassed. I can tell from his actions how into this he is.

I come a third time as he rings my hole and presses one lingering kiss there.

"Shit, Rosie," he mutters, as he staggers to his feet, and the head of his cock nudges against my entrance. "A girl's never wanted me to do that to her before. That was fucking erotic."

"Fuck me," I plead, wiggling my arse against his erection. "Please Alpha."

"Not there," he tells me.

"No, not there." I know I'm not ready for that. He's big and I couldn't take him.

I'm lifted up onto my toes as he thrusts inside my cunt instead.

"But you'd like to?"

"I think ... maybe," I gasp, the air knocked out of my lungs as he pounds me with the force of a man who's on the edge.

"Fuck, Rosie, fuck. You're such an innocent-looking thing. But you're not, are you?"

"No," I say. "I'm dirty."

"A perfectly dirty wee omega. So good for me. So good for Zane."

The words float in the air about my head. Dirty. I'm dirty. But again, I feel no shame. It's freeing to be as dirty as I want. To explore every part of my body. To give every part of myself to these alphas.

Afterwards, I pull on one of his t-shirts, and we lie out on the sun loungers in the massive garden, soaking up the late morning rays. My skin is warm and fuzzy.

"How did it happen between you and Zane?" I ask Duncan. I know the story of how the pack formed, but not how the relationship between Duncan and Zane turned into something else.

He tucks his hands behind his head and stares up at the cloudless sky.

"How do any of these things happen?"

My cheeks redden as always when I find my words difficult to find. I press the back of my palm to one.

"I mean, did you know you were bi before you met Zane?"

"Perhaps. Perhaps I'd registered that I find guys attractive, but I never especially wanted to act on it. With Zane, it was different. We have a similar sense of humour, a similar outlook on the world and with Ollie doing his arty farty crap and Seb off doing his shit, we were often together. One night I'd had a few beers – a bit of dutch courage – and I made a move."

"Oh." I'd always assumed it was Zane who instigated things between him and Duncan.

"Do you love him?"

"Yeah, but I love all my pack mates. Like brothers. With Zane there's a sexual attraction too."

"And is it weird, me being in this too?"

"Nah, Rosie, it feels better."

I hum, the heat in my cheeks fading and a satisfaction spreading through my chest.

"But I don't know what this is going to mean for our pack," he says, and I hear the honesty, the concern in his voice.

And just like that, the warmth in my chest seeps away.

I know this could all end.

Chapter 16

We wanna take you out tonight, me and Duncan. *Zane messages me.*

It's a Monday! I reply.

Just for dinner.

I smile. He knows I'm a sucker for good food.

OK but I'm tutoring until eight in the library.

Duncan will meet you there.

I spend the entire day wondering what a double date with two alphas will be like. I can't help thinking it will be good. They've never been competitive or jealous with me. They are always attentive, and having them both there means I get twice the amount of attention. Something I find I like.

Several times I find my mind wandering away as I sit through my lectures and then my tutoring sessions, and the last of my students has to call my name several times to catch my attention.

Duncan's perching on a low wall beneath a lamppost, a book folded in his lap, when I leave the library. I'm standing right by him when he finally catches my scent and looks up at me.

"Good book?" I ask him.

He lifts it up to me and shows me the cover, an illustration of spaceships and aliens sprawls the cover.

"I'm surprised you can read. It's so dark out here," I say.

"We alphas have good night vision."

It makes sense. I'd wondered how they'd managed to find the right spots in the pitch blackness of Zane's room.

He stares at me and I realise he's waiting for me to make the first move. I suspect this alpha is a little shy.

I sidle up to him, standing between his thighs, and he lifts my chin and kisses me.

"We missed you last night," he says, gliding his hands down to my arse and squeezing.

"We?"

"I. I missed you." He squeezes harder. "I'm not tagging along for the ride here, Rosie. I'm very much into you. And would be whether Zane was in the picture or not."

"Same," I confess. Then I frown. "Is that the way it should be? That wouldn't upset Zane?"

"Aye, it's the way it should be."

They are only words but the way he says them, so assured and confident, I can't help believing them.

It's still late spring and though the days are lengthening, the sky is dark and, above our heads, the first smattering of stars begin to pepper the sky.

"I never get bored with looking at them," I mutter.

He tips his head back. "The stars?"

"Uh huh."

He lifts our conjoined hands and traces his forefingers over the cluster of stars tattooed on the underside of my wrist. "You like stars."

"Yes, always have, ever since I was little. I used to make my parents leave the bedroom curtains open so that I could gaze up at them. I'd build my own spaceships from cardboard boxes and have my sisters help crew my ship out into space." I laugh.

"It's what you still want to do?"

"Well," I say, "I'm not deluded. They'd never pick an omega to be an astronaut." Too weak, too hormonal. "And anyway, I'm not sure being trapped in a spaceship is as glamorous as it is. But I'd like to study the stars. Learn more about what's out there."

I lean my head against his shoulder as we walk into town, immersed in his scent and happy.

The restaurant is a small family-run Italian with chequered tablecloths and candles in old wine bottles. The place is nearly empty and Zane waits for us at a table tucked into a back corner.

"Hey, sugar," he says, drawing back my chair.

"Are you going to let me order for myself tonight?" I ask, picking up a menu and running my eye down the list.

He shrugs. "The lasagna here is really good."

I hate to admit it, but that sounds good, and when the waiter comes to take our order, Zane chuckles when I choose it.

I listen to them discuss training, about Seb's suggestion for a new workout plan. And I can't help thinking about the alpha again. They've told me everything with him is fine, yet since that day on the river, they've made no attempt to introduce me to the pack again. If anything, it seems they've been keeping me away. In the end, I can't help but blurt out what's bothering me.

"Are you going to explain what's going on with Seb?"

"He's very anal about making sure our plan is working," Zane says.

"No, I mean about why he was so rude that day at the river. About why you've been keeping me away from him."

Duncan's forkful of spaghetti pauses in the air, and then he lowers it to his plate. "We told you, he can be a bit of a grumpy git."

I shake my head. "No, it was more than that. Does he have a problem with me?"

Zane reaches across the table and covers my hand with his. "What? No, of course not. Why would he?"

"Come on," I say. "I'm not stupid. The man would hardly look at me."

"It's complicated."

I put down my own fork and swing my gaze from one alpha to the other. My stomach swims with unease. I thought they'd be quick to put my mind at peace like they always do. Now it seems as if they're hiding something. "That doesn't sound reassuring."

"Seb takes his time warming up to people. Especially omegas. He's had his heart broken," Duncan says quietly.

"Oh." I look down at my plate, moving the sheets of pasta around with my fork.

"It's something he should tell you about," Zane goes on.

I peer up at him and his face is serious and concerned, as if he's considering his pack mate.

Duncan reaches over and strokes my hair back over my shoulder. "Don't take it personally and give him a chance. Once he gets to know you, he'll thaw."

"It just didn't seem like he's happy about us." I gesture to the three of us.

"If we're happy, he's happy. And we're happy, very happy." Zane grins.

"He worries things will get messy, that's all. Like it did with Pippa."

My ears prick up at the mention of that name and I open my

mouth to ask about her but Duncan cuts across me.

"Seb's older than us. Sometimes he seems to believe he's responsible for us all."

I saw that at the river. The big alpha appeared to carry more than the boat on his shoulders. And there was an energy around him, as if he was the glue and the bolsters holding the pack together. Maybe that's why his gruffness had upset me so much.

Zane changes the subject after that, making us laugh when he recounts a disastrous encounter with a patient who'd been unwilling to divulge his complaint.

By the time we get to the dessert, I'm relaxed and content again, surfing high on the ripples of their scents.

"We got you a gift," Zane says as I sweep my tongue over my spoon, intent on devouring all of my chocolate mousse.

"You don't have to keep buying me gifts," I say without meaning it. I'm loving every ounce of attention from these men.

Onto the table, Zane slides a black box with a neat silver ribbon tied up in a bow. His eyes flicker with wickedness. "It's not exactly a selfless present. It's as much for us as it is for you."

I throw him a suspicious look and tug at the bow, expecting to find lingerie inside. But when I lift the lid, I find two small objects crafted from black silicone resting in black tissue paper.

I stare at them.

"Do you know what they are, wee yin?" Duncan whispers, leaning in closer and squeezing my thigh under the table.

"I ..." I have a fair idea, but I'm too embarrassed to say in case I'm wrong.

"These are anal beads," Duncan explains as he points to a

row of spheres, "and this is an anal plug."

"Have you ever done things via the backdoor, sugar?" Zane asks, his gaze hot on me.

"Only what I did with Duncan the other day."

"Would you like to do more?"

My eyes spring to his. There's unbridled lust in his eyes and that look has my skin blazing.

"Yes," I whisper. "I want to take you both at once."

The alphas' scents flair and I can taste their arousal in the air.

"You'd like that, Omega?" Zane asks, his voice thick with lust too.

My cheeks are on fire and my underwear wet. These alphas like to play with me, to tease me like this, and fuck me if I don't love it.

"We'd be gentle," Duncan reassures me, "and we'd go at your pace. But if–"

I bite my lip for effect and stare into each set of alpha eyes in turn. "I'd like to try."

Zane growls and I feel it deep in my gut.

"What do I need to do?"

Duncan's jaw is tight and his scent piqued. He doesn't wear his emotions on his face like Zane does, but I know he's just as turned on, just as pleased by my response.

"Like I said, we're going to go slow with you," he says. "So we'll start with the beads. We'll have a play with them so you get used to the sensation. And we'll go from there."

His hand slides up my leg to the wet gusset of my underwear.

"Can we start experimenting with them now?" I breathe, closing my eyes.

Duncan growls and leans forward to nip at my shoulder.

"Get the fucking bill, Zane," he tells his friend.

Chapter 17

As soon as we're out of the taxi, both alphas are on me, Duncan kissing my mouth and Zane my neck as we stumble as one body of entangled limbs towards the house. Zane's forced to break away and fumble with the door, his key slipping from the lock as his eyes keep drifting to his pack mate kissing me, our hands inside each other's tops.

"Fuck," he mutters, "you both look so goddamn sexy. I think I want to fuck you both."

I smile into Duncan's mouth. There was a chance I could feel like an intruder in this thing that exists between Duncan and Zane. But I don't. We are like an equilateral triangle, each a corner of equal weight, of equal force.

I smile harder. I am such a geek.

"What?" Duncan asks, breaking away.

I giggle. "Is it weird I think about mathematics sometimes during sex stuff?"

"Does it turn you on?" Duncan asks as he walks me through the doorway.

"I wouldn't go that far."

"E=MC squared," Duncan growls in my ear, pushing me up against Zane in the hallway.

"You could say anything in that Scottish accent of yours, and it would turn me on," I mutter.

His hand is inside my bra. "Energy is liberated matter," he whispers, squeezing my tit.

Zane nibbles the side of my neck while his hand slides down the back of jeans and into my knickers. He finds my ring and tickles it with the pad of his finger. "Black matter," he growls.

I gasp.

"The Big Bang." Duncan grinds into me and I feel his hard erection on my clit. "Photons and atoms and all that shit."

Zane smears his finger in my slick and then he's ringing my hole, dipping his finger ever so slightly inside.

"Oh," I moan. I know I'm going to find it hard to keep a straight face every time these phrases come up in class from now on. My mind will slip back to this encounter in the hallway.

I hear a click of a door open behind me and then we're walking into the cavernous TV room. It lies in pitch blackness and none of us move to switch on the lights. Instead, Duncan kicks at the door as the three of us tear at each other's clothes. I zip open Duncan's fly and Duncan tugs off Zanes shirt. Zane yanks down my jeans and my underwear and I do the same to Duncan. And then Duncan is unhooking my bra as Zane unbuttons his shirt.

In the darkness, I can just about make out the outline of their bodies, the stiffness of their cocks.

"Where are the toys?" I ask, as Zane knocks me back into the sofa and drops between my thighs as Duncan continues his attention on my breasts, sucking one tit into his mouth as he rubs my other nipple between his finger and thumb.

"You wanna try this now, sugar?" Zane asks me.

"Yes," I say with a hint of impatience. I can hear their combined pants in the silence that follows. "What?"

"It's been a fantasy of ours for a long time," Zane confesses, stroking up and down my thigh. "To think it might – "

"You mean you never did it with ..." I can't bring myself to say her name.

"No," Duncan says simply.

So it's one thing. One thing that will be ours. And not hers. It makes me even more keen to try.

"It might not work," I say cautiously, "But you know ... I want to try it. The thought of both of you inside me at once." They both growl and the sound sets slick trickling from my cunt.

"Ahhh good girl," Duncan says, scrabbling about on the floor, until he finds our pile of clothes and the black box secured in his pocket. He makes quick work of the ribbon and snatches off the lid, lifting out the string of beads. "Do you know how this works?"

"No," I admit.

I hear the puff of air that rushes from his lips as if he's trying to regain some control. I love how much this is turning them on, just the thought of it pushing both of them dangerously close to the edge of their control.

It's tantalising – I'm power tripping with it, getting wetter by the second.

"I'm going to smear these in your slick," he tells me, brushing them lightly down my body, the silicone soft but cold, and then spinning them near my entrance. "Then I'm going to insert them into your," his next word is swallowed up by a growl, and it takes him a moment before he can manage the word, "Arse."

"Yes," I say.

His fingers stroke through my folds and when I peer down

139

at Zane, I can see his attention locked on the work of Duncan's fingers. Then Duncan arrives at my hole and I feel the first bead prod through my tight ring.

"Does that feel OK?"

"Uh huh," I gasp, my eyes fluttering closed as I take in the sensation.

"Then a little more, wee yin." He presses the beads in further. I expect it to burn, but the silicone is well lubricated with my slick and all I feel is this strange fullness and pleasure I didn't expect to find there. "And a little more. Just relax."

I sigh out the breath I'd been holding and sink further into the cushions of the sofa, the pleasure in my backside amplifying when I do.

The beads are about the length of my finger and certainly no wider. Both my alphas are several, several times larger, and I know it's going to take some preparation before either of them will be inside me like this.

"There," Duncan says, bending down to kiss my forehead. "How does that feel?"

"Good," I moan. "But ..." my eyes flick between them. "Is that it?"

"No," Duncan says, "That's not it. Now we're going to make you come. And when you do, I'm going to slide these out and blow your mind."

"Oh," I say, biting down on my lip.

"Zane," Duncan says, and his pack mate tears his gaze from where the end of the beads dangles out of my hole, and brings his mouth down to my clit. His tongue starts achingly slowly, weaving around my nub as if he has all the time in the world, and Duncan copies his actions on my nipple.

"More," I demand, "Please more. It's not enough."

"We know," Zane says against my clit, kissing it gently between his lips. "Trust us."

I groan, lifting my hips, trying to increase the pressure of his mouth against me and squeezing my tits as I do.

"Fuck," Duncan mutters, shaking his head slightly, but staying true to the pace.

I want to come. I want to come badly. But this pace invigorates every single one of my nerve ends, ensuring the sensation between my folds and at my nipples intensifies and intensifies. Soon, my whole body buzzes and my gland throbs. I clench around the beads and a fresh, different sensation spirals through me.

"Ohhhhh," I moan.

"She's close, Duncan," Zane warns and Duncan drops to the floor beside the other alpha. I expect him to grip the beads, ready to tug them out, but instead, he slides one, then two, of his thick fingers up into my cunt and I squeal as he knocks against my G spot.

There's no escape, no hiding. Every part of me is stimulated now.

Duncan pumps his fingers and I hear the sloppy wet noises and the slurp of Zane's tongue as he increases the pace.

My spine arches and the beads shift inside me, sending fresh spasms of pleasure, tripping me over the edge.

"Ohh—" I start to sigh and then Duncan does it, pulling the beads from me, and my orgasm multiplies. I pump slick as my cunt convulses around Duncan's fingers, and my clit gushes straight into Zane's mouth.

I jolt and spasm on the sofa and then I collapse, hot and sweaty and destroyed.

"You gushed," Zane says, licking his lips. "You gushed

straight into my mouth. Fuck, that tastes—"

Duncan grips him by the back of the neck and kisses him hard, and I know he can taste me on Zane's lips.

When they draw back breathless, they peer at me.

"Don't stop," I breathe and I lie there watching as Zane drops to his hands and his knees and Duncan takes him from behind. It's not like it is with me. It's more violent, more powerful, both struggling for dominance. Both wanting to be in control. Once Duncan comes, Zane stumbles to his feet and his cock is in Duncan's mouth in a moment.

I think Zane's going to come in his pack mate's mouth, but at the last moment, he pulls back and stumbles towards me.

"I wanna come on you, Rosie. All over your tits." Duncan's eyes are wide, his hands claiming Zane's shoulders, his mouth kissing along Zane's neck.

"Yes," I groan and hot ribbons of spend stream from Zane's dick in pulses, landing on my chest and my stomach. Marking me as theirs.

Chapter 18

I wake in the night tangled between two sleeping alphas. They are both out for the count, dead weight, which I struggle to move as I slip out in search of water. My mouth is parched, and I know I won't be able to sleep if I don't drink.

I tug on my knickers and throw Zane's t-shirt over my head.

At the door, I pause with my hand on the handle. I could wake one of the alphas and send them out to fetch me water instead. There is something intimidating about creeping through the silent house, but they both look so peaceful, like sleeping lions, and I don't have the heart. So with a steadying draw of breath, I tiptoe out into the hallway, down the staircase and into the large cavernous kitchen.

The moon is bright and pours in through the bifold doors, lighting my path to the shelf with the glasses. I stare for a moment at the moving shadows in the garden, listen to the fridge hum quietly in the corner, feel the cold stone tiles under my feet.

Then I reach up on the tips of my toes, the hem of Zane's t-shirt slipping up my backside. As I do, I sense Seb, his scent seeping into the kitchen.

I freeze, my fingers hovering around the cool glass.

His feet pad on the floor behind me, almost silently, like the movements of a wolf.

I grip the glass and lower back down onto the soles of my feet. I jerk on the tap, trailing my fingers under the cold stream of water as I sense him draw nearer. Closer and closer. Every step towards me forces a fierce beat from my heart.

I can taste his scent more clearly now. Dark, dense, heavy. Like thick, black treacle. The hairs on my forearms prickle and I lick my lips, tasting the scent in my mouth. My gland hums in my neck.

He keeps coming – my heart thumping with each step – right up behind me. Only stopping when the heat of his body grazes mine. An electricity fizzles down my skin.

"What are you doing here, Omega?" His voice sounds full of restrained anger and I quiver despite my best efforts to appear unafraid.

I go to speak but my voice catches in my dry mouth. I lick my lips and try again, "G-g-getting some water to drink."

"No, Omega." His voice is so loud in my head, and yet, I realise he's whispering. "I asked: what are you doing here?" He bends closer, his nose brushing the strands of my hair, breathing me in, his head lowering to where my gland thrums, begging for the touch of his lips. My body tilts toward him. My eyelids drift shut.

I don't answer because I don't know what to say. I sense whatever I say will be wrong.

"You don't belong here," he growls, and I recoil.

I thought ... for a moment, I thought ...

"You'll never be part of this pack." His breath is hot on my gland and air rushes over it as he inhales my scent. "Is that what you want?"

"I-I-I ..." My head spins. His scent is so deep, so overwhelming. I tighten my grip on the glass feeling it slip through my fingers. His tone and his words are so angry and yet ... his scent ... am I imagining it?

"I don't want you," he snarls. A shiver skates down my spine, but it's not fear. It's something else, something in his scent and the heat of his body.

I don't want him, I don't want him either.

"You think you're going to split apart my pack, but you're wrong."

"I don't want to ... I'm just ..." His words confuse me. I can't follow his reasoning.

His lips brush against my neck, so faintly, I blink, unsure if I imagined it.

"You think it wise to walk half-naked through a house full of alphas, Omega?"

I swallow, close my eyes. My gland aches. But he lifts his mouth from my neck and brings it close to the shell of my ear.

"Get ... back ... to ... bed, Omega," he growls. When I don't move, he steps back. "Go!" he barks and I jolt so hard I almost drop the glass.

I spin quickly, trying not to look his way, although my eyes are drawn to him anyway. He's slunk back into the shadows, his face bathed in darkness, but I see the rise and fall of his shoulders, the tension in his body.

I snap my gaze from him and hurry from the room, almost stumbling on the stairs in my bid to get away.

Back in Zane's room, I shut the door and breathe, sucking in the scents of Zane and Duncan, cinnamon and grass, trying to flush the other one away. It's hopeless. He's in my mouth and on my tongue and no matter how many mouthfuls of water I

145

gulp, I can't flush it away.

I climb back into bed and, sandwiched between my alphas, I eventually fall back to sleep.

My dreams are fitful. I'm being watched. A heavy gaze pressing down on me wherever I go. A scent clogging my throat. Words in my ear. *I don't want you.*

It's all such a tangle that by the morning I'm unsure what is real and what isn't. Did I dream that encounter in the kitchen?

So I don't tell Zane and I don't tell Duncan. I have no desire to be part of a pack. If Seb doesn't like me, it's no skin off my nose.

But if he hopes to drive me away, I'm not that easily intimidated. I've been fighting for what I want for too long to be deterred by one grumpy alpha.

No matter how fierce his growl.

Chapter 19

I end up back in Zane or Duncan's bed every night that week, and my arse has never had so much attention. It's been kissed, fingered and stretched, and despite everything I would've believed, I've loved every minute if it. Loudly.

When I'm in bed with these men, I can't help myself. The noises they force from me are raw and untamed. I know it drives them wild, so I make no attempt to be quiet.

The other alphas in the house must hear me. And that, I admit, is part of the appeal. I want them to hear. I want them to imagine me. I want Seb to know I'm not afraid of him.

I don't admit these thoughts to Zane and Duncan, but they seem to guess them.

"I think you are a little exhibitionist, sugar," Zane says, nipping my nipple between his teeth.

"I am?" I say, flat out on my back after another session with both my alphas.

"Definitely. I think you like to be watched and I think you like to be heard."

"I like it when you watch me, or when Duncan watches me." I peer at Zane on one side of me and then at Duncan on the other.

"I also think you like the others in this house to hear you, wee yin."

My cheeks redden and they both chuckle.

"Caught red cheeked." Zane touches my face with a hiss.

"Maybe have some mercy on our poor pack mates, though," Duncan mutters. "Ollie says you've been driving him insane with all your begging and pleading."

"Really?" I think of the beautiful alpha with his caramel eyes and long blonde hair, and I bite my lip.

"Ahh," says Zane. "I think she likes that idea."

"Perhaps," I say, shrugging one shoulder.

Zane props up on one elbow and peers down into my face, tracing his forefinger between my breasts and towards my tummy button. "Do you fancy him, Omega?"

"Ollie?" I say, smiling. "Do you think there is a woman alive who wouldn't find your pack mate attractive?"

Zane peers over at Duncan, and I flick my gaze between the two of them. "What?" I ask.

"He thinks you're pretty."

The blush at my cheeks spreads across my body and straight to my core. "Does he want to ...?" I flick my gaze between my two alphas again. "Because if he did ..."

"I think he'd want nothing more than to fuck you senseless."

I shiver, drawing my hands over my head. "And what would you two think if he did?"

"It feels greedy keeping a delicious omega like you to ourselves. We're used to sharing."

"Besides, we'd get our turn at listening to you being fucked." Both their hands are on me again. This conversation is turning all three of us on.

"Well, then," I say, "let's see what happens."

* * *

At the weekend, Duncan insists I join the Sunday pack dinner.

"It's a tradition, Omega," Duncan says with a tone I know by now means he will not accept any argument. "We all sit down to dinner on a Sunday together. As a family. Seb cooks the best roast. It's about time you showed your face."

"Are you sure I'll be welcome?" I ask, thinking of Seb. Zane and Duncan seem unaware that their pack mate despises me.

"I told you, he just needs to get to know you, and this is the perfect opportunity. Plus, Ollie will be there."

I roll my eyes, smiling. "OK, I'll come. I love a home-cooked roast and I haven't had one in ages."

"Just one thing," Duncan tells me. "You have to promise to wear the butt plug." I've been wearing it most days. To lectures and classes and my shifts in the museum. I don't find it a nuisance. In fact, it's a deliciously naughty way to go about my usual business, when nobody else knows. My alphas find it hot too. They're always asking where and when I wore it.

So I agree, even though I'm racked with nerves. I remember the way Seb scowled at me, his scent full of displeasure, and my knees almost knocking together in fear despite my determination to stay strong. What will he be like at dinner?

And then there's Ollie. We haven't talked about the possibility of me hooking up with him since the other night, but it's been playing around and around in my mind.

I dress in what I hope is a suitable summer dress. It's light and pretty, but not too revealing. Then, I set off for dinner with four alphas, wondering to myself if I am once again walking straight into the wolves' lair.

Zane meets me at the door and, with a big grin, leads me

through to the large kitchen at the rear of the house. The evening is unusually warm and the bifold doors are pulled back, letting in the cool breeze and, with it, the floral scents of the garden.

The long table is set for five people with wine, the roast chicken, vegetables, and potatoes already laid out. Seb stands by the counter stirring gravy, and I notice his shoulders tense as I enter. Duncan is walking around the table setting out cutlery and looks up when we arrive, coming over to kiss my cheek.

"Hi," I say shyly in Seb's direction, and his eyes meet mine for just a fraction of a second, that darkness making my head spin. Then he jerks his chin at me, before carrying the gravy jug to the table and taking a seat at the head.

"Come on, it's going to get cold," he says.

Zane positions me at the centre of the table, sitting next to me and pouring us both a large glass of wine. Duncan takes a seat opposite as Ollie enters the room, his thumbs hooked into the back pockets of his jeans.

"Hey," he says to us all, and I'm struck again by how beautiful he is, seeming to light up the room as he enters. I watch him as he takes the seat next to Duncan, unable to drag my eyes from him. His long golden hair is tied in a messy bun at the base of his skull and I have a strong urge to reach out and run my fingers through the strands. "Nice to see you here, Rosie." I blush pathetically as he loads up his plate and the others follow suit.

"Come on," Zane nudges me with his elbow, "help yourself." And I wonder if there's a double entendre in that statement.

I fish out a couple of roast potatoes from the dish as well as some carrots, peas and kale and slide two thin slices of the roast chicken onto my plate. I look up to locate the gravy jug and find all the alphas staring at me.

"What?" I say.

"Nothing," Zane says, passing me the gravy jug and shaking his head.

"So you're from near Manchester?" Ollie asks me, the full power of his charm aimed directly at me. I answer, and he asks me more questions about myself, smiling and nodding away as he listens intently. It's hypnotic to be the recipient of his intense focus and my skin warms with the heat of his eyes. The others seem happy to allow Ollie to dominate my attention. I hope I'm making a good impression on him at least because Seb keeps his gaze locked on his plate and contributes nothing to the discussion, giving a reluctant grunt whenever anyone asks him a question.

When our plates are clear, I look to Seb hopefully, giving him my most dazzling smile. "Is there pudding?" I ask him.

He jolts, then frowns.

"No, we're training." He slides his chair back. "I'm heading out. You can clear up," he says to Ollie, who nods.

Then Ollie turns to me. "My turn to wash up."

"Don't you have a dishwasher?" I ask, glancing around the huge kitchen with all its shiny appliances.

"You can't put pans in the dishwasher," Seb says as he strides towards the door. "You'll break it."

I want to stick my tongue out at him. My parents have five kids. They always shove as much as they possibly can in the dishwasher until it is groaning, and it does just fine.

"He really doesn't like me," I mutter, once he's out of earshot.

"On the contrary," Ollie says, leaning over the table to take

151

my plate. "He likes you a lot."

I laugh bitterly. "He has a funny way of showing it."

"He's a funny guy." Zane shrugs.

"Can I help you clear up?" I ask, beginning to gather up cutlery.

"You're our guest. You don't have to help clear up," Duncan says.

"Actually, I'd appreciate the help," Ollie says, staring at his pack mates.

They meet his gaze and then peer towards me.

"It's fine," I say. "I don't mind helping."

Something seems to pass unsaid between all of us and then Duncan and Zane are nodding and pushing away from the table.

"Well, we helped with the cooking, so we're going to put our feet up," Zane says, giving my arse a playful swipe as he passes me, and hooks his arm over Duncan's shoulder. "Come find us when you're done."

And then I'm alone in the kitchen with just Ollie, and his scent of leather and orange seems ten times as potent and the room quiet. I can hear the tick of a clock and distant traffic.

"How can I help?" I ask, my voice, that had come so freely throughout the meal, now sticking in my throat.

"Let's load up the dishwasher, and then you can dry while I wash."

I nod and pass him plates as he slides them into the rack.

"So, physics, huh?" he says.

He's asked me about home, my family and my friends, but we're yet to cover what I'm studying.

"Yes," I say, bracing myself for the usual barrage of sarcastic comments. "Before you ask, I'm not a Star Trek fan."

He holds his hands up. "Never crossed my mind. Tell me then, why physics?"

"Why not?" I grab a cloth from the sink and lean over the table, wiping crumbs into my waiting palm. "I've always been fascinated by space and I liked maths and science at school." I meet his eye. "Plus, I've always enjoyed defying people's expectations of me as an omega. We don't all want to study home economics and childcare, you know."

He laughs. "Oh, trust me, I know." I raise an eyebrow. "There are quite a few omegas on my course."

"Are you studying home economics?"

He laughs again. "No, I can't cook. Seb's the cook in the pack."

"So what are you studying?"

He stamps down on the pedal to the bin and the lid pops open. I brush the crumbs from my hand into the waiting sack.

"English Literature. I'm the pack's token arts student." His lips are wet and a piece of hair tumbles forward and sticks to his mouth. Gently he removes it, twining the strand behind his ear and my tummy flips. I've never met someone who looks more like a film star. I wonder if that's why he's studying English.

"Why did you choose that?" I ask him as he turns towards the sink and flips on the tap, clouds of steam soon rising from the faucet.

He twists around, leaning back against the sink as it fills, and crosses his arms, his biceps bulging. "Hmmm." He considers my face. "I should give the usual response about loving reading from a young age and all that crap. But it's not that."

"Why then?"

"I love words." His gaze wanders towards the darkening

153

windows behind me. "It's always fascinated me how people can conjure whole new worlds in my head, make me love or hate characters, with the power of words. And I love how they bend them to their will. Create phrases that slip seamlessly from the tip of the tongue."

"Like what?" I ask him.

His gaze meets mine and his eyes are something I could drown in if I'm not careful. He shakes his head. "Come on." He tosses me a tea towel, yanking the tap off and dropping a pan into the soapy water with a plop.

I stand beside him, and his arm nearly brushes mine as he scrubs away. His scent is much stronger up close, and I notice the light honey notes of it. My gland prickles.

He passes me the pan and I wipe away the moisture.

"Seb will come around," he says.

"To me?"

"To you. To the idea of you becoming the pack's omega." His hand brushes against mine as he passes me the next pan.

I jolt slightly with the electricity of it. My body is so easily seduced by these alphas.

"Pack omega?" I say. "I'm not—"

"You know that's what Zane wants. And Duncan. "

Do they? I've told them I don't want that. But I'm not so sure that's true anymore. At first, I definitely, definitely did not want to belong to a pack. But slowly, slowly, I'm being seduced by the idea.

My eyes meet Ollie's and I wonder if he sees through me. If he senses the truth.

"Seb clearly doesn't want me in this pack," I say. "And I'm not interested in becoming a wedge between you all."

"You haven't asked me what I want?" he says with a pout.

"What do you want?" I ask, a little breathlessly, thinking of my conversation with Zane and Duncan.

He stares at me for one long minute and then shakes his head.

"For you to keep working." He dips his hand into the bowl of bubbles and flicks some towards me.

"Hey!" I protest, wiping at the foam on my chest with the towel. "Anyway, how about me? You haven't asked what I want."

"I think I have a very good idea."

"And how's that?" I ask, resting my fist against my hip.

"I hear quite a lot of begging and pleading going on every time you stay over."

I reach around him and splash the foam at his face. He jumps back, then lunges for my wrist, holding it firmly so I can't dip my hand in the water again. He scoops his hand into the foam and lifts it to my face.

"No," I squeal, but he brushes it against the tip of my nose. Then leans closer and blows into the bubbles, sending the foam flying towards my face in tiny little clumps. I close my eyes and when I open them, he still has a grip on my wrist. He takes the tea towel from my other hand and gently wipes away the bubbles, stroking the rough towel against my cheeks, my chin, my nose, and lastly, my mouth.

I daren't breathe. I'm frozen in place, waiting to see what he'll do. He brushes the towel slowly over my lips, studying them intently, and then he drops the towel and his fingertips find my mouth instead. He traces my lips and tugs down on the bottom one.

"You asked me what I want, Omega." He leans closer. "This is what I want." His eyes flick to mine, and he presses his mouth to mine. Immediately, I sigh, all the tension and anticipation evaporating in that simple movement. I melt against him and he twists my arm behind my back. His grip's still tight on my wrist, and his free hand slides into my hair and finds my gland.

He draws away slowly. "Sin from thy lips?" he whispers, "O trespass sweetly urged! Give me my sin again."

"Shakespeare?"

"Shakespeare," he says, kissing me again. This time he doesn't hold back. He kisses me wildly, his hands everywhere, at my throat, my breasts, my thighs, my arse. I slide my hands under the hem of his shirt and to the warmth of his skin, finding him as toned and as muscular as his pack mates.

His mouth skims down to my neck and he sucks along the tendon, forcing needy gasps from my throat. It does something to him. Before I know it, his hands are hooking under my backside, lifting me up onto the counter, and positioning himself between my thighs.

"You smell so fucking wet."

More of his golden hair tumbles free from its tie and into his face and he looks even more like some mythical creature. I tug at his shirt, wanting to see more of him, and he obliges, shrugging it over his head. And then his fingers are slipping down the waistband of my underwear and sliding between the wet lips of my sex. He glides his fingers through my mess and then tugs his hand free, bringing his drenched fingertips to his mouth. His eyes fall shut as he sucks on his fingers, and his face dissolves into an expression of such unabated bliss it makes my stomach spin.

"You ... taste ..." His eyes flick open so quickly I jolt in alarm. His pupils are blown wide. "I want to eat you out, but first I have to have you, Rosie." He's already fiddling with his fly.

"Yes," I gasp, spreading my thighs wide and making my intent clear as I wriggle my knickers down my legs.

He steps closer, lifting the skirt of my dress so he can see everything. His hard cock strains at the front of his briefs, but he makes no move to free it. Instead, he stares at my bareness and brushes his thumb from my dripping wet entrance to the plug in my arse. He gives it a jiggle.

"Is that what I think it is?"

"Yes," I say.

"Shit," he mutters, and his thumb reaches back to the apex of my lips, forcing me to jolt again as he skims over my clit.

"Oh," I moan, and slowly he rotates the pad of his thumb around my sensitive nub. I want to beg him to fuck me, but already I'm losing myself to the work of his digit. My eyes drift shut and my head tips back, my hands clinging to the edge of the counter.

"That feel good, little mouse?"

"Yessssss."

"Then open your eyes and look at me when you come."

The command is clear and I am powerless to resist it. I gasp when I focus back on him, amazed again at how beautiful this man is. Amazed that a beautiful alpha like Ollie wants me. His thumb continues its work as he hooks himself out of his briefs, and I get my first glimpse of his cock. Unsurprisingly, it's as beautiful as the rest of him and I can't drag my gaze from it as he steps in closer between my thighs, nudging at my entrance with his head.

"Do you want this from me?" he asks as I buck against the electric sensations he's stirring in my clit.

"Yes, yes," I reach for his waist, encouraging him to enter, and then he does, and I squeal as my orgasm rips through my body.

Chapter 20

Ollie is the third pack mate I've fucked and he's just as big, just as skilled, and I am just as much of a mess as I cling to his body and he pounds into me.

"Scream, Omega," he growls, "I want you to scream for me like you scream for them."

Once again, I'm obeying his order before I realise what I'm doing, screaming my way through another orgasm, screaming as his thrusts falter and he comes, screaming as his knot expands and he locks into me.

He hunches forward, nuzzling softly at my neck.

"Fuck, you are a noisy little mouse."

"Mouse?"

"What else am I going to call a little omega who squeaks and squeals so much."

"I'm not that bad."

"You're the noisiest woman I've been with."

How many women has he been with? It's not a question I want to ask.

I brush my fingers through his hair like I've been wanting to do all evening as he continues to kiss my neck. It feels like silk.

I moan some more and his chuckle vibrates against my throat.

He hooks his hands under my backside and lifts me up, his knot still locked inside me. "I'm taking you back to my room."

"And Zane and Duncan?"

"It's my turn now, little mouse. Besides, I haven't tasted you properly yet."

"Ok," I say, wrapping my legs around his waist and letting him carry me through the house and up the stairs.

His room sits at the front of the building with two large windows that look down onto the street. He flips the blinds and drops us down on the king-sized bed. Immediately, he's back to sucking on my neck as I look around the room. A huge bookcase dominates one wall. Books are stuffed onto the shelves and several more are scattered across a desk. The other walls are bare and in the corner are several weights.

His hand comes up to curl around my throat and I notice for the first time the gold signet ring on his little finger. I take his hand in mine and examine the ring, skating my fingertips over the engraved design. He watches me.

"What does it mean?" I ask him.

"It's my family coat of arms."

My mouth drops open. "Coat of arms?"

He grins. "Zane said you were clueless."

I frown. "What does that mean?"

He shifts us up the bed. "My family are the Reese-Hamiltons. Have you heard of them?"

I shake my head.

"That's what I mean. Most people have." He spins the ring around his finger. "Most people have heard about the Amirs too and the Bruces. We get a lot of omegas sniffing around because they're interested in our families, not us."

"Actually, I got warned off you by the girls from the

OmegaSoc."

"What did they say?"

"That you're into dubious shit."

Ollie throws back his head and laughs. "They're pissed because we won't go to their shitty social events. We used to, but the number of gold diggers got old pretty quick."

"So what does your family do?"

"My family doesn't do anything. We own land and titles." He looks at me, clearly judging whether to tell me more. "My grandfather is second cousin to the queen."

"What? Is he a Lord or something?"

"A Duke."

I eye him. "And what does that make you?"

He smiles sheepishly. "An earl."

I gape at him. "An earl?"

His knot begins to deflate and he slips carefully from me and rolls onto his back.

"I can't believe I just fucked an earl," I mutter. "Why does an earl need to be in a pack?"

"Why not? I've found my brethren. I'm happy."

"What does your family think?" I can't imagine an old family like his being open-minded to this way of living. I know mine wouldn't be. "Aren't they really conservative?"

He laughs so hard the bed shakes underneath us. "They pretend to be but the aristocracy, little mouse, is perverted beyond belief."

"But the media ..."

"I'm a minor royal. They're interested in my rowing and that's it."

"How do you know?"

His jaw stiffens. "Pippa," he swallows, "when things with

Pippa broke up, she tried to sell dirt on us to the papers. Zane's family put a stop to that, but to be honest, they weren't interested in what a bunch of students were getting up to."

"She did that?"

"She wasn't the person we thought she was." His eyes soften and flip to mine. "It hurt Seb especially."

I nod. It's what Zane and Duncan have already hinted at.

"Does it change things?" he asks with a hint of a smile.

"Change what?"

"Now you know I'm an earl."

I shake my head. "Although if my mum ever learns of this, she'll have hysterics."

"You're going to tell your mum an earl ate out your sweet little pussy?"

"An earl hasn't," I remind him.

"He is going to now," he says, pouncing on me.

"Wait!" I say as he pins my legs open. "Do you live in a palace?"

"No." He pinches open my labia. "A country estate." His mouth meets my clit and I close my eyes as he goes to work on me, visions of grand houses floating through my head.

He soon has me coming, and then he's positioning me on top of him, and I ride him as I stare down at his beautiful face. His golden hair fans out around his head on the pillow as his caramel eyes glow in the half-light. I feel like I'm in a dream – a very naughty dream — but a dream. He grips my waist firmly and bucks his hips up to meet me every time I slam down on him. He calls me *little mouse*, tells me I have the sweetest tits, purrs that I'm beautiful. The next time I come, it's as he stretches me open with his knot, and his hot spend floods inside me. I collapse down on his body, breathless and panting.

As our rasping breaths begin to normalise, my ears prick. Beyond the door, I hear familiar grunts and groans. I lift my head from Ollie's chest.

"What's that?" Although I know. I'd know those voices anywhere. Zane and Duncan. Do they have another girl in there?

Ollie shifts his head on the pillow. "Sounds like Zane and Duncan enjoying themselves."

"With another girl?" I don't know how to feel about that. I have no cause to complain when I'm in bed with another man. But I guess I'm more possessive of these alphas than I thought.

"I can't hear a girl, little mouse," Ollie tells me.

I listen some more. It's just the two of them. I let out a sigh of relief. "Are they ...?"

Ollie quirks a golden eyebrow at me.

"Now you know what torture it is, little mouse, listening to those sweet groans and moans and not being invited in." He rocks me backward, so I'm sitting over him again and circles a thumb around my pert nipple. Zane and Duncan's grunts become louder, and I can hear the rhythmic thud of a headboard.

"It sounds hot," I admit as my eyes flutter shut.

"I imagine you got them all hot and bothered putting on such a show with me," Ollie says, tweaking my nipple and making me whimper. "I suspect they needed to release that tension."

I rock my hips in time to the thuds, visions of Zane and Duncan tangled together making my core clench.

"Do you know how many times I've wanked off listening to the sound of you being fucked?"

I gasp. Another vision. This time of Ollie fisting his cock. Hard because of me.

Ollie's hand slips down to my clit and he gets me off to the sound of his pack mates rutting.

* * *

I'm up and getting dressed when Ollie returns from early morning training the next day.

"And where do you think you're going?" he asks, hooking his arms around my waist and dragging me towards him.

"My lecture," I say, closing my eyes as he nibbles my throat. I have a littering of love bites down my neck that I've had to disguise under a tonne of foundation.

"I thought we could spend the day together."

"Don't you have lectures?"

"Not until tomorrow." His hand slips under my shirt and brushes against my stomach.

"So you're free all day?" I murmur.

"I can be all yours." His hand reaches for my tit and he gives it a squeeze.

I can't afford to miss a lecture. I shouldn't do it. I'm having to work my arse off to keep up as it is.

But he's so beautiful. His scent so delicious. And so I succumb.

"Actually, you know what, I'm sure missing one lecture won't hurt."

"That's settled then. Today, you're all mine." He walks me to the bed. "Stay here. I'll grab a shower." He grins. "No going anywhere, little mouse."

When he leaves the room, I text Sophia and tell her I'm

skipping today's lecture. Immediately, my phone rings.

"Hello," I say when I answer.

"Rosie? Is that you? Or has someone stolen your phone?"

"It's me, Sophia."

"But skipping a lecture? Rosie Anderson would never ever skip a lecture."

"Well, she is today. If anyone asks, can you say I'm ill?"

"No one is going to ask. Half our course skips lectures." I hear Sophia open and close a door. "And what are you skipping lectures for?"

I shift the phone against my cheek and whisper, "I'm spending the day with Ollie."

"Oh my god, Rosie. What, like as friends, or ..."

"We slept together," I confess, keen to see how my best friend reacts to this news. If she condemns me, there's no hope with anyone else.

I hear her gasp. Her footsteps halt. "You screwed him?"

"Yes?" I squeak.

"Ollie Reese-Hamilton? Did you know he's connected to the royal family?"

"Yes," I squeak again.

"Does Zane know? Or ... does this mean you're in the pack now?"

I pull my fingers through my hair and squirm on the mattress. "I'm not sure, it's complicated."

"So ... you're cheating on Zane?"

"No, NO! It's how things work with this pack."

Sophia whistles lowly. "Ollie Reese-Hamilton. You lucky bitch. He looks like—"

"A Greek god."

"Yep." Sophia laughs. Then she stops. "But just be careful,

OK, Rosie? These guys, they're ... experienced and–"

"I'm fine, Soph."

"OK, good. Well, have fun and I promise not to rat on you on one condition."

"What?"

"Tomorrow you hang out with me."

"Deal." I smile and hang up. When I look up, I find Ollie back in the room.

He puffs out his chest and flexes his biceps. "A Greek god, huh?"

I grab a pillow and fling it at his head. He catches it and then bundles towards me, pinning me to the bed.

"And now you will meet the full wrath of this god, mortal," he roars in a dramatic voice, and before I know it, I'm being flipped over.

I wriggle my arse in encouragement and soon enough he's fucking me.

Afterwards, we discuss what we're going to do with our day.

He wants to take me out for lunch, but I'm still full from the roast last night. He has some other ideas about taking me underwear shopping, but in the end I find an idea.

"Have you ever been to the History of Science Museum?"

"I'm an arts student."

"It's amazing. Let me show it to you."

"It's where you work?"

I nod and then wink. "I can show you behind the scenes."

"That does sound fun," he says, sucking on my neck.

It's late Monday morning by the time we arrive at the museum.

"I've always thought it looks creepy," Ollie mutters as he stares up at the grey Victorian building with its gargoyles glaring down from the roofline.

"Oh, it's much spookier inside," I say. "It's one of the reasons I love it."

Inside, apart from a class of excited school children, the museum is empty. Their speedy chatter echoes off the stone walls and the high vaulted ceiling. But soon they're being hurried away and we have the museum to ourselves.

"Definitely spooky," Ollie says, glancing towards the line of dimly lit glass cases with their stuffed animals. "That is morbid."

"I know," I say. "But look."

I lead him to a case of birds, varying in size from a giant ostrich to a tiny, colourful hummingbird. I point to a squat, dull looking bird about the size of a goose. "It's a dodo," I tell him.

"Wow," he says, crouching down to examine the extinct creature. "I've always wondered what one of these looked like."

"There're quite a few animals in here that don't exist anymore."

"If they hadn't been hunted and stuffed in museum cases, maybe they would still exist," he points out.

"Yep," I nod. "These are all Victorian. But I think most of the extinct animals in here died due to the destruction of their habitats. There are people at the university studying these old animals and applying the findings for conservation purposes."

"Is it all stuffed animals in here?" Ollie asks, gazing at me with amusement.

"No," I say, grabbing his hand. I pull him along to the geology section. "This," I say, rubbing my hand over the giant slab of stone, "is my favourite."

"What is it?"

"It's a piece of an asteroid. It hit earth millions of years ago. Isn't it beautiful?"

Ollie smoothes his own hand over the stone's surface. "It came from outer space?"

I nod.

"What do you think is out there? Is there life?"

"I don't know."

"You're a physicist."

I watch him study the stone. "I think there must be life somewhere. But it might not be as advanced as us."

"So no little green men in flying saucers?"

"Maybe."

"There are more things in Heaven and Earth than are dreamt of in your philosophy."

"More Shakespeare?"

"If you're going to quote anyone, little mouse, it should be Shakespeare."

He fiddles with the tie holding back his long hair and then gestures to a small sign hanging on the wall. "Alphas and omegas."

I peer up at the sign. "Oh yeah," I shrug, "there's a small display on the history of alpha and omega culture."

"Can we see it?"

"I don't really−"

"Come on," he says, grabbing my hand and pulling me that way.

The display is in a small room at the back of the museum, poorly lit and heady with the stale scents of previous omega and alpha visitors. Still, gripping my hand, Ollie heads to the first case and peers down.

"Omega collars," he purrs, examining the three leather Victorian collars on display. "Alphas used to place them on their omegas once they'd claimed them."

"I know," I say, shifting on my toes. I've never liked those things. The way the leather is scuffed and old, the thin, cold chain that trails from one, the silver lock on another. It's a reminder of the oppression omegas endured, of the hard-earned freedoms we've won.

"They make you uncomfortable," Ollie says, smelling the shift in my scent.

"No one should own another person."

"I always thought they were a desperate attempt by alphas to seem in control. Because in reality, an omega owns their alpha as much as an alpha owns their omega."

"You don't have that instinct to submit, to obey, though, do you?"

"I do," he says, and my mouth falls open as I stare at him. "To the leader of our pack. To the head of my family."

"The leader of your pack? I thought you were all equal."

"We try to be. But the truth is Seb is the alpha among us alphas. It's subtle, unspoken, but he is. He doesn't exert it, but if he ever told me outright to do something, I'd have a hard time disobeying." He flicks a strand of hair from his face. "Fuck, I can't believe I just told you that."

I gaze up at him, trying to make sense of his words. What does that mean for me and my relationship with the other alphas?

But then the moment passes. The glimpse of vulnerability he'd just shown me vanishing.

"I'd like to dress you up in a collar and nothing else, Omega." I shiver and he rakes his teeth over my throbbing gland. "You have a very beautiful neck," he whispers into my ear, his hands coming to ring my neck in imitation of a collar. "I think it's my favourite part of you."

We don't stay long after that. We're in a taxi on our way back to his house and his bed before I know it. Afterwards, as we doze together in his bed, I smell Seb's scent, stronger and bolder than the others. I remember what Ollie confessed in that dim room, and I wonder again what it means for me.

Chapter 21

I'm up early with the boys the next day, because as tempting as it is to hang out with Ollie or Zane or Duncan, I can't afford to miss another lecture.

As I step out into the hallway with a large bath towel wrapped around me, I expect to find the house empty. Instead, I hear muffled raised voices from somewhere on the floor below me and the air is tinged with alpha aggression. Creeping to the top of the stairs, I strain to hear.

"You let her skip a lecture," a deep voice growls. I know it's Seb. And my cheeks burn. I had a suspicion this argument was about me, and yet, I'm still shocked.

"It was one lecture," Ollie says. "She isn't Pippa, Seb."

"If you'd just give her a chance—" Duncan starts, but Seb interrupts him.

"But this is how it starts, isn't it? This is how it started with her."

I hear Ollie sigh. "You're right, you're right. I'm sorry. But it was my idea, not hers."

"Rosie is a hard worker, Seb. She wants to make her own way in life. She's not some gold digger."

"Then don't fuck things up for her," Seb snaps and I jump back into the shadows as I watch him storm down the hallway and out the front door, the others following sheepishly in his wake.

I lean against the cold wall as the door slams shut, water sliding down my face. Bile rises in my throat, and I feel more confused than I ever have. I need to talk to Zane. To understand.

But first I have my day with Sophia. I have a feeling some time away from these men, and the power they yield over my body will be a good thing.

* * *

Sophia greets me at the back of the lecture hall with a huge grin and I know as soon as classes are over I'm going to be in for one mega grilling. I try to follow the formula the lecturer scrawls over the white board, but I'm consumed with thoughts of *The Crew* and Seb especially.

Perhaps Sophia senses something is wrong because, as soon as the lecture hall lights flick back on, she's pulling me outside and to the nearest coffee shop, grabbing us two seats and two coffees.

"Spill it," she says, pouring an insane amount of sugar into her latte. I don't understand how she can have such gleaming white teeth with the amount of sugar she consumes. Then I remember she's rich and rich people always have good teeth.

I rest my elbow on the table top and my chin on my palm. I sigh.

"Oh dear." She grimaces. "Something gone wrong in the world of romance?"

"I'm not sure."

Sophia's eyebrow bobs as she swivels a teaspoon around a

saucer-sized cup, clinking it on the rim and depositing it on the table.

"They're not being open with me. There's something going on with Seb."

"Seb Thomas?"

"Yes. Do you know him?"

"I mean, I know of him. But he's the only one of the pack that I hadn't heard of before coming to this college. He didn't go to any of the usual schools."

I roll my eyes. "You mean his family isn't rich."

"I have no idea. I know nothing about them."

"Me neither, it's not like I knew anything about the others anyway."

"So what about Seb?"

I pick up my cup and take a long sip, the liquid scorching beneath the foam. "He doesn't want me as the pack omega."

"Hang on," says Sophia, lifting her hand, and then spinning her finger in a circular motion, "rewind here. Do you want to be this pack's omega?"

I place my cup down on the table and consider her question.

"Rosie, I'm all for you getting your kicks and enjoying yourself, you know that. But you always said getting tied up with an alpha was not for you. You wanted to concentrate on your studies, on making something of yourself. And being an omega to an entire pack, well, that sounds like getting tangled up in a big fucking way."

I sigh. She's right. What the hell am I doing even considering this as an option? Why have I felt rejected ever since coming to the realisation that Seb doesn't want me?

Because I'm fucked up. Being around all those alphas with their sinful scents and their electrifying touch has scrambled

173

my mind.

"I think I need to talk to Zane," I say.

Soph glares at me. "Tomorrow. Tomorrow you can talk to Zane. You promised me a day and I have plans for us tonight."

"Plans?"

"Uh huh. I've been invited to drinks at the Principal's gardens."

My mouth does a little wow. "Who by?"

"Dr Whei. He's holding a drinks party for promising students with some other tutors."

"So what am I doing?" I ask, confused.

"I'm allowed to bring a date."

"Don't you want to take a proper date?"

"No, I want to take you." She takes a long gulp of her coffee. "It's black tie. Have you got anything you can wear?"

I shrug.

She claps her hands together and bounces up and down on her seat. "Yay, shopping time!" Then she frowns and reaches over to pinch my arm. "But no moping."

"I don't mope."

"Good. It's decided then."

We're on our way to the shops when my phone buzzes. Sophia rolls her eyes, but I answer it anyway when I see it's Zane.

"Hi," I say.

"Hey, what you up to? Ollie said you escaped his clutches."

"I'm spending the day with Sophia."

"And you're not stealing her away from me!" Sophia yells towards my phone. "She's all mine today."

"And what are you ladies going to get up to?"

"We're going shopping."

"To buy Rosie a dress," Sophia adds.

"You want me to buy it for you?" Zane asks immediately.

"I have my own money. I can buy my own dress."

"No, she doesn't. No, she can't," Sophia calls out.

Zane chuckles on the other end of the phone. "Let me buy you a dress, sugar. You know I like buying you things."

"You really shouldn't keep buying me things."

"Yes, you should!" Sophia pipes up.

"See," Zane says, "Sophia agrees. That's sorted, I'm paying. But you have to send me photos of the dresses you try on."

"I get to pick my own dress," I tell him.

He chuckles again. "I know. I just want to see." His voice drops a tone lower. "You've never sent me a selfie."

My stomach swoops. "I guess I'll have to change that."

Sophia grins beside me when I hang up. "Oh goodie, our budget just increased. I can take you to this gorgeous little boutique I know of."

"I don't know," I say.

"Don't be silly." She hooks her arm through mine and drags me along.

The boutique is indeed gorgeous, tucked away down a backstreet with all the other expensive shops I've never visited. A bell chimes as we enter the shop, and it's like walking into another world – one with sparkling jewellery and expertly cut creations. I can't help letting out a little gasp and Sophia nudges me in the ribs.

"This looks far too expensive," I hiss at her.

"Your boyfriend can afford it! When we get back to my room, we're going to google your guys' families, and then you can see just how much money these alphas have."

I gulp. I know in Sophia's book that's meant to make me

feel excited or reassured. But it's freaking intimidating. I look down at my skirt and top. Both are items I picked up in the clothing section of the supermarket. If Sophia wasn't standing beside me, looking glamorous as always, I'm pretty sure I'd be thrown out of a shop like this.

Sophia grabs my hand and tugs me over to a display of cocktail dresses. They're made of real satin and the bodices are encrusted with small gems.

We've only just started to rifle through the dresses when an older man with short, bleached-blonde hair and large, tomato-red glasses strolls up to greet us.

"Hello, ladies," he says, clearly addressing Sophia. He can probably smell that she is the one with money. "Can I help you?"

"Yes, please," Sophia says, holding up a dress and examining it. "We're going to a sophisticated cocktail party tonight and my friend needs a dress to wear."

"Aren't you getting a dress too?" I say, with a note of desperation in my throat.

"No, I'm going to wear my red dress. Besides, my mother will kill me if she finds out I've bought more clothes. I'm already in trouble about my last credit card bill."

"So, just for you, Madam?" the shop assistant asks, crossing one arm over his stomach and resting his chin on the knuckles of the other. "You have very pretty eyes, almost a sky blue."

"She's gorgeous, isn't she?" Sophia hums next to me.

"I think we should go for something that brings out the colour." He twirls his hand in front of his face.

"And shows off her figure," Sophia adds.

"But of course. All our dresses do that." The man makes a disgruntled huff and dives into the rack of clothes. Soon, his arms are full and he beckons us to the dressing room at the back of the store.

I've never seen such an elegant dressing area. Waiting back here are heavy drapes, soft chairs, glossy magazines, and water jugs with lemon slices floating near their rims. Sophia flops down in one of the chairs and points to the changing area.

"Let's see then."

I disappear behind the curtain, tugging it closed, and strip out of my clothes, wiggling into the first dress. It's black satin with spaghetti straps. Twisting this way and that, I glance in the mirror, then step out to show Sophia. The shop assistant is there waiting too.

"Hmmm," he says, tapping his fingers against his mouth critically.

"Give me your phone," Soph tells me.

"Why?"

"Your boyfriend wanted pictures, didn't he?" She turns her head to address the shop assistant. "She's dating Zane Amir."

The older man's eyes widen, and he stares at me in amazement, as if he can't quite believe that's true.

I fling my phone at Sophia, and she flutters her eyelashes innocently as she snaps a shot. "Want me to send it to him?"

"Promise you won't send him anything else?"

"No," she says, already typing away. I consider wrestling my phone back off her, but she has it grasped so tightly in her hands I doubt I'd succeed.

"I think this one is too dark for you," the shop assistant ponders.

"Zane likes it," Soph says, reading the text. "Jeez," she adds, "I think the dude needs a cold shower."

"Give me that." I make a grab for the phone, but she holds

it above her head, leaning right back in the chair.

"I'm only joking," she laughs.

I try on a red dress next despite the shop assistant nudging me towards the blue. Soph takes another snap, then I change into the midnight blue. The satin material clings to my curves, emphasising my waist and hips. It has no straps, and the neckline sweeps down in a sweetheart, revealing more cleavage than I'm used to.

Sophia lets out a high-pitched whistle as I emerge around the curtain. "Shit, Rosie. That looks …" She fans herself.

The shop assistant refolds his arms and smiles smugly. "I told you the blue."

"It's a bit …" I twist my head over my shoulder, trying to find a view of my back in the mirror. The dress makes my backside look round and pert.

"Stunning?" Soph says.

"Glamorous?" the shop assistant adds.

"Revealing," I squeak, but Soph is photographing me and sending the images to Zane before I have a chance to say more.

"It is the perfect amount of revealing," the shop assistant says. "And besides, a man like Zane Amir will want a well-dressed woman on his arm.

I'm not sure Zane gives a shit about stuff like that. Then again, maybe that's the reason he's keen to buy me new things.

"Zane wants this one," Soph says. "He's told me to buy it for you even if you refuse."

"What the alpha wants …" The assistant bows his head dramatically.

"I choose my own dresses," I say, staring at each of them in turn. "I make my own decisions."

"So, you don't want this one?" The assistant throws me a

perturbed look.

"No," I admit, "I do want this one." The man is right. It makes my eyes pop, and I don't look like me. I look like someone in a magazine. Someone who could actually date Zane Amir or Duncan Bruce or Ollie Reese-Hamilton.

"Fabulous." The assistant claps his hands.

"We'll need shoes and earrings," Sophia tells him.

"Soph!" I protest.

But she gives me a stern look. "You need the complete outfit, Rosie. Trust me, Zane isn't going to complain."

I peer down at the smooth material of my dress. I've never owned anything like it. My stomach spins in excitement.

Maybe if I look the part, like someone who belongs to a pack like theirs, Seb will change his mind.

Chapter 22

We enter the drinks party through a gate in the old bricked wall. The Principal's private gardens are a sanctuary of blossoms and flowers lit up by hanging lanterns and strings of fairy lights in the branches. Serving staff circulate with trays of canapes and glasses of wine. Groups of people stand chatting in the half light.

It seems like a different world. One from a movie or glossy magazine and not one where someone like me belongs at all. But Sophia links her arm through mine and drags me into the garden, making a beeline for our head professor.

"It's always good to cosy up to the person in charge," she whispers into my ear, and I admire her confidence. Professor Whei, with his thick glasses and spiky eyebrows, has always terrified me because he scans lectures for unsuspecting victims on which to launch deadly questions. It's he who determines my fate on this course.

I also feel exposed in the dress. It covers everything it needs to, falling away to my knees, but my shoulders are bare and the material skims over my form like water. It makes me feel vulnerable.

Sophia engages Dr Whei in conversation about next term's topic and I stand beside her feeling uncomfortable, like a child who's dressed up in her mum's clothes for the evening. The heels are higher than I'd normally wear and my toes ache. The zip of the dress pinches the skin at my back.

I shift my weight from one foot to another and nod and smile at the appropriate moments in the conversation.

Then I feel it.

I feel it before I smell it.

Eyes on me. A hot gaze.

And then that heavy, dominant treacle scent, so potent I can almost feel it slither down my throat.

My skin grows warm from the heat, my pulse races, and I turn my head searching for the source. But I can't see him.

I take a sip of my cool white wine and try to concentrate on what Sophia is saying. The words are nonsense in my head, though, and the sensation of being observed only intensifies.

I scan the garden again, peering into each shadow.

I find him this time, his great frame unmistakable in a corner near the house.

But I'm wrong. He's not watching me. He's not looking at me at all.

I shake my head a little and Professor Whei excuses himself before walking inside.

"Anyone else here you know?" Sophia asks me, eyes scanning the party.

"Erm ... Seb's here."

"Seb?" Her eyes find him. "Oh yeah. Do you want to go over and say hi?"

"I don't think that's a very good idea–" I start to say, but she's already grabbed my hand and started to tug me after her.

"Come on, you shouldn't let him intimidate you."

Easy for her to say; she's not an omega.

181

We stroll closer, and I can spot the moment he senses me coming, his shoulders tightening and his head tipping to the side. But he doesn't turn around. He keeps his back to us and forces Sophia to walk right around him and stop in front.

"Hi," she says with her most charming smile. The alpha scowls at her, refusing, as usual, to meet my eye. "I'm Sophia." He stares at her. "Rosie's friend," she prompts, jerking her head in my direction. "Do you like Rosie's new dress? Zane bought it for her."

His gaze slithers down my figure, electrifying every part of me as it does, and I swallow hard as my gland thrums.

Then his eyes flick back upwards, but he won't meet my eye. Instead, he addresses the wall over my shoulder. "I didn't know you were going to be here," and then, without another word, he stalks away.

Sophia's mouth drops open and she frowns. "What a fucking wanker," she says just loud enough for him to hear.

"Yep," I reply, hoping he hears my agreement too.

It's one thing treating me like dirt because of some problem with his pack, but he could at least have the decency to be polite to my friend. It can't hurt to be civil.

"You really need to talk to Zane," Soph says, "if he's pack mates with this dude ..."

"I don't want to give them up," I say, realising the truth of it for the first time. I'm having too much fun. And I like them. I like all of them and the things they do to me. I've always thought of my body as a cage, a place I'm trapped inside, limiting and confining me. With these alphas, I've realised that my body isn't a prison, it's a paradise.

I'm not going to give that up because one alpha has permanent premenstrual tension.

"Come on," Soph says, "let's get out of here. We can go to *The Lounge* instead."

"In these dresses?"

"Why the hell not! This party is dull."

We link arms and, with our heads held high, march the hell out of that snooty drinks party. I don't belong somewhere like that.

And I ignore the sensation of a scorching hot gaze on my back as we go.

* * *

The queue to the club curls along the pavement, but one look at us in our dresses and the bouncers usher us straight inside, despite the protests from the students at the front of the line.

We head straight for the bar, knocking back a tequila shot each, then we make our way to the dance floor. Some girls Sophia knows from her old school are already dancing in a circle and we join them.

Soon I'm forgetting about alphas and men in general, lost to the beat of the music and the sway of my body.

Somewhere in the recesses of my mind, I know we're being watched again, that guys are circling us, trying to catch our attention. But I don't care. Their gazes don't heat my blood. They can look all they like. They can think about me all they want. I lift my arms above my head, swaying my hips to the beat, closing my eyes. Sophia wraps her arm around my waist and kisses my cheek.

"You look gorgeous, Rosie," she shouts above the music. "No wonder all these alphas are losing their minds over you."

All except one. But I laugh anyway, twining my arms around

her, and we swivel our hips together, giving our group of admirers a show.

Another of Sophia's friends pushes through us with her hands full of shots of tequila and I take one, throwing the alcohol back. My eyes smart as it stings my throat.

Soph grabs my empty glass and walks off to deposit them on a table. When she returns, she's pulling Harrison behind her. She winks at me and links her arms around his neck.

I spin away to give my friend some privacy and continue to dance with her friends until I feel a faint tap on my shoulder. I suspect it's one of the creeps who've been circling us, but when I look around, it's Francesca, the girl from OmegaSoc.

"Rosie," she yells, hugging me and kissing me like we're old friends. "You look sensational."

"Thanks. So do you," I say, noticing her silky black jumpsuit, that looks as if it cost more than my dress.

She smiles. "Want a drink? The barman has a crush on me and I get free drinks here." She flicks her hair over her shoulder.

"Sure," I say, following her through the clammy bodies to the bar.

"What would you like?" she asks.

"Whatever you're having."

She catches the barman's eye immediately. He comes sauntering over, and Francesca orders us two Cosmopolitans.

"Are you going to have to sleep with him for these?" I ask.

"I'll probably just let him sniff my gland later tonight. He has a thing for my scent." I wonder why she's bothering. She can clearly pay for all the drinks she likes. "He's hot though, right?" she says, her eyes slipping down his form.

"I wouldn't have thought he was your type," I say, observing the alpha's stubbled chin and sleeve tattoos. He doesn't look clean-cut enough for someone like Francesca.

"Oh, he's not for anything serious, but maybe for a bit of fun." Her made-up eyes land back on me. "And you?"

"Me?"

"Word has it you've been inseparable from *The Crew*. I'm surprised to see you here without them. I thought they were notorious for keeping their omega on a short leash."

I frown. "What?"

Her gaze flicks across the bar. "Or perhaps I was wrong."

I follow the trajectory of her vision and jolt when I spot Zane and Duncan on the other side, chatting with a couple of girls. How did I not smell them in here?

I watch them, Zane doing most of the talking, as usual, while Duncan listens along. The two girls are melting under their spell, their cheeks flushed, their bodies liquid.

And it hits me. Hits me so hard, I'm surprised I stay standing. A jealousy that floods through me, washing away all reason.

I scowl across at my alphas, and then I'm marching around to where they stand, ignoring the puzzled enquiries of Francesca.

"Zane!" I growl with my arms tight across my chest.

His eyes spring immediately to me. His face flickers from shock to amusement.

"Omega," he says, pushing past the girls like he hadn't been holding them entranced mere moments ago, Duncan close at his side. His arm slides around my waist and Duncan's hand cups my neck.

"Fuck, you look hot," Duncan says in my ear.

"Uh huh," Zane agrees, his eyes darkening as they drink in my form. "I told you, that dress ..."

I toss my head, trying to shake off the strong sensation of desire their combined admiration stirs inside me.

"Who are those girls?" I demand, trying to peer around them.

"What girls?" Zane whispers into my ear, his hand gliding down to squeeze my arse.

"The ones you two were just drooling over."

Zane chuckles and lifts his head. "Seems our little omega may be a tad jealous."

Duncan sweeps his thumb over my gland, purring quietly into my ear.

"I'm not jealous," I say, trying my best not to let my eyes roll in their sockets as Zane's purr joins Duncan's. "You didn't answer my question," I protest, fighting hard to keep my body taut and not molten. "In fact, we need to talk." I twist my head, meeting Zane's gaze and making it as clear as I can that I'm serious.

"You wanna talk," Zane says, grabbing my hand, "let's talk." He speeds off through the crowd, tugging me along behind him, Duncan shielding my body from behind. We cross the dance floor, revellers scattering to make way for the two large alphas and their companion, pass the booths in the dark corner of the club, and slip straight through a door marked 'Private'.

"We're not allowed in here."

Duncan gropes the wall until he finds a switch to flick. Low light reveals a small office, paperwork stacked on a desk and a safe in one corner.

"And who's going to stop us?" asks Zane as Duncan shuts the door and turns the key waiting in the lock. Zane swivels around the leather chair tucked under the desk and points to it. "Sit," he commands, my legs dropping me into the seat.

I cross my arms over my chest again and scowl up at him.

"Are you seriously jealous, sugar?"

"Who were they?"

"Just some girls I know from my course. We are allowed to talk to other girls, sugar." He smirks at me.

"It looked like more than just talking to me." We've never had the conversation about exclusivity, about where this relationship is going. We've been happy to see where the tide takes us. Now I see this was a mistake. I don't want my alphas sleeping with other women. I want them for myself.

No, I want more than that. I want to be theirs. I want to be their omega. Their pack omega.

"If anyone should be jealous here, it's us. That dress is sinful, and here you are in a club without us, for any alpha to just come along and pinch you from under our noses."

"For fuck's sake," I snap, "I'm not your property."

"No, Omega. You're not." Zane rests his hands on either arm of my chair, caging me in, and leans in level with my eyeline. "And we're not yours."

I turn my head away from him, giving my best sulking face. "And what if I want to be? What if I want to be yours, and I want you to be mine? It can't happen, can it, because of Seb." My voice falters and I peer back at him.

He pinches my chin and twists my face back around. My eyes are drawn to his instantly and my body wilts, defiance leaking from me.

His voice is almost a whisper when he speaks.

"You'd like to be ours?"

I nod and his eyes flash.

"Let's be clear here, Omega," he says, our eyes locked on one another's. "You'd like us to sink our teeth into your gland

187

as we sink our cocks into your cunt? You want us to make you ours?"

I close my eyes. My body shakes violently, and I can't make it stop. "Yes," I say.

The music from the club pounds against the door. The floor vibrates.

"Be honest with me, Zane," I whisper. "It can't happen, can it? Not unless all of you want me in the pack."

His touch softens on my jaw, and he strokes the pad of his thumb over my bottom lip. I can sense Duncan's presence and when my eyes flick upwards, I find him standing next to my chair, his hand brushing through my hair.

"It doesn't matter that I want to be yours, does it?" The words catch in my throat. "Seb doesn't want me." The hand under my hair twitches, and I know I'm right. "Be honest with me, please? You said we should always be honest with one another."

Zane sighs and his fingers caress the soft side of my jaw.

"We made a pact after Pippa left. The pack promised we'd never let an omega come between us again."

"I don't understand …"

Zane looks up to Duncan.

"You have to know," Duncan says, "that Seb is different from the rest of us. He doesn't have the money or the family connections. He worked hard for his place at this college. And he demands that hard work, that discipline, of all of us."

"Yes, you told me that before—"

"I'm not finished, wee yin," Duncan says, pinching my gland. "Things went wrong with Pippa. She started to get a bit too comfortable being our pack omega."

"Lazy, you mean," Zane mutters.

"What?" I snark. "Didn't she pick up your dirty laundry and cook your meals for you?"

"No," Zane growls, "she stopped going to lectures and classes, stopped handing in her assignments. She figured we were going to claim her, bond her, and she'd be set up for life. Pampered and looked after in a life of luxury."

"None of us liked it, but it pissed Seb off, especially. They fought about it. He demanded she get her act together. She point-blank refused. She said it was our duty as her alphas to provide for her. He said she was only with us for our money. For *our* money. Mine, Duncan's and Ollie's. Seb doesn't have money like the rest of us."

Zane drops my chin and stands. "Then she tried to come between us." He runs his hand backward, then forward through his hair, rubbing his scalp. "She wanted us to cut Seb out of the pack." Duncan exhales by my side. "When we refused and said she needed to reconcile with him if she wanted to make things work, she started telling lies about him. Making up all sorts of accusations."

"Like what?"

"That he was stealing our money. Using our credit cards. You know how much that would hurt an alpha's pride?"

"But she was just trying to cover her own tracks. And that's when we knew we had to let her go." Duncan leans down and kisses the crown of my head. "She wasn't the woman we thought she was."

"And that's when we made our pact to one another. The next time we choose a member to join our pack – omega or alpha – we all have to be in agreement. All of us. All of us have to be in agreement."

"So if he doesn't want me?"

189

"Do you want him?"

I think of his domineering presence, of the ability it has to both thrill and terrify me. "I don't know."

"You have to want him too if you want to be a part of our pack, Omega." Zane drops to his knees and buries his mouth in my neck. "Give this time, Rosie. There's no rush. Rushing in was what got us into trouble with Pippa."

"Seb will come around." Duncan adds. "You're fucking irresistible, Omega."

I don't know if they're right. I think they want it to be true. Seb seems to despise me. He was abundantly clear about it earlier this evening.

And maybe it's because he senses it about me. Maybe he knows the truth. The one thing I haven't been truthful about.

Unlike the others, maybe he can tell I'm broken.

"And if he doesn't?" For once, they are both silent. "I can never be yours properly, can I? You'll never be able to claim me."

"I didn't think that was what you wanted, Rosie," Zane says, his face pained. "When we started this thing—"

"You hoped it would be, though, deep down you hoped I'd change my mind."

He stares into my eyes and nods. "You know how hard it is to keep from claiming you, little Omega. Every time I fuck you, it's all I can think of."

Zane's pressure on my throat grows stronger and Duncan's grip on my neck firmer. "I think about it too," I whisper. "I think about you sinking your teeth into my neck. I think about you claiming me as your own."

All these wants. All these desires. Bubbling to the surface. I can no longer repress them. No longer hide them. I am who I am. I can no longer deny it.

"There's one way you can claim me," I say.

"No, Rosie, that has to be a pack–"

"Have me together." I look at Zane and then at Duncan. "Both of you."

Duncan drops to his knees beside me. "You still want to do that, wee yin? Even if–"

"You said we should live for the moment," I say to Zane. "That we shouldn't let the fear of the future stop us. You know I want this."

"And you're ready?" Duncan asks.

I nod. As ready as I ever can be. I've been using the plug, we've been experimenting with the beads and their fingers. I know I can stretch wider than before. I lean over and kiss Zane, sinking my tongue deep into his mouth, and then I pull back and turn to Duncan, kissing him too with the taste of Zane still on my lips.

My body trembles with the anticipation of what we're about to do because there is no way I can wait any longer. And by the heightened power of their scents, the lust in their eyes, I know it's the same for them too.

"It's just as well the door is locked, little Omega. Otherwise, every alpha in this shitty club would be breaking through this door to get to you. You smell like sin," Zane hisses, his fingers creeping up my thigh and under the silky material of my dress. "No, underwear." He rocks back, and his eyes are stern. He peers up at Duncan. "Our omega isn't wearing any fucking underwear."

"I couldn't with this dress," I explain.

"We should spank her plump wee arse for this," Duncan says with mischief in his eyes.

"Why don't you fuck it instead, Alpha?"

Zane jumps to his feet and drags me up with him. He slams the chair to one side and leans back against the desk. Then, tugging my dress up around my waist, he pulls me towards him, undoing his fly and releasing his throbbing cock. He grinds into me, his shaft rubbing through my slick folds. Then he snaps me around to face Duncan. He's waiting for his turn, his cock hard and in his hand. He smears himself with my slick and then twists me back to Zane.

I'm giddy, putty in their hands, and before I know what's happening, Duncan's hands encase my waist. He lifts me straight onto Zane's waiting cock and I groan as I sink down onto him, all the way to his hilt.

Zane grins wickedly and yanks down my dress, exposing my tits and squeezing them hungrily, as his other hand steadies me.

"Relax yourself, sugar," he tells me.

"For what?" I ask breathlessly as I rock on him.

"For Duncan. "

I gasp, feeling the nudge at my arsehole, and I peer over my shoulder to meet Duncan's eyes.

"This OK?" Duncan's mouth is at my ear, nibbling on my lobe.

"Yes," I pant. This is what we've been working up to. The hours of play. The hours of gentle persuasion, of stretching and teasing. I've been on tenterhooks, waiting for this, wanting this. "Yes." I pant again, stretching my arm behind me to cup the back of Duncan's head.

He eases in gently. The man is made of steel and yet his touch has always been so gentle, so careful. I'm not sure I'd trust anyone else with this.

Zane remains motionless beneath me, waiting for his pack mate, his gaze locked on my face, drinking up my reaction.

"How does that feel?" he asks me.

"So good," I moan, as Duncan inches in, deeper and deeper and deeper.

I thought I'd felt full before. But now I realise I had no concept of what that truly meant until now. As Duncan glides all the way in, his motion smooth with my slick, I know that I am right. Whatever happens next, we'll always have this. All three of our bodies connecting as one. They've claimed me and I've claimed them. Maybe not in the usual way, in our own unique way.

Duncan purrs with satisfaction. "You have no idea how good this fucking view is. So tight, wee yin, so tight."

Zane groans against my shoulder. "Fuck," he splutters, "fuck, I need to move."

"Gently," Duncan warns him, their eyes meeting over my shoulder as Zane glides from me, and I moan with ecstasy, the sensation so overwhelming I can't control myself.

"I can feel you. I can feel both of you. I can feel your cocks rubbing against one another."

Then Zane's grinding back inside as Duncan slips out, and they begin to find a rhythm, a rhythm that touches every place inside me. A rhythm that confirms these men have me under their control.

Their fingers are tight on my hip bone and my waist, my arse and my ribs, and tell me how hard they are fighting their need to slam into me, to rut me into oblivion.

"Harder," I plead, "you can go harder."

"No," Duncan snaps, as much to Zane as me. "You're not ready for that, Omega."

"I am," I moan and Zane bucks beneath me with a growl so loud I feel his body vibrate.

"No," Duncan says, his nails deep in my flesh, "no," as his hips brush against my backside and I feel him falter.

"Knot me," I whimper as Zane's thrusts stutter too.

And then I feel it, the combined stretch, and my world goes lightening white.

Chapter 23

Afterwards they bundle me into the back of a taxi, both cradling me between their laps, stroking my hair and my cheeks, telling me what a good girl I am, how proud they are of me, how special I am.

At the house, Zane wraps me in his jacket and Duncan carries me upstairs and straight to the bathroom. The room soon fills with steam and sweet aromas as Zane runs the bath.

"I just want to go to bed," I murmur into Duncan's chest, as sleepy as a kitten who just overdosed on full fat cream. But they insist, stripping me gently and lowering me into the warm waiting water.

"Your body just took two alpha knots, wee yin," Duncan whispers. "That's no easy feat. We want to ensure you're not sore tomorrow." Kneeling beside the bathtub, he commands me to lean forward and runs a soft flannel over my shoulder and around my neck. Zane crouches at the other end of the tub, his hand resting on my knee, his thumb circling the soft skin underneath, purring contentedly.

When I've soaked enough, they lift me from the tub and wrap me in fluffy towels, carrying me to Zane's waiting bed and curling up with me. I fall asleep to their calming purrs and their tender touches.

But despite their best efforts, my body feels the previous night's exploits when I wake the next morning. I ache all over and, between my legs, I feel sore and swollen.

Duncan notices the wince as I stagger from the bed.

"Are you hurting, wee yin?" he asks with a concerned frown.

"A bit," I admit.

"Come back to bed. I'll go fetch you breakfast. In fact, stay here all day."

And draw more of Seb's condemnation? No way. I don't want to give him any more reasons to hate me.

"I'm fine," I say, plastering what, I hope, is a convincing smile on my face. "But I think I may need some time to recover."

Duncan growls while grabbing my hand, tugs me back towards the bed. He sweeps my hair from my neck and nuzzles against my gland. "It was good though, wasn't it?"

Zane watches from beside us, his hand idly tracing the contours of Duncan's taut stomach.

"It was so much more than good," I tell them.

* * *

My lectures drag that day, and even though a whispered debrief with Sophia peps me up a little, I'm relieved to flop straight into bed the minute I get home, even if it is the middle of the afternoon. I draw the covers up to my chin, letting the warmth leech away some of my aches. But I don't get any sleep. I'm interrupted by messages from Ollie.

Need to see you, Omega, the first one reads.

I can't. I'm in recovery.

I heard all about it. But I want to hear it from you. Fuck, I wish

I'd been there to see it.

Before I've responded, another message pings onto my phone.

I'll be good, I promise. We can just snuggle. All I want is you naked and in my bed, making it smell divine.

Just snuggling! I tell him.

Just snuggling.

By the evening, I'm pleased he convinced me. I feel shaken, as if I took a giant dose of ecstasy last night and am now dealing with the comedown. I want a pair of strong arms around me again and sweet words in my ear. Fuck, despite my cunt telling me otherwise, I would even like to be rutted and knotted, locked firmly to one of my alphas.

My usual seven o'clock tutorial cancels, so I catch the bus up to the far end of town. Ollie will probably scold me for not taking a taxi and charging it back to him, but it feels too presumptuous.

My forehead rests against the warm glass as the vehicle rumbles through the busy town and out towards the suburbs, the view changing from rows of cramped terraces to vast, detached townhouses.

The evening sun still hovers above the rooftops, casting the street in golden light as I leave the bus and make my way down the avenue of large houses. Around me, windows transform into mirrors and the sun is warm on my face, the breeze frisking my hair. I feel content.

When I reach the packhouse, I skip up to the doorstep and press the bell. The house is silent beyond the door, and I push up onto my toes, attempting to peer through the mottled glass.

It's then I'm hit by it. That dark and dominant scent of treacle. I freeze.

"Move to the side, Omega," he says in that deep growl of a voice, and I practically flatten myself against the wall. He reaches around me, taking care not to touch me, and unlocks the door. The snap of the locks makes me jump.

The door swings back, and he marches through the doorway, leaving it open behind him. "Are you coming in?" he barks.

I attempt to shake off the feeling of fear and step through into the dark hallway, shutting the door quietly behind me.

I gaze up the staircase towards the first floor where Ollie's room is. I could easily make myself comfortable in there. Ollie wouldn't mind. But my eyes fall back to the retreating figure of Seb as he disappears into the kitchen.

I swallow. I'm not going to let him intimidate me. I'm not going to let him ruin this for me. What I have with Zane and Duncan and Ollie is special, and some grumpy arsehole with an unjustified grudge against me can't trample all over it.

So I drop my overnight bag by the bottom of the stairs and follow him into the kitchen.

As soon as I'm in the room with him again though, that momentary flash of resolve and bravery slips away like water down a plughole, and I slither against the wall, my hands behind my back.

He's so big, and everything about him, from his scent to his fierce scowl, screams dominance.

He stares at me for several long seconds. I fight the urge to drop my gaze to the ground with every drop of willpower I still possess. The air between us seems to crackle with tension. I can almost taste it on the tip of my tongue.

In the end, it's too much. I close my eyes.

"Do you want something to drink?" His voice is less menacing. I prize my eyelids open and find he's turned around and is filling the kettle. I let out the breath I'd been holding in a rush.

"Tea, please."

He yanks off the tap and drops the kettle back into its cradle. Then he flicks the switch and turns back towards me.

"Why do you hate me?" I ask, so quietly I'm not sure he hears. But he's watching my lips move.

"I don't hate you."

My nails scratch against the paintwork on the wall behind me. The breath in my lungs feels heavy.

"You don't want me to be part of this pack though, do you?"

The kettle starts to rumble.

"I don't think you're right for this pack."

His words hit me plump on the chest and my heart aches. "Why?"

"Because you don't want someone like me, Omega. And to be in this pack, you have to want every one of us."

I cock my head. Steam rises from the kettle, floating over his head. "Someone like you?"

He takes a step towards me and I see his hands balled into fists by his sides. "Someone who can't spoil you. Can't buy you pretty things." His dark eyes borrow into me. "I can't give you that."

"What can you give me?" I ask, breathless.

"Discipline. Dominance." He steps closer again. His nostrils flair. "Danger."

"Maybe I do want that."

He laughs bitterly. "Maybe you think you do. Hell, maybe you even fantasise about it sometimes. But the reality – the reality you couldn't handle."

I lift my chin. "I can handle more than you could possibly imagine."

Two alpha knots for starters.

He steps in again. He's just an arm's length away now. If I reached for him, my fingertips would brush the front of his shirt.

I can taste that electricity in the air again, the heaviness that comes before a storm.

"An omega of mine would never skip a lecture."

"I know," I croak.

"She'd want my pack for more than just our money."

I nod, although I'm finding it hard to follow his words. His scent and his proximity have my gland buzzing. My heart thumps in my chest.

"If I told her to get down on her hands and knees, she'd get down on her hands and knees."

My knees buckle. My lip trembles.

"Not here, Omega," he says.

I stare up at him. He must be able to see the need in me, to smell it.

He inhales, his nostrils flaring, and his eyes rolling back in their sockets. Then his gaze flicks back to me, and he holds out his hand. "Come with me."

I lift my arm, and he curls his fingers firmly around my hand. Then he's tugging me, yanking me along behind him and back into the dark hallway. He stops beside the door under the staircase. I've never seen it open before. I'd assumed it was a cupboard. But when he snaps the lock and kicks the door, I see stairs disappearing down into darkness.

I have no time to think. To decide whether I want to be led down into the cellar. He's already leading me down.

I try not to tremble. I don't want him to think I'm afraid. What the hell is down here?

But if I'd been imagining chains and whips, I'm wrong.

The large cellar room is an omega's paradise. A nest. With a low ceiling, pale colourings and dim lighting. I can see it's been designed to please an omega, an omega in heat.

I bite the inside of my cheek so hard I taste blood in my mouth.

There are two large beds in the corners and the floor is scattered with cushions and blankets, beanbags and low chaises.

I sniff, wondering if I'll find traces of the omega who came before me. Of any other omega. But I don't. It smells fragrant, yet mellow. Nothing too offensive to a nose like mine.

"A nest?" I say, stating the obvious.

"Yes." He's still holding my hand.

"Did you make it for her?" I say, unable to disguise the hint of bitterness. He must know who I mean.

"No, we made it for us. After she left, we made our pact. And we made this nest. For our omega." He swings around to face me. "You want to be our omega?"

"Yes."

"And you want me?"

"Y-y-yes." The effect he has on my body makes it difficult to form my words.

He scoffs at my answer as if he doesn't believe it. I don't know how to make him see it's the truth.

"I'm not the gentle type, Omega. I'm not going to pander and spoil you. I'm not going to go easy on you."

"That's OK."

He reaches towards my throat, capturing my chain on his fingers, examining the pair of crossed oars, frowning. "Is it?"

"Yes."

"Then on your knees," he says, dropping the chain, the

201

charm knocking against my collarbone.

Eyes locked on his, I drop slowly onto the soft carpet of the nest. I want to lie down, bury myself in the layers of softness, run my palm over the fabrics. But I keep my body rigid and my eyes on him.

He walks around me, coming to tower behind me, his presence overwhelming. He takes a handful of my hair and twists it to one side, revealing the gland throbbing in the back of my neck. Lightly, he wraps his hand around my throat and skims his thumb across the tissue-thin skin.

"When you go into heat, little Omega, we'll bring you down here and rut you together as a pack. One pack servicing their omega through her heat. All of us together. It has to be all of us."

He presses his thumb against my gland.

Suddenly, a stab of panic hits my gut and radiates up through my chest to my throat.

I can't breathe.

He's right. I can't be what he needs. I can't be what any of them needs. I'm broken. Unworthy.

And he knows it. He's always known it right from the start.

That's why he brought me down here. To taunt me. To rub it in my face.

A nest. A nest for an omega in heat.

Something I'll never be.

Perhaps he senses my hesitation in the way my body stiffens because his grip loosens, falling away, and he steps back.

"I can't," I say, dropping forward onto my hands. "I can't."

"I know," he whispers.

I stay there panting, trying to catch some air, his own breaths heavy behind me. And then I scramble to my feet. "I'm sorry,"

I mutter, my face wet, as I stumble to the stairs.

He was right. I can never be one of the pack.

Chapter 24

I walk back into town along the same streets the bus passed only an hour earlier. The sun has vanished now, hidden behind buildings that no longer glow, but loom like sinister shadows. The pavement beneath my feet darkens, colour leaching from the world, and I feel the tears on my cheeks.

I wanted it. I wanted it so badly. To be a part of them. To be a part of their world. To be wedged in the middle of their pack, safe and loved.

But I never really belonged. Instead, I've become what I always feared. The thing I always fought to avoid. A toy. A plaything. Something that's easily discarded once the owners are bored.

Perhaps it's for the best. Seb has forced my hand. Brought this to a halt. Prevented it from lingering on.

Now we all know where we stand. We have our answers. I am not the omega for Seb. So I am not the omega for *The Crew*.

I meander along the road as it darkens further until, finally, I find myself back at my tiny, empty room. I climb into the bed, curling up into a ball, and I lie there, not moving, as evening becomes night, night becomes morning, and morning matures into day. My phone beeps and rings from somewhere on the floor, but eventually, it must run out of battery and falls silent. At midday, Sophia bangs on my door, her voice full of concern. I don't move. I don't answer.

The alphas don't come. They must know by now. They must know it's all useless.

I don't move for twenty-four hours, and then the sun rises on the second day, bright and demanding, and I force myself up.

I won't wallow in my own pity any longer. I fought to get here. I'm not going to throw it all away.

The day I left for university, packing up the last of my things into boxes, I'd promised my little sisters I was going to make something of myself. That I would find my own way in this world. Without an alpha. They'd looked up at me, wide-eyed and in awe. If I could do it, so could they.

My mother had stood in the doorway, arms crossed, silently rolling her eyes.

She'd wanted to send me to a college for omegas, where I'd be paraded and pimped and match-made with a suitable alpha.

"One who can keep you safe and provide for you and your children," she explained, flashing the glossy brochures beneath my nose.

She sneered at my insistence that I wanted to study physics, laughed when I sent off my application to this college, secretly enrolled me in the omega college anyway.

"You won't last five minutes on your own, Rosie," she whispered into my ear as she kissed my cheek and my sisters waved me goodbye.

But I'd proven her wrong, hadn't I? Securing my grades and my place here. Showing I could go it alone. Never imagining I'd be just as vulnerable as every other omega to the charms of seductive alphas.

Fuck!

So I get the hell on with things. Sophia throws me anxious, sideways glances, but I ignore them. I go to my lecture and my class. And when I return later that afternoon, Zane is sitting outside my room, leaning against the door, spinning a pair of sunglasses in his hands. When he sees me, he jumps up, and I note immediately the usual mischief in his eyes is missing.

Or is that wishful thinking? Hoping he feels this pain as acutely as I do.

"Rosie," he says.

I shake my head. I already know what he's going to say. "You've come to break up with me."

For once, he seems lost for words. The man who always gets what he wants can't find a way to make this situation work. He opens then closes his mouth.

"Seb's ... Seb's pulling rank, Rosie."

I nod my head. I knew he would. "He's objecting to our relationship."

"He's convinced you're only interested in us for our money."

I stare at him, shocked. Money? What? Is he trying to keep the real reason for his rejection of me secret?

"You know that's not true," I say.

"Of course, I do." He fiddles with the glasses in his hand, opening and closing the arms. "But there's no telling him. He won't be reasoned with. And I can't go against my pack mate's wishes."

"Especially Seb's." He winces. "I won't come between you and your pack," I tell him. "I won't be the cause of heartache between you."

"Fucking hell, Rosie," he says miserably, "my heart aches

now."

I swallow down a choke that makes my eyes sting. "Don't, Zane," I beg him.

"We can make it work ..." he mutters, but I can see he doesn't believe it. He knows the truth as well as I do. "I could leave the pack–"

"And leave Duncan, destroy the team. You couldn't desert your brothers like that. We both know it. And I won't let you throw away your chances at the Olympics."

He looks utterly crushed. We both know there is no other way. His head drops in defeat. "I'm sorry, Rosie."

I step towards him. Desperate, needy, for one last touch, I reach out and stroke his forearm. "I'll never regret it."

He half smiles, capturing my hand and squeezing it, giving me unspoken words in the pressure of his fingers.

"Tell the others not to come," I say, my words catching in my throat. "I don't think I can do this over and over again."

He nods, drops my hand and walks away.

They do as I ask, and they don't come. Although I find a bunch of purple thistles on my doorstep one day and a book of Shakespeare's sonnets the next. Their way of saying sorry, of saying goodbye.

I keep going.

I hand in my assignments. I tutor my maths students and turn up for my shifts at the museum. I sleep in my little single bed in my tiny dorm room, and I eat meals-for-one that I cook in the communal kitchen.

More days pass in a blur of sameness. I count the days to the holidays until I can escape from this place where I've never belonged and return to my sisters. Where I'll lie about my adventures, editing out all the important events of the last term.

The days grow longer and hotter until I find myself one afternoon in the museum. The Director has opened the giant wooden doors and the ancient fans rotate in the tall ceiling. Yet, it's sweltering. I tie up my hair away from my neck and undo another button of my dress. Still, I'm hot, and I scratch at my skin as I serve cool drinks and ice creams to hyper children and their weary parents in the cafe.

In the rare quiet moments, I sneak opportunities to open the freezer door and stand in the escaping cool air, letting it wash over my burning cheeks. I fantasise of standing under a cold shower back at my dormitory.

I'm nearing the end of my shift, thoroughly sticky and uncomfortable, when that prickle skates across my skin. I freeze, rolling my shoulders. It's that familiar sensation. The one of being watched. Just like in the library all those months ago.

I swing my head around, searching for the observer, but as always, there's no one there. I sniff the air instead, but all I smell is the heady pollen of late spring and the intermingling of a hundred different scents. I roll my shoulders again and shift my attention back to the queue of eager children.

The sensation doesn't go away. Not for the rest of my shift or when it's finally time to close, and I hang up my apron and splash my face with cold water. Even when I step out into the warm air, I still feel those eyes on me. Violent and possessive. I shudder. I must be imagining things. There is no one there.

The streets are full of people out enjoying the sunshine and the heat. The tables outside the pubs heave, and there isn't a green space left to sit on in the park.

It's oppressive; the heat, the people, the eyes watching me.

I turn down the backstreets and out to the quiet paths that run along the back of the houses.

Instantly, I regret it. I'm being followed. I can feel it in my blood and in my bones. And the omega inside me knows it too. She's flitty, nervous, scared. She wants me to run. But I won't be controlled by my designation.

I stumble on. Concentrating on placing one foot in front of the other. I'm sweltering now, despite the shelter of the trees, and my mouth screams for water. My head is giddy and my vision swims.

Then, I catch a whiff of scent on the warm breeze. Alpha. My head snaps around, and I see them through the haze. Not one alpha. Two. Walking together. And another further behind.

They call to me, but I snatch my gaze away and pick up my pace.

I don't understand what's happening, but I know I need to get away.

It's hopeless, though. They're twice as big as me, their stride twice as long, and they've caught me in a matter of minutes.

One reaches out and grabs my arm and I close my eyes.

So dizzy. So hot. So thirsty.

My stomach cramps and I double over with a moan.

The three alphas circling me growl together, and I want to scream, but my mouth is too dry.

And then I know he's here. That scent curling into my mouth. And I sob with relief for no logical reason. He won't help me. He won't care.

"Rosie, stand up," he demands, and I realise I've slumped to the ground. I stagger up to my feet, the pain in my stomach making every movement agony.

His hand closes tightly around my shoulder and I peer up

into the steely eyes of Seb.

"This is my omega," he says.

"We found her first," one of the alphas says, his voice rich with aggression.

"I don't give a fuck what you think. This omega belongs to my pack. If any of you have laid your dirty paws on her, I'll snap your fucking necks."

Seb's whole body radiates violence and anger. I quiver beside him and even the other alphas seem less dangerous than they did minutes ago. They outnumber Seb, but he towers above them.

Still, the three unfamiliar alphas aren't backing off that easily.

"There're more of us than you, man," another says with a crooked smile that he aims at me.

Seb ducks his head down to stare straight into the man's eyes, his grip on my arm so tight it hurts. "And do you know who I am, dickhead? Do you know who my pack is?"

The man attempts to hold his ground, meeting Seb's fierce eyes at first, but soon he submits, his gaze falling to the ground. "We know," he mumbles.

"And you think my whole pack won't come for you if you try messing with me, if you attempt to touch our omega?"

"She's not yours, dude," the last one says, he's a little taller, his head shaved and studs running down the lobe of both ears. "She's not claimed."

"We all know that makes no difference. If I say she's mine, then she is."

"And what does she want?" the man attempts to catch my eyes. "Hey little omega, what do you want? Wanna get fucked? By us all?"

Despite my fear, a little whimper escapes my throat, unbound and unwanted, and the pain in my gut sears deeper.

"She's so fucking ripe," the first one moans, "I can taste it in the air."

"We can share her," the pierced one suggests, appealing to Seb. "She's in heat, she's not going to give a shit."

Heat?

I stare up at Seb, my gland throbbing violently as the dominance of his scent floods my nostrils.

I don't understand. It can't be.

Seb swipes at the pierced man, who darts backwards, narrowly missing a fist to his jaw.

Then Seb snarls, his lips pulling back taut over his grinding teeth, his brow tugged low over eyes that burn. The noise is animalistic, raw and unforgiving. My legs buckle and only Seb's grip keeps me on my feet.

"Fuck off!" he snaps. "I'm giving you to the count of five." The three alphas look at one another, obviously assessing their chances. "One," Seb growls.

The first alpha shakes his head and backs away.

"Come on," the pierced man calls to him. "We can take this motherfucker."

"Two," Seb hisses.

The second alpha strides away too. It's only the pierced one left. He gives me one last lustful glance, forcing another snarl from Seb, and then he spins and hurries after his friend.

Seb watches them go, his body remaining tense until they're out of sight. Then his countenance softens slightly. He curls me against his chest, cradling my head.

"It's OK now, Omega."

I rub my face against his shirt, breathing in needy lungfuls

211

of his scent, my eyes lulling in their sockets and my gland buzzing.

"Alpha," I murmur. I'm drenched in sweat, soaked between my legs, a sticky mess. But my head is so hazy, I barely register anything but the strong body wrapped around mine.

"Come on, let's get you home."

"Nest," I say. I want to be in a nest, somewhere soft and warm and safe. Somewhere I can be rutted and knotted. More wetness floods from me at the thought. I'd been plenty wet over the weeks I spent with Seb's pack, but nothing like this. Is this really my heat? I rub my forehead. "I want a nest."

"Yes," he says, "I'll take you home to your nest."

"Don't have one," I mumble.

He tuts in annoyance, and instinctively, I shrink away. "You don't have one?"

"No." The tears start now. I'm tired and hot and the pain in my gut ... They spill from my eyes and run down my cheeks. "Take me to your nest," I sob.

He's silent. Thinking. The tears fall harder. He's going to say no. I know it. He doesn't want me. He's never wanted me. And now I'm a disgusting, sticky mess, he wants me even less.

"OK," he says simply, and before I know it, he's scooped me up easily in his arms and is striding along the path in the opposite direction to the other alphas. "Need to get you somewhere safe," he mutters, more to himself than to me, as I nestle my head into the crook of his arm, "before your scent has every slimeball alpha out here hunting you down."

I paw at his chest as he carries me, faintly aware of passing rooftops and trees, of being placed in the back of a car. I curl up in a ball, sobbing and moaning in pain, begging him to hold me again, and a deep purr floats from somewhere in the front seat, pacifying me. Then finally, I'm in his arms again, and we're descending the dark stairs into the infinite softness of the nest.

He places me down on the bed, and immediately I'm clawing at my clothes, tearing them from my body and yanking at the sheets, and covers and pillows, arranging them around me, searching out the scents of my mates, wanting their smell in my nose and my mouth and my throat, wanting it smeared all over my skin.

I can feel him watching me and I reach for him. "Alpha," I whine. Why is he so far away?

"I'm going to call the others," he says. "It won't be long, Omega. I know they'll come as fast as they can."

I drag myself up to sit and I note the way his eyes travel down to my breasts, to the drops of sweat that roll between them. His tongue darts over his bottom lip.

"I want you, Alpha," I say.

"It's your heat. You don't know what you want," he says quietly. Then shakes his head, dragging his eyes away from my body, his jaw tightening. "Why the fuck were you out alone in the middle of your heat? Do you have a fucking death wish? You should be taking better care of yourself. If you were my omega–" He stops himself and scowls at me. That all-too-familiar look. Reserved just for me.

"I didn't know," I manage to say as my whole body shakes violently and my teeth rattle. "I didn't know."

"Didn't know what?" he snaps.

"This was my heat."

"How could you–"

"I've never had one before," I say quietly, curling in on myself, unable to look at him anymore. That's why he didn't

213

want me. He knew I was broken. A faulty omega.

"Never?" he says. "But you're twenty."

"Never," I say, I rest my forehead on my arm and the sobs rattle through my body. "I'm broken. That's why you don't want me because I'm broken."

He purrs and I peer up at him. Those eyes have softened. I'm not sure what I see in them now. Pity? "You're not broken, Omega. I had no idea ..."

"I am. They did all the tests. They couldn't find anything wrong. They tried to make it start. But it never came. I waited and waited and it never came."

My mum's face. Glances between my parents. Whispered conversations with doctors. The need to have me bonded before anyone learned the truth.

"Rosie, Rosie," Seb snaps, and my eyes focus back on him. "There's no fucking doubt about it, Omega. You're in heat." There's nothing left of his irises. His eyes are pure darkness, and he drags every breath through his nose. "You smell insanely delicious. Ripe. Primed. Pure fucking sex. Dirty and messy and delicious. All I want to do right now is jam my face between your legs and stay there for the next three goddamn days."

That sounds perfect. Exactly what I'd like him to do.

I roll back down onto the mattress and part my legs, giving him an intimate view. "Please," I beg.

"Omega," he warns, and I glide a finger through my sex, lifting it to show him the slick that trails in glistening ribbons back down to my cunt. "You don't know what you want. You're not in your right mind."

"I am," I say, "and I do. I want you. I've always wanted you. I think you know that. You're the one who's pushed me away."

He's on top of me instantly, towering over my body, his arms caging my head, his face inches from mine. I feel his hot breath rush over my mouth as he speaks, "I've always wanted you too."

"Then why?" I ask him, reaching out slowly to stroke his stubbled cheek. It's like petting the cheek of a wolf. Will he let me, or will he snap at my hand? "Why push me away?"

He closes his eyes. "Because you didn't want me. You wanted those rich boys, not me."

"That's not true" I scrape my nails over the bristles on his chin.

He growls, and then he kisses me, scrambling at the fly of his trousers as he does.

The kiss isn't gentle or careful, it's overpowering and all-consuming. He kisses me hard, like he wants to. Not holding back. Plunging his tongue into my mouth as he thrusts his cock deep into my cunt. I wail as he does, relieved to be filled at last. And fuck, if he isn't the biggest of his pack, so long, I don't think he'll fit all the way in. But he's undeterred. He promised me this. I knew what to expect, and he meets my resistance with little care, lowering himself further, forcing me to take more, until we're flush against one another.

"Such a wet cunt," he groans, taking a hold of my leg and forcing my knee into my chest, angling my hips so that he can plunge further. He keeps my leg locked there and, with his other arm, he pushes himself off the mattress and braces himself above me. The muscles in his biceps bulge and strain, but his face is all soft pleasure. He lets out a low, guttural groan and fucks me hard. Harder than I've ever been fucked before. Using my body exactly as he wants. And I take it. I take it all. I meet his violent thrusts, lifting my hips to accept him in, rewarding him with the noises I know all these alphas love.

"Such a good omega, such a good omega," he murmurs and these words of praise are enough to send me soaring. The unbearable pain in my gut morphs into pleasure.

I've never come in a heat, never known what it would be like. I've read plenty of accounts, stalked the omega discussion boards. I know the pain and the frustration is enough to drive an omega to the edge, but the pleasure ... the pleasure is like nothing imaginable.

My orgasm rips through my body and every other orgasm I've had pales in comparison. My body wants this alpha, it wants to be fucked and knotted and filled with his come. I tell him. Tell him that's what I want. That I want him to bite me, make me his. That I want my belly filled with his seed.

I'm wild. Wild with lust. And I have no control over my mind, my body, or my mouth.

Thank goodness he does. Although I can see it takes every last drop of his self-control. He groans every time I make my demands, thrusting harder, fingers digging deeper.

"You think I don't want to, little Omega? You think I don't want to bite you and taste that sweet-smelling gland of yours? The one that's been driving me out of my mind for months. Your scent is like a drug to me. You know how hard I've worked to keep control around you. To not grab you by the hair and drag you to the floor and fuck your brains out. Shit! Shit." He stutters, his thrusts frantic, and then his body spasms, and he fills me like I want him to, his knot expanding immediately. The usual pain I feel as I'm knotted in this way is missing – another advantage of the heat – and all I feel is satisfaction and the need for him to hold me close.

He releases my leg and lowers himself down on top of me.

We're both coated in sweat now, his T-shirt sticking to his body. He wriggles it off, and I see the tattoo scrawled across his left pectoral. Over his heart is a pair of oars crossed at their centres. A mirror image of the charm Zane gave me.

He glances down at me, fingering the charm I'm still wearing, uncertainty in his eyes.

"I'm OK," I say, before he can ask. "In fact, I'm more than OK." I wrap my arms around his neck and kiss him. It's a little more tender now, an action that tells me how he's feeling.

After a moment, he tips his head away and smooths the damp locks of my hair from my face. His eyes are a dark brown. So dark they've often appeared jet. But now I see the depths of the colour, the way it lightens to the hue of young wood at the rims, the golden specks that float in his irises, catching the light.

Then I realise. I blink. How had I missed it?

"It was you," I whisper, "in the library. It was you watching me." All that time, I thought it was Zane. But it wasn't. My body has always responded to Seb's presence. Aware of his domineering proximity, heating my blood, electrifying my skin, even though my mind hadn't understood it.

He rubs the calloused pad of his thumb along my cheekbone. "Yes. It was me."

"Why?"

"Zane told us about his ... encounter with you." He smiles, and I realise it's the first time I've seen the expression on his face. It softens his features, brightens his eyes. "That there was this new omega we'd not met who smelled like heaven. I went to check you out for myself. I meant to introduce myself. But then I got a lungful of your scent and," he looks a little sheepish, "it drove me wild. I didn't trust myself."

"So you didn't introduce yourself …"

"No, but I couldn't stay away either. You were fucking intoxicating. So I sent Harrison as a go-between instead. I wanted to do things properly, the old-fashioned way." He flicks his gaze away. "But you said no."

"You sent Harrison?" I frown in confusion.

"And then Zane asked you out, and you said yes to him. And to Duncan and to Ollie. You wanted the rich boys."

I shake my head. "Harrison never said who sent him. I always assumed it was Zane."

His eyes meet mine again, and he peers into them as if he's searching for the truth.

"I'm not her," I say. "I'm not here because of money. I'm here because of you."

"Yes," he closes his eyes and groans and a fresh shot of his come floods inside me, "And the others?"

"I think I'm falling in love with them," I admit.

I want to ask him more. About what this means for us and for the pack. But I don't get the chance as several pairs of footsteps come thundering down the stairs.

Chapter 25

"Is that smell what I think it is?" I hear Zane call from the stairway.

"It certainly smells like it," Ollie groans. "So fucking sweet."

Seb yanks a sheet over our bodies and rolls us onto our sides. We both glance towards the doorway in time to see the other three members of the pack halt at the bottom of the stairs.

"I got a whiff of her in town," Seb says to them all as they gape at us, "as well as the scents of some alpha following her."

"I'm not surprised," Duncan drawls, "she smells so ripe." The others growl in agreement, their eyes hungrily assessing me.

"I found her in some back alley–"

I don't want to relive the hazy details of that right now. "I wanted him to bring me here. I wanted him to rut me," I say. I want to make it clear to all of them that I'm knotted to Seb of my own free will, my own free desire.

"You're going to have to share, you know," Zane says to Seb, already shrugging off his shirt and strolling into the nest.

Ollie follows, but Duncan lingers by the door. "Does she need anything? Water, food?" he asks.

"Water, please," I say, snuggling against Seb.

"Get all the snacks in the cupboard too," Seb tells him. "I have a feeling we're going to be down here awhile." He grins at the others. "She's never had a heat before."

"Fuuuuck," Ollie mutters, sliding into the bed and coming to lie at my back, his hard cock nudging at my arse, and his tongue searching for my gland. "Didn't we tell you she had a delicious little cunt?" he says to his pack mate.

"I haven't tasted it yet," Seb says, meeting my eye as his knot begins to deflate. I whimper not wanting him to slip away, but soon both men are rolling me onto my back and Seb's face is between my legs. He slurps his way up my thigh, dragging his tongue and finding every drop of wet slick that rolls down my leg. When he reaches my labia, he sucks the swollen flesh between his lips and kisses me there like he had done my mouth. I dig my nails into his scalp and tug at his hair, guiding him to my clit. I'm starting to go under again, the heat taking control. I'm aware of Ollie and Zane lying either side of me, watching as Seb devours me, punishing my sensitive nub with his tongue.

Ollie fondles one of my breasts, tugging and tweaking the nipple. I reach down and find his cock with one hand and rub my fist up and down his shaft. I have no rhythm, I'm too lost to Seb's attention, but Ollie curls his fingers around my hand and takes control.

I peek up at Zane. The smile on his face is the wickedest and wildest I've seen it.

"I've been waiting for you to go into heat, to have you in our nest, for all of us to rut you like this."

"You're ... not ... rutting ... me," I huff out in frustration.

"Well, let's change that, shall we?" Zane smirks.

"Not yet," Seb snarls, "I'm not finished." And he thrusts

his tongue into my cunt.

"I ... need ... a .... knot," I snarl right back.

"You can have one when I say," he growls, dragging his tongue back to my clit and swirling around it, making me dizzy with need. "You taste fucking criminal. And I'm not done."

With that, he flickers the tip of his tongue over my clit, hissing like a snake, and another of those earth-shattering orgasms hits me. When I come back down to earth minutes later, my alphas are manoeuvring me onto my hands and knees, Seb lying beneath me, a tight arm around my waist. They lower me onto his waiting cock, and then I feel another at my backside.

"Can you take us both?" Ollie whispers from behind.

"Yes," I plead.

I'm not sure one alpha's knot will ever be enough for me now. I think I'll always need more. Seb's more careful this time, restraining himself as he ruts me from below and Ollie from above. I bounce between them, crushed by their powerful bodies, and they slide in and out of me with ease, lubricated with my slick. Zane kneels beside us, watching, and I beckon him forward, meeting his mouth with mine. Our kiss is sloppy, knocked around by the movement of the other alphas, but I hang onto his shoulders, not letting him go.

Then I catch the sound of Duncan returning to the nest. I call him over, and soon I feel his hands on my breasts, massaging and kneading them, tweaking my nipples.

I feel worshipped. I feel like something divine. All these alphas want me. All these alphas are here for me, to see me through this heat. To keep me coming and pumped full of their come.

It's all for me.

Just me.

* * *

If I thought I was a needy, debauched omega before, then I was wrong. Because this heat transforms me into some other creature entirely. A creature who's passed between alphas, rolling from one orgasm to the next.

Whenever they dare to leave me, I whine and snarl, snap my teeth and bare my canines, begging and pleading for my next touch, my next kiss, my next knot.

There are no windows down here in the basement and I lose all track of the hours; time flowing away from me.

At some point, Seb forces me up to sit, caging me against his chest, and the others force water down my throat and tiny pieces of energy bar into my mouth. I scowl at them all, nipping at their fingers and attempting to squirm around into Seb's lap.

"Stop it, Omega," Seb hisses, his hand twisting in my hair and tugging hard.

"I don't want to eat," I sulk. "I want to be fucked."

"You need to stay hydrated, and you need to keep your energy up. Your heat is showing no sign of abating, and I don't want a lecture from a puffed-up little doctor when we have to take you in for dehydration and exhaustion."

"We have our own doctor right here," I say, pointing towards Zane.

"And the doctor says to drink, sugar."

I open my mouth and let him pour more water between my lips. When I've gulped down what he obviously considers a decent amount, he leans forward and kisses my forehead.

"You're doing so well, Omega."

I dart my gaze between all of them, and they nod and hum in agreement.

Every single one of them is in rut now, permanently aroused, desire singing in their alpha eyes. They're also naked, and I cast my eyes over each of them, admiring how magnificent each of my alphas is, beautiful in their own way, but all strong and powerful.

I slink low against Seb and fresh slick gushes from me.

"Enough food," Ollie insists. "Time for more fucking."

My gazes flits between them wondering who will have me this time.

"Who do you want, sugar?" Zane asks with his usual grin.

But the truth is I'm greedy. "All of you," I say, crawling from Seb's lap on my hands and knees. I give my arse a little wiggle in Seb's direction, and he slaps my cheek hard.

"Cheeky little tease," he growls, and then his hands are tight on my hips, and he's kneeling behind me, and thrusting deep inside. The others watch wide-eyed.

"I can take more," I say, licking my lips.

Duncan reaches out and cups my chin, his fingers stroking over my lips. "How were we so lucky to find you?"

"Her scent," Zane chuckles.

"I'm just glad you're back, wee yin," Duncan whispers, kneeling before me and feeding me his cock.

Seb's fingers slip to my clit, and soon he's fucking me through my orgasm as Duncan releases into my mouth. I swallow as much of his seed as I can. It's more warming, more filling, than any of the snacks they've fed me. When I've taken all he has to give, he pops from my mouth and Ollie is there next.

223

He crouches down to kiss me, even though the pounding Seb is giving me means my own kiss is sloppy in return. He tweaks a nipple.

"You still hungry?" he asks me, and when I nod, he draws up on his knees and I take his cock in my mouth.

He tastes different from Duncan – they all have their own flavour – and I marvel at how closely their scents and tastes match their personalities. While Duncan's scent has always reminded me of mountains and forests, Ollie's reminds me of warm sunshine and heady flowers.

Soon I'm gulping his seed down too and Zane's straight after, all while Seb continues his steady, forceful pace behind me.

At last, my arms give way and I collapse down on the mattress, only my backside held aloft, and Seb knots me with a roar that sends shivers skating all over my body.

"I haven't tasted you," I mutter with a whine as he gathers me up in his arms and settles us down on the mattress.

"There's plenty of time for that, Omega," he whispers as I drift off to sleep held against his chest.

When I awake again, it's to find myself tangled up in a pile of limbs and bodies. Seb's arm rests under my shoulders and Zane's trails over my waist. Ollie's head rests on my stomach and Duncan's on my thighs. They are all passed out, their sleepy breaths synchronised, their chests rising and falling together.

I run my fingers through Ollie's hair, and he shifts slightly, murmuring something incomprehensible.

The pain in my gut tugs and I know that soon I'll be pawing at them for another orgasm. But right now, I have enough of my wits to soak in my situation.

The aroma in the nest has shifted. It's laced with all our

scents now, tangled together like our bodies, and I think I like the smell better than anything else before. In fact, I like this whole damn situation better than anything I've experienced before.

I'd been so fearful of ending up here. A plaything for alphas. Something my mother had always warned me against. But I'd been wrong about that. This isn't being used. This isn't being abused. This is what it's like to be cherished, to be worshipped, to be loved.

Maybe part of my fear had always been my own belief that I was faulty. That I could never provide what an alpha craved: a heat. But maybe my body had just been waiting – waiting for the right alphas to see me through it.

I smile to myself, Ollie's golden strands soft against my fingers.

And then I nudge my alphas awake and set them to work all over again.

Chapter 26

After that, the heat starts to wane, and when Duncan leads me up the staircase and back into daylight, I realise three days have passed.

"How do you feel, wee yin?" he asks me as he leads me up another flight of stairs and to the bathroom. It seems he has taken the lead in overseeing my aftercare which I'm happy about. He's always been the most gentle with me and the deep tones in his Scottish accent are soothing.

"Fine," I say smiling, "surprisingly fine, although a little sore and tired."

He inspects me in the giant shower, kissing each little bruise, scratch, and love bite. When he's washed me to his satisfaction and patted me dry, he smoothes arnica cream into every mark.

"What day is it?" I ask, rubbing at my forehead.

Duncan stands up and places the pot of cream back in the medicine cabinet.

"Sunday."

I let out a sigh of relief. No lectures or shifts today. Which is just as well. I know Seb won't humour any excuses about skipping those. Then I remember all the shifts and tutoring sessions I have missed. "Shit!" I mutter.

"What?" Duncan asks, resting his hands on my shoulders.

"The heat came on so suddenly, I never got a chance to tell work, or my students or – "

"All taken care of."

"Really?"

He nods. "It's our job to take care of you, Omega. And that means in all things."

He finds me a pair of shorts and a T-shirt, then we go to join the others in the TV room.

Each alpha sprawls out on a sofa and a tower of pizza boxes balances on the floor. The others have already tucked in, devouring slices, and Duncan snatches one of his own and flops next to Zane with a groan. I see now just how hungry and exhausted they all are, and I can't help a little giggle.

"What?" Seb asks me with a mouthful of dough and cheese.

"I must have worked you hard."

"That, Omega," Zane says, resting his feet in Duncan's lap, "is a fucking understatement. I want to sleep for a fucking week."

"Well, you can't," Seb snaps, 'training tomorrow."

"And is pizza really the best diet for you all?" I ask, helping myself to a piece and then sinking into the sofa with Seb when he raises his arm signalling for me to curl up beside him.

"Probably not," Ollie says, reaching over the arm of his sofa to tickle the sole of my foot, "but that heat was harder than any training session. I think we earned the right to load up on greasy crap."

"I'm wondering if you just don't have the stamina," I say, twirling stringy cheese around my forefinger and then sucking it into my mouth. "It doesn't usually take four alphas working together to see an omega through her heat."

"You're not most omegas, Rosie. I told you, you are a needy, greedy little thing," Ollie counters.

Seb growls and nuzzles at my neck, seeking out my gland and raking his teeth over it.

I close my eyes and sigh. "You're right. I can't help myself."

There is silence for a flicker of a moment and then all of my alphas burst out laughing and I think that sound is better than any groan or grunt or growl I've drawn from them so far. I snuggle deeper into Seb's arms and draw my hand under his taut t-shirt.

Seb returns to his pizza, but his hand strays back to my gland. He strokes his thumb across it as we eat our food, the others discussing the training schedule for the week ahead.

Their words drift through my head, but I don't take them in because all my attention is focused on Seb's fingers on my gland. The way he caresses and strokes it. I'm sure it's only an absent-minded action, and yet it sets my pulse racing.

For the whole of those three days of my heat, all I'd wanted my alphas to do was bite me there and make me theirs permanently. I'd begged them multiple times, but they'd all stoically resisted.

The instinct to be claimed with a bite to the gland is overpowering in a heat and only a dickhead alpha would take advantage of an omega like that. Maybe things happened like that in the old days. But now there's a thing called consent. And I'm grateful my alphas know the boundaries.

And yet, here I am, my heat over, and that throb in my gland and that longing to be bitten is just as powerful.

"What's wrong, lass?" Seb whispers.

"Nothing," I say, swallowing, and immediately he shifts me around so he can make eye contact. The others fall silent. Seb glares at me, and I relent. "I guess I'm just wondering where we all stand now. We haven't discussed it."

"What's there to discuss?" Zane says, lunging at another piece of pizza. "You're pack now."

"Am I?" I say, peering into Seb's eyes.

"Yes," he says, tickling my gland lightly as he does and making me gasp. "We're committing to you, Omega, if you're willing to commit to us."

"Yes, I'm more than willing," I beam.

"You can have the attic on the top floor," Ollie says. "An entire floor to yourself. It has its own bathroom."

"What?" I drag my gaze from Seb's to Ollie's.

"Well, you're moving in, aren't you?"

"I am?!" I ask, thinking of my shitty dorm room back in the centre of town.

"Of course," Ollie says, "you're our omega, one of us. This is where you belong. Your home."

"And besides, I've never been happy about you living in that shithole," Zane adds.

I lick the grease from my fingers. If I move in, then everyone is going to know the truth about me and this pack. I'm going to have to tell my family too. Then there's my own security to think about. What happens if this doesn't work out? If they tire of me? I'd literally be homeless. Am I willing to take that risk? I take a deep breath, their mingled scents rushing down my throat, and I know that, yes, I am. Being with them all the time is far too good to resist.

"OK," I say and Seb purrs his approval beneath me. "But," I counter, raising my hand, "we need to talk about how this is going to work – this relationship between all of us."

"With honesty and openness," Zane says, and I raise my eyebrow at him. "I know, I know. I haven't always been as upfront about things as I should've been. But it's the only way this can work."

Seb nods seriously. "You have to tell us how you're feeling and we have to do the same."

"We're already used to sharing," Duncan adds, obviously picking up on some of my uncertainty. "Things work differently in a pack; there isn't the usual territorial bullshit and possessiveness."

"I think I might get jealous sometimes," I admit.

"It's natural," Seb says.

"And besides, I like it when you get jealous," Zane chuckles. "It leads to good things."

I stick my tongue out.

There's one other question I want to ask. One burning in my gland. My stomach churns as I consider how to put my question into words. But I have to. They said we needed to be honest.

"And the future?" I mumble, unable to look any of them in the eye.

They are all silent and my stomach spins so violently I might vomit.

Then Seb soothes his fingers over my gland. "We're in this together for the long run, Omega. There is the option for you to be too."

My heart thumps into life. My gland pulses against his touch. "Claiming?" I ask.

The scents of the four alphas seem to intensify. I can hear them drawing air into their lungs.

"You know we want to," Ollie whispers finally. "But you're young, Omega."

"So are you," I point out.

"And you've only just started your studies. There is plenty of time." Seb caresses my gland again as if underlining his words.

"Don't think it means we don't want to," Duncan adds softly, "But it's important for us that you have options."

"I have plenty of options right here," I murmur sulkily.

"You haven't even talked to your family about this yet, have you, wee yin?"

I shake my head. That is one conversation I am not looking forward to.

Seb twists my head around so I'm eye to eye with him. "Things went wrong for us before, Rosie. If we'd made the mistake of bonding her, imagine the unhappiness we'd be embroiled in now. We need to take things slowly, for our sakes as much as yours. Do you understand?" I do, but I can't help feeling down-hearted. I guess I was caught up in the romance of it all and my little omega heart feels slighted. Yet, rationally, it's the right decision.

"So what does that mean?" I ask. "Am I pack or not?"

"Ahhh," says Zane, his lips curling into that familiar smile, "There's one final test you have to pass first."

A test? To pass? And a final one at that? Have these alphas been testing me the whole time?

"What test?" I ask with a frown.

"Bob," Zane says simply.

Who the hell is Bob?

Chapter 27

"This is Bob. Our coach," Zane says, squeezing the brakes of his bicycle and bringing us to a halt outside the boathouse. He's promised to buy me my own bike, but I have a feeling he's going to drag his feet about it. He enjoys having me balanced on his handlebars, displaying me like a hunter his latest catch.

Bob is not, as I expected, a middle-aged man. Bob is, in fact, a woman who, judging by her lined face and bobbed grey hair, is nearing her sixties. She's dressed in a tracksuit, a whistle dangling round her neck and a baseball cap pulled over her crown.

"Bob, this is Rosie," Zane explains as I slide from the handlebars.

"Hello, Rosie." Bob gives me a curt nod and gestures towards the bench at the side of the river.

The alphas lock up their bikes and unbolt the double doors of the boathouse, disappearing within.

"Can I help set up or something?" I ask Bob.

"Nope, it's part of the commitment the team made to each other. They each have their own part of the boat they are responsible for checking, maintaining and setting up. The boat is the fifth member of the crew and needs to be in the best shape."

"OK," I say, now sure I definitely don't want to interfere.

Bob jangles the keys clipped to her waist and then vanishes inside the boathouse too.

I tuck my hands between my knees and gaze out across the river. Summer is in full bloom and down here by the water, the vegetation is fresh and lush. Dragonflies skim over the water, their rainbow wings catching the early morning light, and from the corner of my eye I see a flash of vivid blue I think must be a kingfisher.

Behind me, I can hear clangs and clashes and then the pack appears one by one, carrying oars and the boat down to the river. I watch them set up, Bob standing over them, her hands on her hips, offering instructions.

She's a beta, I can tell by her scent, and a woman to boot, and I imagine she must be pretty good at her job for a pack of alphas to accept instruction from her. In some ways, she holds herself like an alpha, with confidence and ease, but perhaps that has come with age.

Soon, my four boys are climbing into the boat and Bob tells them to row a few lengths to warm up before they do a timed trial.

Like before, they push off from the bank and float in the centre of the river, readying themselves, before Ollie gives the signal for them to start.

Bob comes to sit beside me on the bench, her set of keys jangling as she lowers down, and for a moment, we watch them together.

"So you're responsible for my team's absence the last few days?"

"I am," I confess, preparing myself for a berating. "Has it

233

thrown you off schedule?" The college rowing championships are only a few weeks away, and I can sense how important it is to the pack. Not only a pride thing, but an opportunity to qualify for the Olympics if they win.

"Ahhh." Bob leans back, crossing her arms over her chest, eyes still locked on the boat. "Actually, it gets rid of all that pent-up sexual energy at once and allows them to concentrate on training. Just don't go and have another heat before race day, OK?"

That's not exactly something I can guarantee. But now that I've had my first heat, I intend to talk to the doctor about pills to control how regularly I have them. Quite frankly, I'd be content to be in heat with my alphas rutting me for the rest of my days, but that is not exactly practical.

"So, are you a permanent addition?" Bob continues. "These boys don't exactly keep me abreast of their personal lives, as much as I like to pry."

"They said it depended on you. Although I think that may have been a joke."

"Me?"

"Apparently I have to pass the Bob test."

Bob snorts. "Like they ever listen to a word I say." She turns her head and examines my face. "But actually, for what it's worth, I think it's a good thing for a pack of alphas to have an omega. It seems to keep them out of trouble, increases the bond, sees them working better together. That's been my experience working with boat crews anyway."

"You've had other boat crews who were alpha packs?"

"A handful in my time, yes."

The boat disappears around the bend in the river and I watch the ripples it leaves behind on the surface of the water.

"But – I'm sorry if this is intrusive – is it right for you, Rosie?" the woman beside me asks. "I've worked with young men and women all my life. I'm not bothered what people get up to in their private lives as long as it does no harm, and they give me the best out there on the water. But I know it isn't always as tolerant out there. Especially for omegas."

"You mean everyone will think I'm a ..."

I don't want to use the S word. But that doesn't mean other people won't. A man, especially an alpha, can have as many women as he likes, and people will pat him on the back and congratulate him. The hypocrisy of it makes me sick.

I smooth my palm down the cotton skirt of my dress.

But, as hard as I'd fought not to think like my mum, hadn't I thought that way too? Isn't it one of the reasons I was so reluctant to get mixed up with this pack in the first place? I feared what it would mean for me, of losing control over my life. But I was also scared of harming my reputation. Would anyone take a pack's omega seriously? It's hard enough to fight against people's prejudices as it is. Belonging to a pack would make that uphill struggle all the more challenging.

I've kept the thought of these consequences pushed to one side. A reality I haven't wanted to face. Being an omega already comes with a shitload of assumptions and prejudices. Being an omega to a pack of alphas, rather than one, will mean I'm exposed to curiosity at best, derision at worst.

"Have you told your family?"

I shake my head. I know what my family will think. What they'll say.

"Oh, love," Bob says, placing a hand on my shoulder, "I'm not meaning to put a cat among the pigeons. I love these boys. And they are good boys too."

"They are," I say, "and I'm not ashamed of what we have."

Bob squeezes my shoulder. "Ahhh, you're a little fighter. I can see why they've fallen for you."

The slap of oars on water captures our attention, and the boat swims around the corner.

Bob cups her hands around her mouth.

"Time for a time trial," she calls. "Let's see what you got."

Chapter 28

I've watched the boys train twice now, and I know from listening to them talk they spend a lot of their time perfecting their actions and synchronisation, but, so far, I've not seen them at their full power and their full speed.

I get to my feet as I watch them ready themselves; a sense of anticipation in the air. My gland tingles in a new way at the back of my neck, and my stomach flutters with butterflies.

Through the breeze, I smell their tension, their determination, their power. All four sets of alpha hands are tight on the handles of their oar, all four brows pinched in concentration.

Bob blows her whistle and they start. The boat rocks on the water for a millisecond, and then it's dragged through the water by the strength of my four alphas. Their arms and legs straining with everything they have. At first, the water is resistant, barging them back, but more tugs of their oars, more slicing through the surface, and they win the struggle. Before I know it, they're soaring, their bodies a blur of motion, the boat a rocket.

Their grunts, as they punish their bodies to the max, are almost painful to my ears, but I can't drag my eyes from them. They are mesmerising, all of them. Raw alpha power. I see now how careful they must be with me every second. How easily they could snap a thing like me in two. How much power they possess in every fibre of their honed bodies. A sense of pride courses through me as they tear through the water. I'm on my toes, my hands at my mouth. These are my men, my alphas.

"Come on!" Bob yells to me and I see she's already on a bike and pedalling fast after the boat.

I start to run, but their pace far outstrips mine and before long I lose sight of them in the bends of the river.

When I finally catch them, they've finished. The boat hovers on the water and all four are collapsed over their oars. Their great shoulders heave as they drag oxygen back inside their bodies, and sweat pours down their faces. They look utterly and thoroughly spent.

"Not bad!" Bob calls from her bike, punching the air. "Not bad at all."

* * *

"We need to be faster," Seb says later as we sit around the kitchen table.

"Fuck, man." Zane scrubs his hand through his hair. "I gave it everything I had. I haven't got any more than that."

Seb shakes his head. "We're going to have to find it from somewhere. Look." He holds his phone up, and I squint at the screen. The picture and the display mean nothing to me, but the others all groan or mutter obscenities under their breath.

"What?" I ask, swinging my gaze around.

"That's *The Sharks*' social media feed," Duncan explains. "They've just posted a time."

I pull a face. "Who are *The Sharks*?"

"They're our main opposition. The ones most likely to beat

us at the championships."

"And what's with the name?"

"Alpha bullshit." Ollie grins. "They think it makes them sound tough."

"And so what about their time?" I gesture towards Seb's phone.

"It's two seconds faster than ours," Seb replies flatly.

"Oh." My earlier elation droops. I can't believe anyone could be faster than them. They looked like something supernatural out there on the water. But then what do I know about rowing, about any of this really.

"It could be bullshit," Zane says, "Just trying to get inside the other competitors' heads."

"Possibly," Seb tosses his phone onto the tabletop, "But it's not like we can afford to take that risk. We're going to have to find those extra seconds."

Zane groans.

"You will," I say to them all, "you'll find it. I have a feeling about it, right down deep in my gut."

"Are you sure that's not some other kind of feeling," Zane asks with a smirk, reaching over to squeeze my thigh.

"No," I tell him, punching his bicep and then flapping my hand about when I crunch my knuckles in the process. "But," I add, "talking of that, maybe I better not move in just yet."

Four alpha growls rumble in four sets of throats. I raise my hand, pleading for them to hear me out. "You need to save your strength and your energy for the race. Not be wasting it on ... you know what." I blush. I've done all sorts of dirty things with these men, yet I still find it hard to put those things into words.

"Sex actually helps," Ollie says.

I raise an eyebrow sceptically. I may know fuck all about sport, but I have at least heard that footballers and other athletes usually get put on a sex ban before a big match.

"He's telling the truth," Duncan adds. "It helps with the alpha adrenaline. Keeps us pumped."

I look to Seb for confirmation, and he nods.

"Fine!" I laugh. I'm hardly capable of turning down my alphas, and if it's going to help, I don't need any more persuasion.

"So you'll hand in your notice on your room?" Seb asks.

"Yep."

"Now?"

"Now?" I repeat, flabbergasted.

"No time like the present."

"But I need time to—"

"Let's show her the room," Ollie says, lumbering to his feet. I can see they're all sore from earlier despite the giant ice bath they subjected themselves to as soon as we returned to the house. Ollie crooks his finger and beckons me up onto my feet. "Come on, little mouse. Let me show you to your burrow."

I glance at the others, and they all grin back. Now my curiosity is definitely piqued. I've never been up into the top floor of the house. To be honest, I've been so occupied with my alphas on the others, it's never even occurred to me to investigate what's up there.

Ollie hums as we climb the stairs, and my excitement grows with every step upwards.

Finally, we emerge on the top floor, and straight away I'm gobsmacked. Attics, I thought, were dark and dingy places, but this floor is flooded with light, the windows prized wide open and a summer's breeze rushing through.

The space up here runs the entire width and length of the house. A giant space just for me. There's a four-poster bed built from driftwood, light, gauzy material hooked around its frame; several deep, cozy-looking armchairs; rows and rows of bookcases; a desk with a computer already set up; and to the side, a bathroom screened off.

"Obviously, this is your room, so you can change it however you like."

"I don't think I want to change anything," I say, strolling into the space, lifting my arms and letting the sunlight fall over me. "It's so big."

"We can divide it up if you don't like it," Ollie says, coming to join me and wrapping his arms around my waist.

"No, I like it." I grin. "I always had to share a room with my sisters growing up, and then, well, you've seen my dorm room. I feel like I could breathe up here." I step away from him and spin around, my arms stretching wide.

"And," Ollie says, taking my elbow and guiding me around, "did you see this?"

I halt, my mouth falling open, and I blink. A choke rises in my throat.

Resting atop a tripod of spindly legs sits a telescope, angled up towards one of the overhead windows.

"Is it for me?"

Ollie nuzzles my ear. "Of course it is, little mouse. We bought it for you. We never want you to stop reaching for the stars."

"I won't," I whisper, my eyes wet.

"Unfortunately, you can't play with your new toy now. You'll have to wait for nightfall," he nips at my throat, "but there is something else we could christen."

"Are you sure you've got the energy?" I ask, reaching around to run my fingers through his hair.

"For you, Omega. Always."

Our lovemaking is lazy and languid. He's exhausted after training and I am more than happy for him to take his time, allowing me to gaze into those caramel eyes as he holds me close and whispers sweet words in my ear.

Words that turn profound as he comes and knots me.

"You have a pretty way with words," I tell him afterwards, combing back his hair from his face.

He chuckles. "I don't know what you've done to me, Rosie. I can't stop all these words from pouring out of me when I'm inside you."

"You should write them down."

He shakes his head.

"Why? They're poetic."

He peers into my face to see if I'm serious. "You think?" he asks.

"Yes."

"Sometimes I write," he admits.

I smile at him. "I thought you probably did. Do the others know?"

"No, I haven't shared any of it with anyone." He twists his head and kisses the palm of my hand. "You're the first person I've told."

"What's it about?"

"Shit. All sorts." He wraps his arms around me, bringing me closer, his knot still firm inside me. "Some of it's about this little mouse who kept driving the big bad wolf to distraction with her squeaks and her squeals."

"Until finally, he caught her in his big paws."

"And then she squeaked and squealed for him."

He kisses my neck, a trail up and down. "I'm glad you're home, Rosie. I'm sorry all that heartache happened with Seb. But now it's better than before. Now that we all belong together. It feels stronger."

"See," I say, aware I'm sniffling. "You could be a writer."

"I want to win a gold medal at the Olympics." He grins. "Just got to find those extra seconds."

I smile back at him, my eyes wet, my heart full of emotion.

"And what do you want to be, little mouse, when you grow up?"

"If I can get a good degree and Dr Whei puts a word in for me, I'm hoping I can get a job at the International Space Agency."

He squeezes me tight.

"Our omega is fucking awesome," he roars, tilting his head to listen. "Did you hear that, boys?" he yells again towards the staircase. "Awesome."

"Very poetic," I giggle.

Chapter 29

"I can't believe you're leaving me," Soph moans face down on my bed, making no effort to help me pack up my stuff like she'd offered.

"I'm not leaving you," I say from my position cross-legged on the floor, where I'm stacking my books into boxes. "I'm only moving to the outskirts of the city."

"It's so far!"

"It is not. And I'm going to see you every day in lectures. And you can come for sleepovers in my room and actually have somewhere to sleep."

Soph props herself up on her elbows. "You mean your room in the roof? Like Cinderella. Are they going to make you cook and clean?"

"Cinderella lived in the cellar. Disney got it wrong. She didn't live in a massive, designer attic room."

"You're so lucky."

"Soph, you have a designer apartment."

"But I don't have four men."

"I'm sure you could get some if you tried."

"To be honest, it sounds amazing, but in reality, I don't think I'd have the energy." She rolls over onto her back. "Besides, Harrison is keeping me busy enough."

"Uh huh," I mutter. I've already had the details. Harrison and Sophia are now a thing. For the time being, anyway. Until their brothers find out and probably put an end to it. In fact, I think the sneaking around is half the appeal for Sophia.

"Have you told your folks yet?"

I sigh and drop the textbook I'm holding into my lap. "No, I haven't told them."

Soph slides off the bed and drops beside me. "I thought you were going to do it last night?"

"I was," I bury my face in my hands dramatically, "but I wimped out."

"Urgh, Rosie. You're going to have to tell them sooner or later."

"I don't want to," I squeak from behind my hands.

Soph peels away my fingers. "Why? From what I've heard of your mum, she'll be dancing on the rooftops. Not one, but four eligible alphas."

"Exactly, four!" I shake my head miserably. "She's not going to approve."

"How about your dad?"

I lean against the bed and tip back my head. My dad? I'm not sure about my dad. It is always my mum lecturing us girls about the way things should be, always my mum I'm fighting against to be something different. My dad just lets us get on with things, never really declaring a side.

"Surely, if your mum is an omega, she can't disown you without your dad's permission."

"Thanks, Soph. That's really reassuring."

"I'm just saying, maybe talk to him first if you think he's less likely to freak out." She lifts a book from the ground, turns it over in her hands, examining the spine, then drops it into the writing box. "Why don't you invite him to the race?"

"Maybe," I say noncommittally, because I'm not sure.

And so I put it off. The alphas come and move my belongings up to their house, and I say goodbye to my old room once and for all. June arrives, and I spend more and more time up by the river, lying out on the bank, revising and working through my assignments. Sometimes, Sophia comes to join me. Pinching me every few minutes and reminding me how lucky I am as she gazes out at the boys working on the river. Other times, I fall asleep in the shade and only wake when one of the alphas comes to find me and snuggle up with me in the grass.

It's blissful. Dreamlike. And I don't want to break this perfect bubble of existence by telling my parents. Maybe Soph is right, and they'll be OK with it. But maybe they won't, and then what?

But the bubble is broken anyway, despite my best efforts and from an entirely different direction.

I'm home alone in the house, the boys out at training, when the doorbell rings. I'm up in my room and have to call that I'm coming as I race down the steps. I'm breathless by the time I swing back the door and find myself face to face with a woman I don't know.

For a moment, I wonder if it's another member of the OmegaSoc come to check up on me – or nose about – but the look on the woman's face tells me she's just as surprised to see me.

"Hello," she says slowly, examining my face critically. Her floral scent engulfs me, too much for my sensitive nose, and I'm forced to breathe through my mouth, the taste of her too sweet on my tongue. "And who are you?"

Me? Who is she?

"I'm Rosie," I answer, my fingers gripping the door handle as if I'm scared she'll wrestle it from me. "Can I help you?"

"Are any of the boys in?" She attempts to peer over my shoulder, flipping her designer sunglasses off her head, and letting her jet-black hair fall across her face as she does. Her eyes are very blue, almost violet. She is the ideal version of an omega, all petite and perfectly curved.

"They're not."

"Will they be back soon?"

"No, not for a while."

"Well, never mind," she says with a smile she obviously hopes will disguise her annoyance. "I just came around to collect some things that I left behind." She steps up towards the door, pushing against the wood.

I don't budge. "Excuse me, who are you?" I ask, even though I know. I know exactly who she is. Her scent is even more suffocating in my throat.

"Oh, I'm Pippa." Her fake smile widens. "I'm sure they've told you about me."

I wish – oh, how I wish – I could say no. Instead, I nod.

"So, if you'd just let me in, I can grab my things and get out of your hair. Of course, it would've been nice to say hi to the boys. I'm sure they'd love to see me. But—"

"You'll have to come back," I say, "when they're here. I can't just let you in to rummage through their stuff."

The woman laughs. "Oh, they won't mind, sweetie."

"I think they will. And I think you should've called before you showed up."

"Oh, I did. I was messaging Seb last night. Didn't he tell you?" She looks at me with fake sympathy, and I've never wanted to reach out and strangle someone as much as I do

247

right now. "Didn't he mention I'd be dropping by?"

"No," I say, trying not to grind my teeth, "and I've got to go." She starts to protest, but I close the door before she gets a chance. I hear her mutter something about my rudeness, and then her heels click on the path as she walks away.

I wait a few minutes and then creep to one of the front windows, peering through and searching the street. She's gone.

Immediately, I rush up to the bathroom, searching through the cabinet until I find mouthwash. Snapping off the cap, I chug back a whole mouthful, swilling it around my mouth, desperate to remove the sugary taste of the other omega. I don't know why it repulses me so much, but it does, turning my stomach and making the fine hairs in my nose bristle. I wash my mouth out three more times and blow my nose twice before I'm satisfied. Then I scrub my hands and my face, even though I didn't touch her.

Her scent hangs in the hallway like a bad smell, though, slowly curling up the stairs and to my room as if she's invading the house.

When the alphas return, I come to lurk in the hall, ready to read their expressions. They smell her immediately. I see the way their nostrils twitch and the knowing glances they throw at each other.

"What the hell?" Zane mutters.

I step forward. "She was here," I say before any of them can dash away.

"Pippa," Ollie states.

I nod my head. "She wanted to come and pick up some stuff. I wouldn't let her in."

"Good," Zane snaps, dropping his bag to the floor with a

thud.

"But she said you knew she was coming, that you'd arranged it."

Zane's eyes leap to mine in shock, and he points to his chest. "Me?"

"No," I say, peering over the others to Seb lurking by the door. "Seb."

The others snap their heads around to stare at their pack mate. "You've been talking to her?" Ollie asks in clear disbelief.

"No." Seb stomps towards me, stopping right before me. "She's been talking to me." I go to open my mouth, but he cuts me off. "You know we're not interested in that omega. Are you seriously concerned about this?"

"No," I say, feeling foolish. The girl hurt them, Seb especially. And I'm their omega now.

"So, what exactly has she been 'talking' to you about?" Zane asks, the tension clear in his voice.

"She's been texting me. Saying she made a mistake. That she wants us back."

"For how long?" My voice is weak in my throat. "For how long has she been texting?"

"A couple of weeks. I ignored the messages. Then I got pissed off with them and told her we have a new omega and to leave us alone." He reaches up and places his palm on my shoulder. "I am guessing that sparked her curiosity, and she wanted to get a look at you. If I'd known ..." I frown. "She's so far from my mind now, Omega, it didn't seem worth mentioning it. To you. To any of you," he adds, turning to look around at his pack mates.

"It wasn't." Duncan pats Seb on the back and walks through

to the kitchen.

"It was!" I glare at Seb, that same stab of jealousy I'd experienced at the bar returning tenfold. "You can't be having conversations with another omega behind my back, especially with your ex."

"Are you telling me what I can and can't do?" Seb asks, a slight warning growl to his voice.

"When it comes to her, yes," I say, lifting my chin in defiance and meeting his stern eyes. The woman's scent is still thick in the air, and it's driving me to distraction.

"You know you're mine, Omega," he says lowly. "You want Ollie and Zane to pin you against the wall so I can claim you, bite you, here and now?"

"Seb," Ollie warns softly. We all know that would be a bad idea. Claiming me would tip me into heat and my alphas into rut, and the championships are only days away. Besides, it's not what we agreed. We agreed we'd wait.

I drop my gaze to the floor, but Seb tilts it up to meet his with the curl of his finger.

"I will talk to her, make it damn clear she's to stay away from us, all of us. OK?" I bite my bottom lip, and nod. "But you can't talk to me like that, Omega. You know that's not how it works with me."

I open my mouth to protest but, before I've had the chance, I'm lifted off my feet and flung over his shoulder.

I squeal, lifting my head to find both Ollie and Zane grinning at me.

"I'm taking you to my room," Seb tells me, "and spanking your arse."

Chapter 30

"Are you sure we couldn't have gone to a tattoo studio in a nice part of the city?" Sophia asks me, clutching my arm, eyes flitting about the street, over the rubbish at the curb, the graffiti scrawled on closed-down shops and the worn paintwork of the ones still open.

"This studio has an omega artist. There's lots of chat about her on the omega online community."

"Does it matter who does your tattoo?" Sophia asks.

I look her hard in the eye. We've been good friends for nearly nine months now, but she still struggles to see what it's like for me as an omega. "Most tattoo artists are alphas," I remind her. "That's not exactly a great situation to be in. That's why this woman is getting so popular."

Sophia nods, and we stop outside the door of the studio. The windows are covered in large tattoo designs, and it's nearly impossible to see through into the shop.

"Are you sure about this?" Sophia asks. "This little tattoo right here." She points to one on her wrist, "hurt like hell. And I have tough beta skin. I'm not as sensitive to pain as you are."

I thrust out my arm, and remind her of the constellation of stars I have tattooed over my wrist. Sure, it hurt and my mum refused to talk to me for a week after I got it done, but it was worth it.

Soph shudders. "Oh, I think I'm going to be sick."

I roll my eyes and push my shoulder against the door. "It'll be fine," I tell her. Besides, I want this. I want a way to prove to the boys that I am theirs.

Despite Seb's words of reassurance, I'm still spooked by Pippa's appearance. Perhaps I'll always feel like this. The omega inside me always insecure until we're bonded. But for now, I think this permanent ink on my skin will help.

My eyes adjust to the dim electric lighting, and together we stroll to the counter where a woman waits on the other side, flipping through her phone. Her cherry-red hair sits in a high pony at the back of her head, tied with a ribbon, and a curled fringe frames her face. She wears lipstick that matches her hair and a tight 1950s-style dress, her bare shoulder covered in a pattern of inks.

"Hi," she smiles, "Rosie, right?" She addresses me, probably picking up on my scent under the blockers.

I recognise her voice, but I can make out her scent under blockers too. I nod. "And you must be—"

"Connie."

We've been in email contact as well as talked on the phone, and I've sent her several designs and ideas.

"Let's go out back," she says. A large man who must be an alpha works on a young beta man on the other side of the shop, and I spot their glances towards us from the corner of my eye. "We have a special room out the back for omega clients. Nice and fresh smelling, no contamination from alpha scents." She jumps down from her seat, and we follow her behind a beaded curtain and through into a small room. She gestures for me to sit on the large dentist-like chair and for Sophia to take the plastic seat to one side.

The lighting in here is softer and rather than the rock that blasts out in the main shop, it's sultry love songs.

"So," the woman says. "I've worked up a couple of plans for you." She opens a drawer and lifts out several sheets of paper, passing them to me. Sophia peers over my shoulder as I flick through them. "Like any?" the woman asks, crossing her legs.

"This one, I think," I say, alighting on the third and lifting it up for Sophia to inspect.

"Yeah, that's gorgeous," Sophia says. "Makes me wonder whether I could stomach another. I've tried to tell her it's going to hurt." She jerks her head in my direction.

"Where are we doing this again?" the artist asks.

"Here," I say, tugging down the waistband of my skirt and pointing to the soft skin of my stomach, just by my hipbone.

"It will hurt." She nods, chewing at gum. "But it's always more painful for us omegas. It isn't bone, so it's not as bad as it could be. And I have some numbing gel that can help."

I take a deep inhale, suddenly nervous.

"You sure about this?" the older woman asks, a smile hovering on her lips.

"Yes," I say with all the self-assurance I can muster. She tells me to take off my skirt and wriggle down my underwear, and then she cleans the skin.

"So, what's the meaning behind the design?" the woman asks as she prepares her equipment.

"She's in love," Sophia says.

The woman frowns slightly. "Is it about an alpha because you know this thing is permanent?"

"So's what we have."

The frown on the woman's forehead grows deeper. "But you're not bonded, right?"

"No, not yet. That's why I want to get this."

"Maybe better to keep it that way," she mutters, snapping shut a drawer. "In my experience, an alpha is only good for one thing."

"What's that?" Sophia asks.

"Cock."

Sophia laughs and I find myself doing the same. I lift a hand to my cheek, finding it cool. A comment like that used to have me blushing. Not anymore.

"Yeah," I say, my gaze flitting between the two other women. "The cock is good, but there is other stuff too."

"What?" the artist quips. "Like their arrogance, dominance and control-freakiness."

I smile mischievously. "That can be fun sometimes."

"Oh," Sophia says, wiggling her eyebrows.

"But I was thinking of stuff like having someone that cares for you, someone to talk to, someone to snuggle up with at night."

"See," Sophia points her hand in my direction. "I told you, in love."

Is Sophia right?

As I lie back in the chair and grit my teeth against the pain, I mull it over. It does feel like love. This warm fuzzy feeling in my chest. This sensation like I'm floating in a safe and secure bubble. The little butterflies I still get whenever one of my alpha looks at me.

Yes, I think I am in love. With all of them.

Chapter 31

I f it's love, then maybe it's about time I tell my parents.

The boys spend more and more of their evenings at training in the run-up to the competition. I don't mind. I haven't had a lot of time to myself since we fell into this relationship together, and I enjoy the opportunity to listen to true-crime podcasts while I unpack my belongings and rearrange them around my room.

When it's dark, I play with my new telescope, exploring the stars above our city and losing myself for hours. Sometimes joined by one of the alphas when the hours draw late, and I teach them all the different constellations, showing each of them their Zodiac sign in the sky.

I wait for one of these evenings alone and I message my parents, telling them I need to talk to them on Zoom. I sit staring at my face on the laptop screen, waiting for them to join. I can read my nerves in my eyes.

Then the second black box appears and the image of my parents side-by-side flicks up. The sound follows a few seconds later, and I wave and smile as best as I can while we wait to speak to one another.

"Hello, darling," my dad says. "You look well."

"She looks skinny," my mum says. "I suppose you're not

eating properly?"

"I'm eating fine." My father's still dressed in his shirt from the office, although he's wearing no tie and his top button is loose. He leans back slightly in his chair, whereas my mum sits straight-backed, her hair curled behind her ears, her blouse buttoned to her throat.

I look at them both and wonder if they've ever experienced the type of passion I have. If they're happy. In love.

"So what's this all about then, Rosie?" my mum asks, patting down her hair as she glances at her image on the screen. "I want to catch the news in ten minutes."

"You're not in any trouble, are you?" my dad adds.

"No, no trouble." I take a deep inhale. "I have some news I want to tell you."

"You're pregnant," my mum gasps, her hand flying to her throat.

"No, I'm not pregnant. But I have ... I have had a heat."

My mum's shoulders sag in relief and her hand drops to her lap. "Oh my, well, thank goodness for that." She turns to my dad. "That is good news."

"Very good news," he repeats, looking flustered.

"And I met someone." I can see my mum's going to speak again, so I cut across her. "Actually, I met more than one person. I've met a pack."

My parent's brows crease in confusion. "A pack?" my dad says.

"What do you mean, you met them?" My mum examines my face. "Are you dating several men at once, Rosie?"

"No," I straighten in my seat. "I'm in a pack now with four alphas." I see the look of horror on my mum's face, but I force myself to keep going. "And these are the four alphas I want to be with for the rest of my life."

My dad hesitates, then speaks. "That's good news, Rosie." He peers at my mum. "That's good news, Francis. That's what you want, isn't it? For Rosie to find an alpha."

My mother's jaw tightens and her mouth forms a tight line. "An alpha, Christopher, not four." She glares at me through the computer screen. "What did I say? What did I say would happen if you went off to this college? I knew you'd end up in trouble, and now here you are, caught up with a pack. Rosie! What on earth do you think you're doing?"

"I'm happy," I say. "More happy than I've ever been before. They're good guys." I appeal to my dad. "They come from good—"

"Happy?!" My mum scoffs. "And how long do you think that will last? You'll be shunned. Shut out of all respectable society. A pack omega!" She rests her hand on my dad's shoulder. "Christopher, what will people say? About us?"

I keep my back straight, my face blank. I don't let her to see how much her words wound me.

Is she right? Things aren't like they used to be. There are more freedoms now. More opportunities for alphas and omegas to be who they want to be. To live the life they want. No more collars. No more chains.

She turns back to me. "And what of your ambitions? Now you're just throwing them to one side, I assume."

"No, that hasn't changed."

She scoffs. "A prestigious institute like the International Space Agency won't hire a pack omega."

Her words hit me in the gut, but I don't show it. I stare back at her.

"This is what I want. I've made my decision." I hang up. My

257

mobile buzzes on the table, but I ignore it.

Outside, a storm whips up, and the wind swoops around the rooftop and howls down the chimney. Suddenly, I feel very alone in this big, old house.

I'm used to having my sisters around. Perhaps this is why being in a pack appealed to me. I like the noise and the bustle. The constant chat and someone always being here.

I huddle in one of the armchairs, trying to read a book, but in the end the noise of the wind and the voices in my head freak me out completely, and I trot downstairs to the first floor. There are still a few hours before the boys will be back, and so I stand on the empty landing and gaze through their doorways. Then, with my book still in my hand, I walk through into Seb's room.

It may be my favourite of all the alpha's rooms, probably because his scent is so rich in here, and just stepping inside has my skin tingling. My body has always reacted most potently to his scent. But also because it isn't the bare, orderly room I'd expected. This is a room of a man who cares – about his family, about his pack mates, and now about me too.

Photos are pinned across the walls. Some he's taken with his phone, some with his camera. Photos of his mum and his grandparents. Photos of his pack mates. And a few additions of me. The most recent a black and white shot of me lying against his pillow, peering up at the camera and smiling sleepily.

But my favourite is the large framed photo that hangs in the centre of the room. It's one of his pack mates sitting in their boat, laughing, the water glistening around them as if they're floating in some other mystical world. Somehow, it reflects all their personalities. Ollie, stunningly beautiful; Duncan, sensitive and quiet; Zane, cheeky and fun.

I walk around the room, examining each of the photos like I've done a million times before, and then I climb into his giant bed and snuggle down into the sheets. It's hot, and I don't really need the cover, but I like to be cocooned in his scent, for it to brush against my skin.

I read my book, happier now, less lonely, less frightened. My eyes grow heavy, and I must fall asleep because the next thing I know, a warm body slides into the bed next to me.

"Seb?" I ask, rolling towards him. He wraps his strong arms around me, dragging me towards him.

"Shhh, lass," he says, "it's me. You can go back to sleep."

I wriggle in closer to him, resting my head on his shoulder and sliding my legs between his, and drift back to sleep.

In the morning, he's still there and I'm still encased in his hold.

"Don't you have training?" I murmur when I look up and find him awake.

"Yes, but I couldn't drag myself away."

"Are you feeling well?" I ask him, yawning and pushing myself up onto my elbows. "That does not sound like Sebastian Thomas talking."

"It doesn't, does it?" he admits. "But you looked so peaceful. Ollie persuaded me we've been working hard enough and one morning's rest wouldn't make or break us."

"Ollie is a bad influence on both of us."

"That's what bloody earls are like. No idea what it's like for us mere peasants."

"I think it's good, though," I say, sweeping his hair away from his eyes. "You work so hard, you're so dedicated. You don't want to burn yourself out. You don't have to prove anything to anyone."

He shakes his head. "I have a responsibility to keep our team and this pack together."

"But you can share that responsibility." I stroke his rough cheek. "You know, I'd like to care for you sometimes too."

"Oh yeah?" he asks, eyebrow bobbing up and his eyeline dropping down my body.

I lean down and kiss him and as that kiss deepens, and he tries to flip me over onto my back, I resist.

"No," I say, "my time to care for you, remember, Alpha?"

"How?" he says, his voice descending lower. "How are you going to care for me?"

I kiss him again, sweeping my palms over his torso until I find the V of muscle at his abdomen. I follow the line until I discover the coarse curls at his groin, and then lower still to his stiff cock. I grasp it in my hands and stroke along his long shaft, twisting my hands when I reach the head.

His head lifts off the pillow to peer down at the work of my hands and I take my opportunity to lift my knee over his body and come to straddle him.

"Hmmm," he purrs, "I like this."

"Going to give you more, though, Alpha," I murmur back, and resting up on my knees, I hover about him, before lowering slowly onto his waiting cock. He watches me swallow him up, watches me sink lower and lower, watches as I come flush against him.

"I want to make you feel good," I say, feeling him twitch inside me, knocking against my spot.

"You are making me feel good," he says, reaching up to rest his hands around my waist.

I grind my hips in circles, and his fingers flex.

"Is that good?"

"Fuck, little Omega, watching you take my cock is always good. Finding you in my bed, smearing your goddamn delicious juices all over my sheets is good. Everything about you is good."

I smile down at him, grinding him harder.

"You belong with us, lass. You're perfect for me. Perfect for this pack. We're alike, you and me."

"We don't really belong here, do we?" I say. "Not like the others."

"No, we don't. But we're going to be here any-goddamn-way," he grunts, lifting me up, allowing his cock to drag from my entrance and then slamming me back down.

I throw back my head and wail, and then we work together. I bounce up and down on his shaft until my thighs burn, and he helps me along, lifting me up and down.

When we come, we come together, my cunt clenching around him and milking his cock and his grip loosens and his face relaxes.

When we're both silent again, still a little dizzy and out of breath, he opens his eyes and stares into mine.

"This pack is better, I'm better, with you here, Rosie."

"Is it love?" I ask him.

"Yes," he says, "This is love."

And I trust him. I trust him the most.

If Seb says this is love, then it is.

"I spoke to my parents," I admit to him. They've all been encouraging me to tell them the truth, Seb more than any of them.

"And what did they say?"

I trace the outline of the muscles on his chest with my fingertip. "That I'm ruining my life." I swallow hard. "That everyone will shun me. That I can kiss goodbye to my dreams."

"They said that," he says, the constrained anger clear in his voice.

"Not in so many words."

"You know they're wrong though, Rosie? You know that, don't you?" I glance up at his dark eyes. I want to believe that too.

I'm not ashamed of what I am, who I am. Not anymore. But I am afraid that others will think like my mum. That choosing this path will hamper the few chances I had. That this will end my dreams of the space agency.

"The world is changing, lass. We're changing it. You can be ours, we can be yours, and you can still be all you want to be."

"It almost sounds too good to be true," I admit. "Too greedy, too lucky."

"You deserve it." I smile at him. "You know who already loves you before she's even met you?" Seb says, stroking my hair and kissing the crown of my head.

"Who?"

"My mum. Are you ready to meet our parents?" he asks me.

I flip my head around to look at him. "Parents?"

"They're going to be at the race. They're all curious to meet you. Especially my mum." He chuckles. "She's been threatening to hop on a train and come down here to meet you for the last few weeks. I told her she has to be patient."

"You guys told your parents about me? What did they say?"

"They're pretty damn delighted." He strokes his fingers through my hair. "You're pack now."

Chapter 32

The night before the race, the college has paid for the boys to stay in a hotel close to the course. Strictly speaking, I'm not sure I'm allowed to be staying too, but there's no way my alphas are going to let me spend a night away from them. Especially when that night is the night before the biggest race of their lives. They want me close by, my touch, my scent, my calming presence.

Most of the day is lost to race officials talking the boys through the arrangements, interviews with members of the press, and weigh-ins and drug testing. After it's all finished, Bob takes them for a carb heavy meal, and then it's check-in time.

It seems we're not the only rowing team that's chosen to stay close to the event. The lobby is full of oversized men, the air con circulating many alpha scents.

Duncan draws me into his body as we wait by the reception desk. "Stay close to us, wee yin," he tells me as he eyes the other crews milling about the lobby.

I can understand his worry. That familiar feeling of alpha eyes on my body troubles me. I slide my hand into his and note the way my alphas come to stand around me, forming a barrier with their bodies.

Once Bob's checked us all in, we move as one towards the lifts, but then, as the boys haul their bags through the opening doors, I get a whiff of that scent. Sickly sweet.

I freeze, an icy shiver running down my spine. What's she doing here?

I swing my gaze about, searching for her through the throng of people, and then I'm pushed.

One minute I'm standing waiting to step into the lift, the next I'm bundled through into the adjacent one. The buttons on the walls are slammed and the doors crash shut.

I grapple for the handle and look up, finding myself alone in the mirrored box with four large alphas. They all wear matching green polo shirts, tiny embroidered sharks swimming across their left pecs. And I understand immediately. These are *The Sharks*. My boys' competitors.

They circle me, each grinning toothily, and I slink back against the wall.

"She smells fucking delicious," the largest ones says, his eyes travelling down my form slowly like I'm something he'd like to devour.

"And unclaimed," the fair man to his right chuckles. He steps towards me and I flinch away. "They not giving you what you need, sweetheart?"

"I have everything I need, thank you," I manage to spit out, edging towards the row of buttons. Another man steps forward, blocking my way.

The lift keeps rising; the motion pushing my feet into the floor and my stomach into my lungs.

Surely, the lift will stop any second now.

The man blocking my path leans in towards me, his nose finding my neck. "Definitely unclaimed. Bunch of fucking pussies. Or maybe they just don't want you." The pack of alphas move as one group, closing in on me. "But we'll have you. Wouldn't you rather be with winners, not a bunch of losers?"

"They're going to crush you," I whisper, just as the lift comes to an abrupt halt and the doors are ripped open. Seb crashes through, pinning the man at my neck to the wall, his arm pressing into his throat. Duncan follows right behind, fists clenched, backing the others up, and Ollie and Zane grab me by a wrist each and haul me out of the box, my feet barely touching the ground.

"If you ever," Seb growls, leaning on the other man's windpipe, "ever touch her, we'll rip your fucking throats out."

"Please don't," I call to Seb, as Ollie and Zane drag me along the corridor. "They're just playing games with you." I can see the grin of the man Seb has pinned. He whispers something to Seb I don't catch, and Seb snarls, his whole body fighting the instinct to pound his competitor.

But then what? He fucks up his hand at best, at worst the team gets disqualified for fighting.

"Seb! Duncan!" I yell, digging in my heels and trying to tug free from my other alphas' grasps.

Seb's head snaps my way and as our eyes meet, I see the madness leave his face. He breathes, loosens his pressure on the man's neck, then takes a step back. Duncan joins him, and after more snarled words I don't hear, they turn together and follow us down the corridor.

"How the fuck did that happen?" Zane asks with annoyance as they usher me into our hotel room. "You were right with us."

I remember that scent. But I decide not to mention it.

265

They're already rattled.

"Fuckers," Ollie says, starting to pace the large hotel suite with its four double beds.

Duncan has his hands on my shoulders, examining my face. "Are you OK, wee yin? Did they hurt you?"

"No, I'm fine, honestly." I plaster on the best smile I can muster. Getting all flustered and emotional over this isn't going to help my pack. And it's exactly what the other team had in mind when they'd pulled that stunt. Rile *The Crew* up, pump their adrenaline into overdrive so they're running on empty by the time the race comes.

I stroke Duncan's cheek, then lead him to the bed by the window, the view falling away to the river beyond. I jump up onto the bed and the others lumber on reluctantly.

"Everyone just breathe, OK?" I tell them. "I'm fine. I've been dealing with alpha arseholes all my life." Inside, I'm shaking, but I suppress it, steadying my scent so that I appear calm on the surface. "Don't let them get inside your heads."

"We're going to beat those fuckers," Ollie hisses, kissing the crown of my head.

"Yes," I agree, "you're going to blow them out of the fucking water."

Chapter 33

I can't sleep. The adrenaline from my encounter with the other boat team streams through my veins despite my best efforts, and I'm racked with nerves.

Nerves about the race. Nerves about that conversation with my mum and dad. And nerves about meeting the parents of my alphas. I lie in bed staring at the ceiling, listening to the soft whistle of breath from the alphas around me.

The race plays out in my head again and again – sometimes my boys winning, sometimes them losing. The hours tick by, and eventually the dawn crawls in and the alarm goes off.

The next hour is a blur of rushing to get ready and Bob ensuring everyone has eaten and drunk the right things. Then we're whisked away to the racing venue, and the anticipation in the vehicle is palpable. My boys aren't nervous like I am. They're pumped and ready to go. Pride blossoms through my chest as I watch them talk through their game plan for the ten-millionth time.

All four sets of parents are waiting in a line in the family section when we arrive. I take a deep breath, squeezing Ollie's hand as he leads me down the row behind the others. He introduces me to three smart couples, all immaculately dressed in expensive designer outfits, the wealth dripping off their wrists and ears.

Each parent shakes my hand politely, a hint of curiosity in their eyes, until I reach the end of the row. There waits Seb's mum, a tiny omega woman who pinches my cheeks and tells me I'm beautiful before enveloping me in a bear hug.

"I'm so nervous," she mutters into my ear, "won't you come and sit with me, love?"

Seb comes up behind me and carefully pries me from his mother's grasp.

"Easy, Mum," he grins, squeezing the older woman's shoulders, "don't break her."

"Isn't she just beautiful?" she repeats to her son this time.

"We think so, yes," Seb says, meeting my eyes, and I'm surprised his Mum doesn't melt into a puddle then and there. "We've got to go get set up now, lass."

The others come and stand around us as he kisses my cheek and I squeeze him tight.

"We'll see you after the race, OK?" Zane says, kissing me too.

I'm such a jangle of nerves I can hardly speak, but I kiss each of my alphas in turn and wish them luck, crossing my fingers and my toes as they leave.

I watch them stroll away, my heart in my mouth until I lose them in the throng of competitors and officials.

"Rosie!" A voice calls from the crowd behind us, and I spot Sophia jumping up and down on her toes, waving at me frantically. I beckon her over, and we take up the chairs to the left of Mrs Thomas. My friend engages the older woman in a cheery conversation about college, and I am eternally grateful. I'm so nervous I can hardly speak.

The river lies mere metres in front of us, and despite the clear summer's day, the wind is frisky, the water lapping violently against the moorings. Watching its backward and forward motion only adds to my nausea.

But then my eyes are dragged away as applause trickles through the audience, growing in enthusiasm and volume, and I spy the competitors carrying their boats to the water, my pack somewhere in the middle.

"They look good, don't you think?" Mrs Thomas whispers to me and Sophia. We both nod. They do, confident, relaxed, and for a moment, I feel a million times calmer.

They place their boat down in the water and chat among themselves, Zane saying something which makes the others laugh as they wait for the official.

But then something changes.

I see it almost immediately. Tension ripples through all their bodies, their respective shoulders stiffening. I smell it a second later. And I understand.

That scent. That sickly sweet scent.

Mrs Thomas sniffs beside me.

"What is that gold-digging hussy doing here?" she mumbles, shuffling on her chair. I follow her line of sight to two crews along the bank.

Pippa stands with *The Sharks*, hugging and pawing over the boys, advertising to everyone that she is their omega. I notice it in her scent too, the flavour of it has changed. Deepened. Darkened. Something I hadn't spotted yesterday.

They've claimed her. Pippa belongs to that pack. Bitten and bonded.

"What's going on?" Sophia asks, registering mine and Mrs Thomas' discomfort as well as the sudden change in countenance of my boys.

"That's their ex-omega," I whisper to her.

Sophia's eyes float over the other woman. "She's with a rival crew now?"

"Worse. She's bonded to them."

"Shit," Sophia mutters.

"*The Sharks* have done this on purpose," my hands ball into fists on my knees, "trying to get inside their heads again."

"Well," says Sophia pointedly. "I think it might be working."

I stand and stare at my alphas. They're rattled. It's clear. And they need to be focused. Not distracted by that crew and that omega.

I swing my head around looking at the growing crowds on both sides of the river banks, at the TV crews and the journalists, at the parents of my pack.

If I go to my alphas now, everyone will know. There will be no hiding. It will be clear to the world that I belong to all these alphas. All four. That I am a pack omega.

And what then? Is my mum right? Will I be shunned? Ridiculed? Will I lose my opportunities, my dreams?

A prestigious institute like the International Space Agency won't hire a pack omega.

I close my eyes, fighting the voices in my head.

You know they're wrong. You know that, don't you? The world is changing. You can be all you want to be.

I open my eyes and gaze at my alphas. They are whispering tersely to each other, Zane and Seb's bodies betraying their rage in their boiling countenances.

This is their dream. To race, to win, to be in with a shot at the Olympics. And I can see it all drifting away from them as their focus and energy drains away.

I know how important dreams are.

I can't sit back and watch. I start walking, one foot in front of the other.

"Where are you going, love?" Mrs Thomas calls, but I don't answer. I pick up my feet, my pace increasing until I'm jogging, pushing through the crowd and past the officials, ignoring the attempts by people with badges to stop me.

I reach the jetty; the boards wobbling beneath me, and race along, skidding to a halt by my pack.

"Rosie?" Zane says, "You can't be here."

Screw that. If that other omega can be here, then so can I.

"I didn't get a chance to say," I pant, trying to catch my breath, "that you can win this. I feel it in my blood and in my bones. You're better than them, than her, than all the other competitors. I know you all, know how badly you all want it, how hard you've worked. It's yours. You only have to reach out and grab it."

All four of my alphas smile at me, and I can see some of that tension leaching away, the determination returning. "So go out there and show those bastards, show that dumb bitch, what you're made of. Alphas, go win this for me, your omega."

Zane laughs and wraps me in his arms and lifts me off the ground. "We'd do anything for you, Omega, you know that," he whispers in my ear.

When he places me back on my feet, I raise my hand to stop the others from mauling over me too. "Wait, there's something else. Something I wanted to show you." I lift the hem of my top and tug down the waistband of my shorts, revealing the tender skin by my hip bone. It's been bandaged for the last few days. I told them I'd grazed myself.

Now I show them the truth: a little tattoo of a pair of crossed

271

oars. Identical to my pendant, identical to Seb's tattoo on his chest. Around the tattoo are the initials of each of my alphas.

"I wanted a more permanent way to show I belong to you," I say, peering up at them, suddenly concerned they may be cross. "I want you to know how much I love you, all of you."

"Fuck," Duncan mutters, "you really are ours."

"Yes," I say, "I am."

And then I find myself in the middle of a group hug, a very potent, solid and muscular hug, in which I'm dwarfed. More words of love are muttered, and soon tears are streaming down my cheeks.

"Rosie's right," Seb growls. "We've got this. Screw everyone else and their crappy mind-fuckery. We're going to smash them out of the water. Are you with me, pack?"

"Yes!" the others yell together, and then I'm being ushered away by some irritated official.

It's time for the race to start.

Chapter 34

An eerie silence hangs in the air as the boats float out on the wide river, waiting for the starter's gun.

My heart thumps so violently in my chest it shakes my whole body, and my palm is damp in Mrs Thomas' hand.

The wind rushes through the leaves. Someone in the crowd coughs. A cloud moves across the sun.

And the gun explodes.

For a moment, the boats bob, unmoving, as oars are dragged through the water. Briefly, we hear the groans of men working with all their might and then the crowd comes to life, cheering and shouting around us.

The boats begin to move, slicing through the water, nudging forward with every pull on the oars.

I can't drag my eyes from my alphas. They are something magnificent out there. Pure power, pure exertion, pure will. I urge them on with every rotation of their oars.

"Come on, come on," I mutter, seeing how they nose ahead, gradually, gradually leaving the others behind.

Nearly all the others. Two boats down, I see the nose of *The Sharks'* boat, neck and neck with *The Crew*.

Soon, both are pulling away, a whole boat-length ahead of the other competitors, the gap widening all the time.

It's just the Sharks and my boys now.

I'm on my feet, Sophia and Mrs Thomas beside me.

"Oh God, it's so close," Sophia mutters. "I can't watch." She closes her eyes and rests her forehead on my shoulder.

Mrs Thomas yells, her language turning bluer and bluer by the second.

I've lost the ability to speak, to think. All my focus, my entire being, is locked on them. With everything I have, I will them on.

The finish line comes into view. It's nail-biting to watch. One second, my boys nudge ahead. The next, *The Sharks*. There's nothing between them, nothing at all.

Until suddenly, there is. *The Crew* seem to find a last blast of energy from somewhere. Ollie yells, and they heave with even more power, with even more muscle, hauling the boat onwards, smashing it through the water, pulling ahead, first the bow, then a quarter, then a half.

I bounce up and down on my toes, screaming each of their names with all my might.

The finish line is within touching distance. Right in front of them. Just there. Just there.

The front of the boat nudges against it, then streams through, the Sharks lost behind them. Zane crosses the line, then Duncan, then Seb and finally Ollie.

I punch my arms up into the air, jumping up and down, tears streaming from my eyes. Mrs Thomas sobs beside me and I hug her, then Sophia, then Mrs Thomas again.

Duncan, Zane and Ollie's parents are hugging and crying too. All their earlier reserve vanished.

"They won," I yell to nobody in particular, "they won."

Out on the water, the boys are heaving for breath, their

shoulders falling and rising rapidly, but huge grins stretch over their faces as they slap each other on the shoulders, linking hands and roaring their approval.

Then Zane struggles to his feet, standing in the belly of the boat as it rocks madly. He's peering out at the crowd, his hand beckoning someone, and I can see the word on his lips: "Rosie!"

"Go on, love," Mrs Thomas says, giving me a little nudge. "They want you down there."

I make my way back through the crowd, tears of joy streaking down my cheeks as I see Ollie knock Zane off his feet and into the water, and then they're all standing and leaping into the river, hugging each other and knocking their fists against the spray.

When I meet the edge of the water, they spot me and start racing each other to see who can reach me first. Soon their heads are bobbing at my feet.

"We did it," Zane grins up at me. And all I can do is smile and nod back, the tears still coming. "Get down here and give me a kiss, then," he tells me.

I crouch down by the water's edge, but four pairs of hands are on me in a moment, and I land in the freezing water with a splash.

"Fuck," I scream, as I break back through the surface, the cold knocking the air from my lungs. But I can't be mad, not at the joyful faces circling me. Seb grabs me first, twining his arms around my waist, holding me afloat and kissing me, and I feel Ollie at my back, his arms around me too, his lips at my throat.

I'm surrounded by all four, caught up in their embraces and their passion. No one watching this will be in any doubt as to

275

what we are, as to what I am.

My secret's out.

I belong to not one alpha, but four.

I'm pack.

"Claim me," I say to their exuberant faces as they circle me. "Claim me."

"Rosie," Seb says softly.

"I don't want to wait any longer. I can't wait," I plead.

"We can't do this here," Seb says, his eyes swivelling to the crowd around us, the cameras, the reporters. "Let's talk about this later, alright?"

I nod, my pulse still thumping in my throat. Maybe he is right, maybe it's the adrenaline and the occasion talking.

Except it isn't. There's an anticipation buzzing, crackling, in the air between us for the rest of the day. The alphas won't let me leave their side. One or other of them has his hands on me for the entire day. Through the award ceremony and the debriefs. Much to my dismay, and Bob's, I'm even dragged into the recovery ice bath once all the formalities are done.

I hope there'll be time to talk then, but the boys are still full of the race, wanting to go over it again and again.

"How did you find that extra bit of oomph at the end?" I ask, sandwiched, shivering in the icy water, between Duncan's legs.

"You, sugar," Zane says with that teasing twinkle in his eyes.

"Me?" I raise my eyebrow sceptically at him in our usual game.

"Ollie said ..." he gestures to Ollie.

Ollie sits up straight in the giant bathtub, puffing out his chest and lifting his chin. He swings his fist through the air. "Once more unto the breach, dear friends. For Rosie, England,

and Saint George!"

Duncan snorts at the England reference.

"You're all so full of bullshit," I laugh.

"It was always part of the game-plan," Duncan explains. "Leave a bit in the tank for the end."

"Genius," I tell them, and they grin at me like puppy dogs. Very big, muscular puppy dogs. I'm just about to bring up the claiming thing again when Bob thumps on the bathroom door.

"Time to get out of the bath! Come on, we've got a press conference to get to."

"Press conference!" I groan as Duncan helps me out of the bath and into a robe. I'd forgotten we had somewhere to be next.

"Yep," Ollie says, "I guess we're going to have to get used to them if we're going to the Olympics." He laughs and they cheer all over again.

I giggle, flopping onto one of the beds with my phone in my hand. I glance at the screen. A message from my dad runs across the centre.

The boys continue to roar and cheer around me, smacking each other on the shoulders, wrestling one another. Silently, I click on the message, opening it up. My heart thumps in my chest, my hand trembles.

At first, the words won't focus, but then I force them to, force them to line up neatly, so I can run my eye along them and take in the meaning.

They appear to be good lads, Rosie. You all seem very happy together.

I stare at the words, a choke bubbling in my throat, wetness sliding down my face.

"What is it?" Duncan asks, and I glance up to find my alphas all staring at me with concern.

"My dad," I say, my gaze sinking back to my phone.

"You need to ignore their—" Seb begins, his brow furrowed.

I shake my head. "No. I think …" I look up at them and smile. "I think it's going to be OK."

Chapter 35

wo weeks later

T I sit sandwiched between my alphas at a table bigger than my old dormitory room. Above us, a giant crystal chandelier glistens, and throughout the ballroom, voices murmur and glasses tinkle. Across the crisp white tablecloth are the discarded dishes we've made our way through, half-emptied bottles of champagne and lipstick stained glasses.

The boys had all moaned at Bob about the need to come to this dinner. It's held for all the teams that competed in the championship. But I'd wanted to come. I admit I enjoy the opportunity of dressing up for my boys, of soaking up their hungry stares. Tonight, I wear a black cocktail dress, strapless and made from soft velvet, and I pinned my hair up, exposing the back of my neck, which I know drives them mad.

Ollie's hand rests on my thigh, skimming circles on the soft skin, drawing ever closer to the gusset of my underwear, and Seb's arm rests around the back of my chair, his fingers tracing over my hot gland.

Clearly, the pair of them are winding me up, stoking the fire of my desire, teasing me with these lazy touches. Touches they pretend to pay no attention to, but have shivers racing up and down my skin.

My words out there in the water two weeks ago haven't been forgotten. Over the days that have passed since, there's been an awareness between all of us – in our scents, when our eyes meet – it's coming. The moment is coming.

My pulse flutters and my gland tingles. I'm primed with anticipation. I have been for the last fourteen days.

When will it be? When will it happen?

I realise they will not refuse me. I know their restraint has been stretched to its limit, and now it's going to snap, flinging us all together in an explosion of want. There's no holding back this tide.

I lift my glass to my mouth, my hand trembling, and pour cool water onto my lip.

"OK?" Seb asks, his breath hot on my ear, his grip suddenly tight. His voice is tight too. I can hear the strain, the beginning of the break.

"Yes," I say, hardly hearing the breathy word over the buzzing in my head. I shudder hard when he rests his lips on my shoulder.

His head remains bowed. Almost as if he's fighting himself. I count the beats of my heart.

One.

Two.

Three.

And then he's slamming back his chair, dragging me up onto my feet.

His hand is tight on my wrist as he pulls me along behind him, the others soon catching us, surrounding me in a circle.

There are no words. Only ragged breaths and raised scents.

We know what this is. We all know what this is.

Seb crashes through the doors of the ballroom and out through the lobby.

The hotel sits alongside the river on which they raced. It shimmers in front of us now as we hurtle out into the night.

"This way," Seb grunts, his pace increasing so that I'm trotting behind him, stumbling in my heels.

But no one asks him to slow, not even me. I want us to arrive. I want us to arrive wherever we are going as quickly as we can.

We snake along the darkened river, until Seb swerves, pulling us in his wake, up the bank to an old boathouse, the door missing, its belly empty. Grass has infiltrated the building, soft beneath our feet, and the hulk of an old boat rests near one wall.

Seb halts, swinging around to face us all.

"We're going to do this? Now?"

It's not a question for me. It's a question for his pack mates. His eyes flick from one to the other, first Ollie, then Zane and then Duncan, and one by one they nod.

"We're going to make her ours."

Duncan growls and I shake so hard I can barely stand.

This is it. The moment.

The moment all others have been leading to.

We've reached the crossroads. After this, there can be no turning back. We'll be bonded together for life.

Seb reaches for my throat, forcing my chin up with the nudge of his wrist.

He is all alpha. Monster. Power. Mate.

"Are you certain, Omega?" His voice is so deep it seems to reverberate off the damp walls. His eyes are dark, but I can see the outline of his face, painted silver by the moon behind us.

"Yes," I say, meeting his gaze. Then I grip his wrist with

both my hands. "Claim me."

And in that moment, it snaps.

Everything.

We are no longer the civilised peoples of our century. We are our ancestors. Instinct. Adrenaline. Life. Death. Sex.

We are four alphas and one omega. All pretence that we are anything else evaporates.

"Pin her against the wall," Seb grunts and hands scrabble at me, grabbing my wrists and my arms, my shoulders and my waist. I'm manhandled deeper into the boathouse, thrust into the shadows and held against the wall, my cheek pressing into the damp wood. Then my dress is ripped away, followed by my underwear and the cold air nips at my skin.

I shiver.

"Are you frightened, Omega?" Seb asks by my ear.

I have no words. I wriggle my arse against him, trying to lower my head and expose the back of my neck.

A rough hand squeezes my arse cheek and I mewl, slick dribbling from between my thighs.

"She's ready," a voice says, and I squirm some more, trying to break free of the grasps and find one of my alphas.

Another hand slaps my arse cheek and I freeze. "Still omega."

And then I'm driven up onto my toes by the force of a thrust deep inside me.

I moan with pleasure, my legs turning to jelly as I'm held aloft by the strong hands.

"She needs to come," another voice says. And fingers find my clit and my nipples, stroking and tweaking and teasing.

Another hand squeezes my throat and fingers slip into my mouth.

I come with lightning speed; my body waiting for this. It takes but a few of their purposeful touches, and I'm falling apart, pleasure sweeping through me, drowning every part of me.

Seb thrusts in deeper, and then I feel the first pinch of teeth at the base of my neck.

My gland thrums, so violently it's almost painful, tears stinging my eyes.

"Pleeeaaaase," I whine. "Pleeeeaaaasssse." His pace doesn't falter. His tongue is wet on my gland, bathing it in the warmness of his spit. I hear the rasp of his breath through his nose, the grunt as he spills. Then there's the blissful stretch of his knot and his teeth plunge through my skin.

I scream as blinding pain shoots from my neck to my brain and to my chest. Desperately, I try to pull away, struggling, but I'm held firm, by his knot, by his teeth, by his pack mates' hands.

They growl at me, another hand whacks at my arse. "Hold still, Omega," I'm ordered.

I go limp at the command, the pain throbbing in my neck as I catch my breath. And then it subsides, replaced by a tingling. Something that's faint and indistinct at first but builds and builds, rippling through me gently but growing in intensity until it sweeps through my whole body and I'm moaning in pleasure.

And then something else. Something forming in the pit of my stomach. A bond that I almost see in my mind's eyes, a golden ribbon reaching right from within me and ending in Seb.

I could stay here, pressed against the wall, his weight heavy on my back, his teeth deep in my neck forever. But the other alphas are impatient. They want their turn.

They're snapping and snarling at him as he sucks at my neck, swallowing down the sweet taste of my blood.

"Seb!" Duncan growls, and I feel Seb yanked from me, his teeth leaving my flesh.

I howl. It's nothing compared to the feeling when he wrenches his half-deflated knot free of me. I try to thrash around but the next alpha, Duncan, is at my back, sweeping his cock through my folds, making himself nice and wet before he plunges into me, fucking me into the wall.

I wonder if I'm tipping into heat. I feel wild. Primed. So turned on, swollen and wet, that I'm coming again in seconds, the alpha right behind me, wanting to bite me and claim me as quickly as he can.

His teeth find the wound left by his pack mate and, as his knot expands, he empties into me. As he sinks his teeth even deeper than before, I sigh with the pain and the pleasure. Another bond locks into place inside me.

I'm already ruined, destroyed, my body wrecked, and there are still two more to go. Two more knots. Two more sets of teeth.

Duncan has no time to relish his claiming bite. He's pushed aside, and I feel the tug in my gut as he moves away.

I whine, but the bodies around me hush me, calm me, and Ollie takes his place, his long hair tickling against my shoulder.

"I'm going to bite you, little mouse," he whispers, snapping his teeth by my ear as he starts to pound into me.

My response is nonsense, one long, pleading syllable. I want his bite too. His teeth, his bond. I want to be tethered to him too.

284

The hands don't stop their work, teasing and taunting me, rolling me back up to orgasm so that my alpha can sink his teeth into the fresh wound at my neck and make me his.

"My bounty is as boundless as the sea,

My love as deep; the more I give to thee,

The more I have, for both are infinite," he murmurs before his teeth snap through my skin, his tongue swirling against my torn flesh.

"So good, Omega," Seb says, sweeping wet strands from my face and wiping away the tears on my cheek. "You're doing so well for us. Just one more."

"Zane," I moan. My vision is hazy, faces swimming in front of my own, but I see his vivid green eyes piercing through everything else and finding mine.

Zane.

He moves in closer, his hand palming my arse cheeks. "From the moment you knocked me off my feet, I've dreamt of this, Rosie. I've dreamt of claiming you, of making you ours." His fingers dip into my soaking hole, already full with his pack mates' come. "I've never wanted anything more," he says breathlessly, as he slides his cock into me. He's gentler than the others, less rushed. He grinds into me and the hands on my body respond, pinches and pulls morphing into strokes and kisses.

The orgasm rolls in lazily this time. I'm already high, and it lifts me higher, right through the roof of this old boat house and up into the star-littered sky.

Where I've always wanted to be.

I don't feel the bite at my neck, his teeth, the pain. This time I just feel that bond. The final one, slotting into place like a perfectly crafted puzzle piece.

I am full. And I am done.

I sink to the floor, my alphas coming with me. We are a sweaty mess of limbs and lips, kissing and touching, wanting to be as close to each other as we can.

The moon rises higher in the sky, and the boathouse darkens.

We sit as one, catching our breaths, an interconnected bundle of flesh and blood.

Pack.

Chapter 36 - Epilogue

Three years later — Seb

The sauce simmers on the stove and I add a pinch of cumin, dipping the wooden spoon into the liquid and scooping some out.

"Rosie!" I call, and I hear her skip down the hallway and into the kitchen. Her scent drifts into the room before she does, and after all this time, it still heats my blood, still sets a pulse thumping in my gland.

"How's it going?" she asks, sliding her arms around my waist and peering around my shoulder.

Behind her, Duncan and Zane follow in her wake, pulling out a chair each around the table.

I rest my hand over hers, squeezing them. They are still cold from outside. She only returned home with Duncan a half hour ago. Now we're in the depths of winter, we won't let her travel home alone. Of course, Zane offered to buy her a car of her own, but my lass is insisting on saving up to buy it for herself. I imagine she has her eye on something bright and impractical.

"Would you try this?" I ask her.

She sidles around me, and holding her hair back from her face, bends over the saucepan as I lift the spoon to her mouth.

"Blow it," I tell her, and she bristles a little at the order. She knows I like that. Knows I can't get enough of the little mischievous omega act. Just enough to push my buttons, but not too far.

She lets out a breath of air, and the sauce ripples slightly on the surface of the spoon, then she sips it into her mouth, sighing as she does.

"Delicious," she says, licking her lips and straightening.

"Does it need more spice? How do your parents like it?"

Rosie's twin sisters are coming to stay for the weekend and her parents are driving them up tomorrow. They've agreed to stay for lunch. It's another gradual step, steps towards accepting the pack and Rosie's position. I'm going all out to impress them. We all are. Duncan spent an hour cleaning the kitchen before work this morning, and Zane came home with an armful of fresh flowers. Ollie's planning to woo them with yet more tales of trips to Buckingham Palace.

Rosie would like nothing more than for her family to support her, to support us. We're going to make it happen, no matter how long it takes.

"I think it's perfect," she says.

"OK, then butter up the dish, lass."

I've already prepared and rolled out the pastry, so I switch off the gas and turn around to watch as she fetches the butter from the fridge and runs the block around the sides of the dish.

"How was your day?" I ask, folding my arms and leaning back to listen as she recounts the data she's been analysing from a telescope far out in the depths of space.

Duncan asks her a few questions from the table. I don't follow a lot of her answers, but I love listening to her talk about her work, love the way her eyes light up, how the pace of her words quickens, the way she swings up on her toes in excitement. It makes me want to encase her in my arms and smother her in kisses. Instead, I smile, nodding along.

"Actually," she says, wrapping the paper back around the butter and spinning to face all of us. "My supervisor pulled me to one side today."

I lift my eyebrow. "And?"

"They want to fund me to do a PhD." She grins, those pale blue eyes shimmering, and I can't resist her any longer. I reach for her hand and tug her towards me.

"I am not surprised, little lass. You've been working so hard, and you are possibly the cleverest person I know."

She crinkles up her nose. "I'm not sure about that."

"You chose this pack, didn't you? Seems pretty damn clever to me."

The others bound over, Duncan and Zane both kissing and congratulating her.

"I think this pack picked me," she says with a giggle once the kisses have subsided. She rests her palms against my chest as I draw my hand up under her hair and trace the teeth marks on her gland. They've hardly faded, still as strong, still as vivid, just like this pull towards her.

"Does this mean you'll be back at the college?" I ask her.

"If it all works out, then yes, it does, Professor Thomas."

"That is definitely something worth celebrating, Miss Anderson," I say, imagining all the illicit hookups, all the opportunities to bend her over the desk in my shiny new office.

My hand drifts down to her ripe arse and I give it a firm squeeze, leaving her in no doubt of my intentions. Then I kiss her, and she melts against me, the fingers of her hands spreading wide across my chest.

"Something smells good," Ollie says, strolling into the kitchen and coming over to sniff the sauce.

"It's for tomorrow. Don't touch."

"Looks good, though," he says with a nod, moving to stand behind Rosie and kissing her neck. "And how's my little mouse? Nervous about tomorrow?"

"It seems your little mouse," I say, "is going to be a doctor."

Ollie gives me a puzzled look, and Rosie twists her head around. "The Agency is willing to fund the PhD I want to do."

He squeezes her tight, then nibbles her shoulder. "Congratulations, little mouse."

"Two doctors and a professor." Duncan whistles.

"And a writer and an engineer," Zane adds, massaging Duncan's shoulder.

"And a team of Olympic rowers," Ollie grins, then pauses. "Rosie, will you still be able to take the summer off?"

Rosie steps out from between us and passes me the dish. I give a nod and pour the creamy chicken in before covering it in the pastry.

"Of course," Rosie tells Ollie, watching as I trim the pastry top to fit the dish. "You think I'm going to miss the opportunity to visit Madrid?"

Ollie prods her soft waist. "Or the chance to watch your alphas win gold at the Olympics?"

"That too," she says with a mischievous grin.

It won't be long before we'll be relocating out to Spain and starting our training out there. The Agency has agreed to let Rosie come with us. We make a neat little media story for the country; rowing team with a shot at a gold, bonded to a woman working for the space agency. But she won't be working for the two weeks of the actual competition. She's very clear. She wants to be by our sides, giving us her full attention.

I'm glad of it. While I don't want any of us getting in the way of her and her dreams, we need our omega, need her more than ever in those moments where everything hangs in the balance. I know we'll row harder, faster, with her by our sides.

Rosie snuggles up against Ollie as I roll the off-cuts of pastry into thin sausages and arrange them over the top of the pie, spelling out the pack's name. As I do, my eyes keep straying back to Ollie and Rosie. I can't help but watch his fingers stray beneath her top and his lips press against her neck.

I catch Zane's eye, and he winks, taking Duncan's hand and leading him from the kitchen, the stairs creaking a moment later.

Growing up, I'd never imagined I'd want to share an omega, that I'd want to live in a pack. I'd often felt excluded. The clever, serious one at school who never fitted in. Then the poor kid in a college full of rich ones. But I don't feel that way anymore. Even when I'm watching from the outside, as I do now. There is something erotic, something irresistible, about sharing my omega with another alpha, about watching one of my brothers drive her into pleasure, about knowing the other two will soon be rutting. We're all one bundle of love and sex in this pack, mixed and tangled together.

When I'm finished with the pie, I glaze the top and place it in the fridge. We'll cook it tomorrow before Rosie's parents arrive. I already know what I intend to say to them. The same thing I've been saying for the last three years. That I will take good care of their daughter, that I will spend every day of the rest of my life making her happy. Just like every other alpha in this pack.

And I'm going to do that right now.

I wipe my hands on the towel and stalk towards my omega.

She's moaning softly, enjoying the way Ollie plays with her tits and sucks on her throat, but her eyelids flutter open as she senses me draw closer.

"What?" she whispers, those sky-blue eyes meeting mine.

"Nothing," I grin, sinking to my knees and wrapping my hands around her calves.

"You have that wicked glint in your eye," she says.

"I always have a wicked glint in my eye when you are near, lass, you know that."

"Yes." She sighs as I run my hands up her legs and under her skirt. "I do."

"Are you going to make her come?" Ollie's words are muffled against skin.

"Would you like that, lass?" I ask her.

"Yes," she gasps.

I stare up at her as I roll down her tights and her underwear and help her step out of them. Ollie's hand has pulled up her top and I see the soft skin of her abdomen. I have that urge, deep in my gut, to fill that belly, to see it rounded with my child, with all our children. I'm looking forward to the day when this house is filled with them.

Not yet, though, there's still time. Time for all of that.

I duck my head under her skirt and my nose fills with the sweet scent of her. She smells like her name, like summer roses, beautiful yet strong. I take a deep inhale, my gland buzzing with pleasure, and then I press a kiss to her sex.

Above me, she moans and my cock, always hard in her presence, jerks inside my pants. There's time for that later too. First, I'm going to make her come.

I dip my tongue between her folds and her flavour hits my

taste buds. My eyes roll back in their sockets and I groan. Her taste is like nothing else. Nothing I have the words to describe. Maybe someone like Ollie could, with his poetic turn of phrase, or Zane, with his free flowing words. But not me. All I know is there is no better place in the world than here, between her thighs, kissing the most intimate, most raw, part of her.

She moans as I drag my tongue around her clit and then glide through her folds until I come to her entrance. I slip inside, my tongue soaked in her completely now, my mouth full of her swollen, slippery flesh. I suck her into my mouth, clit and all, and her legs shake in my hands.

I suck harder and then I withdraw.

"Hold still, Omega," I instruct her.

"Make her squeal, Seb. You know I love it when she squeals." Ollie's voice is almost a growl, and I know we'll both be rutting her here in the kitchen.

"I'm going to," I tell him, returning to her clit. I sweep around it languidly and as I do, I slide my finger up inside her, finding that spot that makes her squirt.

I massage my finger against that swollen spot as I continue to circle her clit. She's sensitive, my omega, and I know I need to build her up, lead her to the crescendo. Just enough pressure, just enough stimulation.

Her little nub quivers against my tongue, and her cunt clenches around my fingers. I groan, knowing how good that action feels around my cock, wanting to sink into her now, but holding back, giving her this first.

I skim over the top of her clit, brushing over the surface, and her hips buck. She whimpers and those pleading words start streaming from her mouth.

"You wanna come, little mouse, you wanna come," Ollie

293

mutters.

For a second, I'm stabbed with jealousy. She's other worldly when she comes. So damn gorgeous. And Ollie will have the perfect view as her skin flushes, as her eyelids flutter, as pleasure cascades across her face and those teasing noises spill from her mouth.

But the feeling vanishes as quickly as it comes as more of her slick finds my mouth, and I drink it down, my mouth soaked in her flavour.

I hum my approval against her, and she jolts harder, so close, so close to the edge. Just a couple more flicks of my tongue. Taunting her. Bringing her so near and then, just as she's about to come, I pause, leaving her hanging. Suspended. I want to draw this out for her, to make it one long, never-ending orgasm. Then I stroke my tongue over her clit, and she comes, comes on my tongue, in my mouth and around my fingers.

"You're a work of art, little mouse," Ollie tells her. "A goddamn masterpiece."

And my heart strains in my chest, beats so hard. I never believed someone like her – so beautiful, so clever, so perfect – could love someone like me – too caught up in my own head, too stuck in my ways, too blind to see what's there in front of my nose.

But she does.

"Seb," she murmurs, and I give her pussy one last lingering lick, then stand. She wraps her arms around my neck and kisses me. Despite the mess on my face, she kisses me hard.

"I love you," she says.

~ THE END ~

Want to read another sweet reverse harem omegaverse in

the *In With The Pack* series?
Read on for a look at Sophia's story — *In Control*

Need more Rosie and her pack?
Download their steamy bonus scene from my website
www.hannahhaze.com

Join my VIP reader Facebook group, Soft and Steamy
omegaverse, for all the latest news and goodies.

Thank you so much for reading. If you enjoyed this book,
please consider leaving a review or rating — it's a great help
to indie authors like me!

In Control

S ophia

My breath hovers in my throat, my gaze captured by the figure spinning across the stage.

One dancer in particular. The lead. He's formed of densely packed muscle, his thighs and his torso rippling with every move he makes. And yet those movements are graceful, considered, and beautiful. As he lifts and spins his partner, drawing her close to the stage floor one minute and high into the air the next, it is him I can't drag my eyes from. It's as if she weighs nothing, as if it costs him nothing to glide her through the moving spotlights.

When finally he exits the stage, leaving his partner for her solo dance, I lean back in my seat, the velvet brushing against my bare back, and catch my breath.

It's then I sense it. An awareness. Someone is watching me.

The sensation is not unusual. I catch people's eyes. I know that. In fact, I like it – most of the time anyway. It's why I'm wearing this dress tonight – a deeply seductive purple made of silk that swims over my body and pools at my feet.

I'm curious, though, as always, to see whose eye I've caught this time. Is it a catch worth pursuing, or one to discard back into the sea?

It's opening night, and one of my mother's latest beaus has wangled us tickets. All the great and good of the city of Studworth are gracing the theatre tonight. Some I'd like to meet, others I most definitely want to avoid.

Subtly, I lift my gaze, and it's as if it's drawn there. Drawn there by a man sitting in one of the boxes high above me. A man I don't recognise.

He sits at the front, chin resting in his hand, and he's staring right at me. He makes no attempt to disguise it. He's dressed in a dark suit, although, unlike many of the men here at the ballet tonight, his white shirt is open at the neck. He has no bow tie. Even through the layers of his jacket, I can tell he is as well built and as powerful as the man I've been watching dancing across the stage. Although he's larger, making the seat he's crouching on seem minuscule.

And then there are his eyes. Dark and swirling and mesmerising. Capturing my attention and refusing to release it.

My breath stalls in my throat again.

Alpha.

The man is an alpha. And an alpha staring at me with obvious interest.

I quirk my head to one side.

I catch people's attention all the time. Men and women. Old and young.

Not alphas' though. I may be something worth gazing at, but I'm one thing no alpha wants. A beta.

Perhaps he can't tell over the distance. Perhaps he's mistaken me for the one thing every alpha does want: an omega.

I stare back at him. Meeting those intensely dark eyes with my own.

He'll look away now. He'll lose interest.

An omega can't meet an alpha eye-to-eye. Something in their ancient instincts stirs and they're compelled to look away. I don't own those ancient instincts though. I have no problem staring right back at this man, the corner of my mouth curving in a seductive smile.

Most men like that. A little flirtation has their blood stirring. This man will be different though.

I wait for him to turn away.

The music on stage erupts. Trumpets blare. The pitter patter of many feet vibrates the sprung-floor.

He keeps his eyes fixed on mine and the corner of my mouth drops. A shiver traces its way down my spine. His hair is dark too, and his brows and the stubble that runs across his square jaw.

His tongue darts between his lips and traces along his bottom lip.

Then, eyes still locked on me, he stands, watching me as he side-steps his seat.

There's a command in the way he's looking at me. I'm no omega. I can't read it, but I can give it a damn good guess.

I stand too, and for a minute his eyes leave mine, skating across my bare shoulders, lingering at the cleavage of my dress, warming my blood.

Slowly, his eyes rake up my throat before returning to meet mine. His brow lowers and my knees turn to jelly.

I've never been at the mercy of an alpha before, never piqued one's interest. It is ... intriguing.

I tear my eyes from him and lean down to whisper in my mother's ear.

"I'm going to use the bathroom."

As much as that dancer has held me entranced, I never wanted to be here. But wanting and having to be here are two different things. There was a time when I jumped at every opportunity to attend an event like this. But now there's always that doubt lingering in the back of my mind. Will he be here? At an event like this, it's always a possibility.

My mother slides her knees to the side and I squeeze along the row of people, conscious the entire time that the alpha is still watching me.

In the aisle, I gaze up at him again, meeting that stare which now seems hungry. Then I lift the hem of my dress and saunter towards the exit, hips swaying, giving him my best show.

Out in the foyer, it's cool and goosebumps raise along my arms. I take a deep breath. My skin tingles with anticipation.

Have I caught my fish?

The long elegant bar with its mirror running the full length of the room stands empty. I stroll that way, anyway, finding a jug of water and several glasses.

I pour myself some, half watching the mirror.

I know immediately when the alpha enters the room, before I spy his warped reflection in the dimly lit mirror, before I hear his feet pad across the plush carpet. I sense him. His presence. If I was an omega, I'd know by his scent, but it's not until he's closed the space and I can see his dark eyes in the reflection, closer now, even darker, that I catch the faint whiff of his scent.

Dark too, like treacle.

I inhale, sucking his flavour across my tongue.

I take another sip of water, leaving a red imprint of my lip on the glass, and lower it to the bar.

Turning slowly, I find him so close we're almost touching.

Warmth and dominance radiate from his body, and, despite my heels, I have to tip my head back to meet his eyes.

"I'd ask you to buy me a drink," I say, a smile hovering on my lips, "but the bar is closed."

"I don't think you came out here for a drink, little one." His voice is deep, reverberating in his broad chest. It's like a growl, a growl dipped in honey. It has that shiver shimmying down my spine again.

"No, I didn't."

"No, you didn't," he repeats, bending so our eyes are level.

Up close, I observe the colour of his. Not jet like they'd appeared in the theatre. A mahogany brown with a rim of gold.

"You're very beautiful," he tells me, reaching out to trace a fingertip down the column of my throat. "Do you taste as good as you look?"

I go to open my mouth, to give him one of my quick retorts, but his mouth has replaced the pressure of his fingers and he kisses my throat.

I guess we're skipping the small talk, sliding straight past the flirtation, heading straight for the seduction.

I certainly don't have a problem with that.

The man smells like something I'd like to eat and his lips are plush and tender on my skin. Tender, with a hint of power.

I'm only mortal. Like every other woman on the planet, I've fantasised about an alpha's mouth on my throat, about his strong alpha teeth snapping through my flesh.

I sigh, tipping my head back, leaning against the bar. His large hands come to claim my hips and he holds me still as he kisses up my neck to my ear, nipping at my lobe before whispering in the shell.

"Come with me, little one."

No pretence at asking me if this is what I want. No ...

He's an alpha. He's used to getting his way, to having his orders obeyed.

In any other situation, it would piss me off. I'm not some pushover, some little girl to be bossed about by men.

But in this situation, I'm more than happy to play along.

He takes a grip of my hand and walks us across the dimly lit foyer to a door marked PRIVATE.

I guess I should be thankful he didn't try to rut me right there against the bar. Then again ...

The door snaps open as he leans his heavy shoulder against it and he drags me along behind him as we enter a pitch-black room. No window. No light.

I want to protest, but then he's pushing me up against the cool wall, my head knocking against the smooth plaster.

With his alpha vision, I assume he can see in this darkness because he finds my ear and whispers, "Such a pretty thing." His hands glide over the silk of my dress, caresses the curve of my waist and my hips. "And this dress."

"You're quite pretty yourself," I tease.

He snorts, his hand travelling down the outside of my thigh until he discovers the slit in my dress. He growls.

A noise that, now it's directed at me, has my core spinning.

"I'm not pretty, little one. I'm not careful. I'm not gentle."

"What are you then?"

His hand slips inside my dress, his knuckles rubbing against the inside of my thigh. Higher and higher until he finds the gusset of my thong. His thumb skates against my mound.

"Dirty," he growls.

Continue reading here

A Guide to Hannah's Omegaverse

I write soft and steamy omegaverse romances — stories that are on the sweeter side — mixing the sauciness of omegaverse dynamics with contemporary plots.

My omegaverse stories are set in a modern world just like ours, except people can be one of three kinds — Alphas, Betas and Omegas. Betas are just like you and I, but Alphas and Omegas are slightly different biologically. In my stories, the characters are often battling with their biological urges, needs and instincts, and trying to fit into a modern world which can be judgemental and sometimes prejudiced.

Alphas

Alphas are generally larger, stronger and more aggressive. Their instincts can make them domineering and controlling. Alpha males are also a little anatomically different where it counts the most. Yep, I'm talking the peen — at the base there is a knot which expands when an Alpha comes, locking him into his partner where they remain stuck together for a period of time. Biologically, this increases the chance of pregnancy. Some Alphas can control the expansion of their knot, others can't.

Omegas

Omegas are smaller and their instincts can make them more submissive — especially towards an Alpha. Only an Omega can 'take' an Alpha's knot. An Omega has regular heat cycles where they are especially fertile. During this period they become hot and horny and very uncomfortable unless they are fucked and knotted frequently by an Alpha.

Heats, ruts and bites

Similarly to menstrual cycles, the Omegas in my world have differing heat cycles. Some have very regular heats, some have them less often, and others control or suppress them with medication. A heat typically lasts three or four days. When an Omega falls into a heat, their scent alters and they become especially alluring to any Alpha close by.

An Omega in heat can drive an Alpha into rut. An Alpha in rut isn't hindered by the usual biological restraints that your average guy is. I'm talking about permanent erections, no recovery, and the ability to come multiple times! (Sounds like fun, huh?)

Both Omegas and Alphas have glands at the back of their necks, the source of their scents. These glands are especially sensitive when the Omega or Alpha is turned on. Biting this gland is known as claiming and binds the pair together, often irreversibly. It also leaves a scar and changes the

Alpha or Omega's scent which signals to others that they are 'taken'. During a heat, when an Omega is at the mercy of their biological urges, an Omega can often beg for an Alpha to 'claim' or bite them.

Scents, blockers and suppressants

Both Omegas and Alphas have heightened senses of smells and distinctive scents. An Alpha and Omega can recognise another Alpha or Omega by their scent alone, often over great distances. Their scents can also signal how they're feeling — especially when they are aroused or aggravated. Omegas and Alphas can mask their scents using blockers. They can also try to quell their Alpha and Omega instincts with the use of suppressants — for example an Alpha might take an emergency suppressant to stop themselves responding to an Omega in heat.

Soft and steamy Omegaverse

In my world, Alphas and Omegas are rare and viewed as a source of fascination by Betas. Alphas are often struggling to fit into a society where aggression and violence isn't tolerated, and Omegas are torn between their desire to be independent and their instinct to be controlled. It is often true love and the perfect partner that allows them to find the balance, acceptance and happiness they need and deserve.

Happily ever afters guaranteed!

About the Author

Hannah writes soft and steamy omegaverse romances, sure to get your pulse racing and your heart fluttering. Her couples are destined to find each other – and when they do, oh boy!

Hannah Haze loves long romantic walks in the countryside, undisturbed soaks in a hot bath and even hotter stories.

Hannah lives close enough to London to take advantage of city delights, but far enough away to explore muddy woods and fields with her husband and children.

Subscribe to my newsletter:
✉ https://www.hannahhaze.com/about

Also by Hannah Haze

More Soft and Steamy Omegaverse. All available on Amazon and Kindle Unlimited. Find out more at www.hannahhaze.com

Contemporary RH omegaverse series — *In With The Pack*
  In Deep
  In Trouble
  In Knots
  In Doubt
  In Control

Contemporary RH omegaverse - *The Rockview Omegaverse*
  Pack Rivals Part I
  Pack Rivals Part II
  Pack Choice

Contemporary MF omegaverse series — *The Alpha Rock Stars*
  The Rockstar's Omega
  Rocked by the Alpha
  Fourth Base with the Alpha

Contemporary MF omegaverse standalones
  Oxford Heat
  The Alpha Escort Agency
  Omega's Forbidden Heat

Contemporary MF omegaverse novellas
  The Omega Chase
  Online Heat

Christmas Heat

Alien omegaverse MF romance series — *The Alpha Prince of Astia*
  Alien Desire
  Alien Passion

Visit Hannah's website for more details: www.hannah-haze.com

Printed in Great Britain
by Amazon

23677832R00175